INHABITED

Ike Hamill

INHABITED

ISBN: 0692754725
ISBN-13: 978-0692754726 (Misdirected Books)

For my mother, whose help was invaluable.

Chapter One — Preface

1978

"DON'T MOVE," CLARENCE whispered. He blinked his eyes and then returned them to wide open. It didn't help. He had never experienced a black so profound. There was *nothing* to see.

"I can get us out," Joan said. She sounded perfectly calm and rational. "If we follow the right wall until we get to the big gap, all we have to do is..."

"Shh!" Clarence said. He reached out to touch her, but his hand found nothing but emptiness.

"Is this some ruse to frighten me?" she asked. Her voice sounded like it was only inches from his face. Something about the carved rock around them reflected the sound and played tricks on his ears. "I have three older brothers. When I was little, they used to lock me in the cellar with the lights off to try to frighten me. It never worked."

"Listen," Clarence said. He returned his voice to a whisper. "Something shut off our lights. *Something*. It wasn't me, and I'm assuming it wasn't you. I brought a lighter, matches, a flashlight, and a damn candle, but *those* are all gone. Unless *you* have the bag, then maybe that same *something* took our backup lights as well."

"It wasn't me," she said. For the first time, she sounded uncertain. The confidence returned to her voice quickly. "Regardless, sight is only one sense. I can still hear, and I can still feel. This isn't a cave, where we have to be concerned about slipping down into some endless chasm. All we have to do is follow the walls until we get out. You said it yourself—this mine isn't even very deep."

"No," Clarence said. "What I said was that this is a shallow ore chute. Ore was dropped in from above and carted out through here. As chutes go, it's not very deep but it does connect to the rest of the mine."

"Connects how?"

"Up through a vertical shaft."

"Oh!" Joan said, giving a little laugh. "So as long as we don't stumble *up a vertical shaft*, I think we're okay."

Clarence heard the slide of her shirtsleeve just before her hand grabbed his. He managed to not scream or jerk away. He yielded to the tug of her warm hand.

"Come on," she said. I can get us out of here.

Clarence let his feet slip forward over the rocky floor. There were puddles in places, but he had given up on dry feet some time ago. Besides, he had fresh shoes and socks out in the car. He stumbled on a rock and had to lean on her grip to stay upright. At the moment, nothing was more important than the feel of his hand in hers. If he had only known that utter darkness was what it would take to feel her touch, he would have dashed his light against a rock twenty minutes ago.

Clarence ran into her back.

"Shhh!" she said, stealing his line. He heard her hair swoosh as she turned her head from side to side.

"What?" he whispered. He honestly didn't care. For the first time in a long time he thought he had a shot at something more than friendship with Joan, and that was way more important than being a hundred yards down an ore chute. After all, it wasn't even a very deep chute. Holding hands in the dark wasn't much, but it was more than he had expected.

"I guess it's nothing," she said. She shuffled forward a few more feet and then stopped again. This time, she squeezed his hand to alert him to stop, instead of letting him run into her. "Here's the gap."

"What?"

"The gap in the wall. When we came in, there was that room on our left. If we just follow straight across this gap, we should pick up the other wall, right? I mean, correct?" She laughed at her own confusing statement.

"Yeah, I see what you mean," he said. But was she sure? It was way too soon to find that gap. If they were passing the room, then they were close to the entrance. This close to the entrance and they should be able to see moonlight. His eyes were still registering exactly nothing.

He started forward again when she tugged on his hand.

"Oh!" Joan said. She stopped once more. "I think I found the bag." Her hand descended as she knelt down. He heard her fumbling with something for several seconds. "No. It's not the bag. It feels like a shirt or something? Do you remember passing a shirt?"

"No," Clarence said.

"Gross," she said. She pulled on his hand more as she lowered down. Clarence heard water flowing and wondered what she was up to. Her grip tightened and then slacked. She did it again and then her hand went completely limp.

In the dark, Clarence tilted his head and smiled as he wondered what she was up to.

"Joan?" he whispered. "Joan!"

He tugged at her arm. She offered no resistance.

Clarence knelt and took her hand in both of his. The fingers didn't grip back. He worked his other hand over to her shoulder and shook. From what he could tell, she was basically laying on the ground.

"What are you doing?" he asked. His smile became expectant. He moved his hand up her shoulder and towards her face. She didn't stop him. He pictured her in the dark, laying down, and waiting for his touch.

He reached his shaking hand out towards her chest. Even if she objected and pulled away, he would still get the thrill of one fleeting touch. It was worth the risk. When his hand landed on her soft bosom, she didn't react at all.

"Joan?" he asked. The corners of his mouth began to turn down. He felt on her wrist for a pulse—it was weak. He moved his hand up to her neck to check her pulse there. Perhaps she was having an episode and needed resuscitation.

When his hand touched her neck, Clarence froze. Her skin had been parted. So had the muscle and sinew underneath. His hand touched an artery that was pumping out the last of her blood. Clarence pressed his head down to her chest and heard the final beat of her heart.

He popped his head back up and spun it around rapidly, desperate for any light or sound. He heard nothing but his own breathing and his own hammering heart. Clarence let go of her hand and rose silently to his feet. His knee clicked and inside his head he cursed the noise. He didn't have time to worry about her body, and he certainly didn't have time to panic. Something was loose in the mine and he would be its next victim if he didn't act decisively.

First things first—he had lost his sense of direction and no longer had any idea which way was out.

Clarence patted his pockets. He had his keys, a knife, and some change. Everything else was back in the car. He opened the pocketknife and held it out against the dark. With his other hand, the hand sticky with blood, he used two fingers to pull a single coin from his pocket. He tossed it towards where he thought the wall might be. The coin sailed through the air and reported back with a little clang. Clarence tried to get a sense of the place based on the reverberation of the noise. He also hoped that the sound might draw away whatever had... He shook his head. He didn't want to think about Joan.

He slid a foot to his left. There was a wall over there somewhere. Clarence shifted his weight and moved his right foot to join the first. He repeated the process several times. Each time, he expected the wall. He remained disappointed for a while.

The toe of Clarence's sneaker finally scraped on the rock wall.

He heard another sound immediately after. From off to his right, he heard something that sounded liked a breathy sigh. Clarence froze. He closed his eyes to the darkness.

With calm, even breaths, he set his mind to the problem. He remembered the details of their entry. They had walked in casually, pointing their headlights at chains hanging from the supports, looking at the graffiti from a thousand trespassing vandals. Joan had never been in a mine before, and she was thrilled by every detail. Clarence had played the magnanimous guide. He had explored many abandoned mines. Back East, he had been a caver. Mines were off-limits in the Smokey Mountains because they would fill up with poisonous gasses. Out here, they were fair game.

They had made two turns. The shaft turned left and then right. There was one big room to the side. Clarence pictured it from the top down, like a map. He imagined the two of them going deeper and deeper, around the two turns, until both of their lights had gone out for no reason. At first, only Joan's light had gone dark. Clarence moved to help her. A second later, his had gone out too.

He pictured where they had stood and then tried to guess the direction they had gone after she took his hand.

Clarence nodded to himself in the dark.

He figured it out. If they had headed the wrong direction, her right hand would have lost the wall quickly as the tunnel curved away. That's what happened. She had assumed that they were passing by the big room, when instead they were going deeper into the shaft.

Clarence reached up and touched the wall. He knew what he had to do.

He turned around and began a very slow walk away from Joan. He moved like Scooby and Shaggy would when they were trying to tiptoe around a ghost. He reached out, toe first, and set his foot down like he was trying to balance on eggshells without breaking them.

Clarence was rewarded with silence. Except for his breathing, he was unable to detect the sound of his own movement.

He heard another sigh behind him and he froze. The sound was from back down the shaft. He decided to sacrifice some of his stealth for speed.

Clarence gained confidence as he strode into the dark. He trailed his fingers down the rough wall to make sure he kept going in the correct direction. Using his mental map of the mine, Clarence held his other hand out in front. He led with the knife. He expected to run into...

He found it! Now he was certain that he was on the right trail. His hand found the wall before his face hit it. All he had to do was follow this shaft for a little bit and then he could make his final turn. Clarence held himself to a medium pace. He only slowed down when he scuffed his foot. He still didn't think he could afford to make that much noise.

His wall ran out. This was more good news. That meant he just had to make one more turn. Everything was lining up. Clarence wanted to run, but this would be the worst time. It was in this shaft that chains hung down from some of the support beams. If he ran into one of those, it would make a terrible racket. He brushed by one of the posts and could picture how it would look. The ground got softer towards the mouth of the mine and these supporting arches were spaced every ten to fifteen feet.

Clarence blinked and peered as he walked. He imagined a dark-blue rectangle of night sky in the distance, but it could just be random firings of his optic nerve. The only way to tell would be to keep going.

After two more support columns, he was sure of it. There was the faint glow of moonlight in the distance. He could see the hanging shapes of a couple of the chains. As long as he kept close to the wall, he might be able to run without hitting them.

He ran out of wall.

Clarence stopped. It was the room. There was a gap in the wall where the shaft led to the big room. He'd heard that at one time the room had stored supplies for the civil defense shelter. If that was true, the supplies had been completely cleared out. He had searched every corner of the room and never found anything more substantial than the skeleton of a bat.

Compared to the glow at the end of the shaft, the room was a return to pure black. He didn't like standing next to it. It felt as dangerous as the deep darkness behind him. Clarence rushed past the opening to the room and his hand found the wall again on the far side. He rushed to be closer to the moonlight. Soon, he could see the shadow his legs were casting on the mine floor. His heart soared to be so close to freedom.

His hand rested on the final support post, just below the "No Trespassing" sign emblazoned with a skull and crossbones. Clarence turned back to look into the darkness. Guilt swept through him. Somewhere back there, Joan was lying on the floor of the mine in the dark.

She had committed the crime of curiosity. Was he even sure she was dead?

He shook his head. Of course he was sure. Her heart had stopped and her blood had been everywhere. He had touched it and smelled it.

Maybe it was a joke.

If so, it was a very elaborate and mean joke. Hell, if she was going to play a joke like that, she deserved to be left in the mine. His mind was made up—he would drive home as fast as he could and he would wake up his father. His old man worked for the fire department, but he was nearly a doctor. If anyone could help Joan, it was him.

Clarence folded his knife and tucked it back into his pocket. He reached for his keys. They were gone. A thin film of sweat jumped instantly to his skin and Clarence began to frantically pat his pockets. He looked back into the black hole of the mine and remembered where he'd last had them. He had been standing right next to Joan's body. There was no way he could go back. Even if there was nothing in there, even if Joan's death had been a complete accident, he would never find his keys in the dark.

With desperation taking over, he shoved his sticky hand deep into his front pocket. Hope washed through his veins when his fingers found something hard. Below the change, he found his keys, right where he had left them. Clarence fished them out and squeezed them tight in his fist. He turned towards the trail that led to where he had parked.

He nearly made it.

Clarence took one step out into the safety of the night before the thing slinked out of the dark and looped twice around his ankle. It jerked back, sending Clarence towards the ground. He smacked into the hard rock and the keys bounced from his grip. He reached for them as his body was dragged backwards into the darkness of the mine.

Chapter Two — Basement

"Where else?" Justin asked.

"I don't know... Anywhere?" Travis asked.

Justin shook his head. He pushed open the gate and let the spring pull it back. As he descended the concrete steps, he felt the difference in temperature. It was a stifling night. It almost hurt to breathe the hot air. He knocked twice on the basement door.

"Come on," Ryan said.

Justin was already halfway through the door anyway. He left it cocked open for Travis.

Ryan was sitting on the couch. He fired up his lighter and touched the flame to the bowl of his bong as he inhaled. Travis pressed the door shut behind him. Justin and Travis took chairs as Ryan turned his face to the side and exhaled into a pillow.

"What's happening?" Ryan asked. His voice produced little more than a croak.

"We need a new hang," Travis said.

Justin shrugged.

"Where else?" Justin asked again. "And what's wrong with this place anyway? Ryan's got his own entrance. It's private enough."

Travis didn't answer. He wrinkled his nose and shook his head.

"He's right," Ryan said after clearing his throat. "This place just has that oppressive parent vibe seeping down from upstairs. I feel it." He coughed again.

"They're not even home half the time," Justin said.

"Yeah, but which half?" Travis asked. "The point is that you

9

never know. We should get out of here this weekend, you know? Let's do Vegas. We can try to get comped and eat at shitty buffets."

"Come on," Justin said. "It's a day's pay up and back. And it's only cheap there if you have money to spend. It's oxymoronic."

The door banged open. When the young man slipped through he slammed it shut behind himself and then pressed back against it. "Holy shit, holy shit!"

They all just stared at him.

Eventually, Ryan said one word. "What?"

Ryan slid over and made room on the couch. Miguel took a place in front of the bong. He put up a finger to ask them to wait while he took a hit.

Travis raised his eyebrows and tapped his foot impatiently. Miguel waved for the pillow and then coughed into it. On the couch next to him, Ryan frowned and scratched his nose as he watched.

"Listen," Travis said, clearing his throat. "Nothing *ever* happens here. Nothing is interesting. Nothing is exciting. Barstow is a fucking desert that doesn't even know how to be a decent desert. So when you come in here like you've got big news and then you leave us all hanging, you're really just making a bad situation worse. So just spit out your shitty news and quit making us wait for it."

"Yeah," Justin said. "Suspense requires reward."

"What he said," Travis said.

"There's gold in Old Hang," Miguel said.

The room was silent for several seconds.

Everyone erupted at once.

"Bullshit," Travis said.

"Fuck you," Ryan yelled. He smacked Miguel's shoulder.

"I'm serious," Miguel said. "Totally serious."

"This is a work, right?" Justin asked. "Just admit it now and we'll all stay friends. You and Travis are trying to work us."

"What are you talking about?" Miguel said.

"Travis had that stupid story last week about how some guy named Cameron," Justin started.

Travis interrupted him—"Clarence."

"Some guy named Clarence took his girlfriend into Old Hang and they both got eaten by some monster. Then you show up and start talking about gold. Then one of you is going to say, 'I think we should go looking for gold down there.' And we end up underground while Jordan or Carlos jumps out and scares the shit out of us, right?"

Miguel shook his head. "I didn't even know about Travis's story. Some guy and his girlfriend died?"

Justin rolled his eyes. "This is a work."

"It wasn't his girlfriend," Travis said. "And this was back in the seventies. They're missing and presumed dead, but since they never found the bodies, nobody knows for sure."

"Yes," Ryan said. He picked up his bong and used a set of tweezers to pick through the char in the bowl. "This is definitely a work. I agree with Justin."

"Tell me about the couple," Miguel said to Travis.

"Like I said, it was the seventies. Some guy named Clarence was trying to get with this girl named Joan. They went down there, but they were never seen again. His car was found up by the Nook. That's how they know they went in the mine," Travis said.

"That's creepy," Miguel said.

"Let me ask you something," Justin began. "If they never found the bodies or anything, how did you have all that detail about exactly what happened to them down in the mine? Were there cameras? Did psychics reconstruct the details of the doomed expedition?"

"It's just basic storytelling, man," Travis said.

"So these people could be anywhere then. They could have moved to Alaska to work at a salmon packing plant. They could be in Georgia, selling peanut butter door to door," Justin said. He shifted in his chair to face Travis.

"You never believe in anything," Travis said. "You're so pessimistic."

"Me? You're convinced that every moment of every day has to be torture. You're convinced that you live in the shittiest place in the world, and you're never going to have the life you want. And you call me pessimistic?"

"I'm open to new experiences," Travis said. "But I'm not going to sugarcoat reality."

"It's so frustrating to be around such a negative attitude all the time," Justin said. "Maybe I will take a hit off of that bong." He leaned forward and Ryan pulled the bong back towards himself protectively.

"Wait," Ryan said. "First tell me about the peanut butter."

Both Travis and Justin laughed.

"There is no peanut butter, man," Justin said. "Never mind, I don't want to get that fucked up. Miguel, tell us more about your bullshit gold story."

Miguel shook his head. "It's not bullshit, man. I found out all about it. They're going to start mining on it pretty soon and then everyone is going to know. But if we could get in there before they start up, we could grab some of the easy stuff right off the walls and we would clean up."

"Old Hang was a gypsum mine," Justin said. "There's no gold in a gypsum mine."

Travis surprised Justin by agreeing with him. "He's right. Besides, why would they just walk away from gold in the walls? At the very least, high school kids would have snarfed that shit up years ago. Why would it still be there for the taking?"

"Two reasons," Miguel said. "Wait, is there peanut butter?"

Ryan looked up, hopeful.

"No," Justin and Travis said.

"Anyway," Miguel said. "You can't get to the spot easily. There's no lateral entrance for the shaft—you have to either climb up from the tailings, or rope down from the winze."

"Does he know what he's talking about?" Justin asked Travis. Travis shrugged.

"Second," Miguel started, "most people think that area is haunted and dangerous. Maybe that's because of that Clarence guy who died."

"That was a bullshit story," Justin said.

"Third," Miguel said, "it's not in the gypsum part of the mine. It's from where the mine shaft intersected with a natural limestone cave. In the limestone there was a vein of quartz. In the quartz, there was gold. The miners didn't trust the cave so they never went in there."

"So on the dozens of expeditions that have been in that mine over the years, how come nobody knows about this?" Justin asked. "And that was *three* reasons. You said *two*."

"You don't listen," Miguel said. "They *do* know about it. They're getting ready to start mining on it pretty soon. We have to get in there before they get all the permits and everything. Right now, it's government property. Every citizen has the right to go down there. Once they get all their permits, it will be illegal for anyone else to go in there and take gold. We're screwed once that happens."

"I don't think it works that way," Travis said.

Justin nodded. "You can't just take gold. And that place is condemned. It's trespassing to go in there."

"Oh yeah?" Miguel asked. Before anyone could answer, he lifted his butt off the couch and began digging his hand into his pocket. He fished out a plastic baggie and dropped it on the coffee table with a hand flourish. "Then what's that?"

Justin twisted his mouth into a scowl.

Travis reached forward and picked up the bag.

"Gross. It's all sweaty," Travis said.

"That's right," Miguel said. "The world is sweaty. It's a damn *sweatpocalypse* out there."

Travis lifted the bag and held it up to the overhead light.

"The moisture you feel on that bag is one-hundred percent Venezuelan ball sweat."

"Ugh," Travis said, dropping the bag back to the table. It thumped when it hit.

Justin leaned forward and picked up the bag by the corner. He teased apart the plastic zipper and shook the bag to rearrange the contents. Most of the rock was cloudy grey and white quartz, but he saw distinct threads of shiny gold. Justin pulled the biggest chunk from the bag. It was a golf ball of rock. He picked at the quartz and pulled off a flake to reveal a big deposit of gold.

"Hey," Miguel said.

Justin picked up Ryan's tweezers and used the point to dent

the metal.

"Where did you get this?"

"Do you listen to anything I say? It came from the mine. Technically, the cave attached to the mine, but close enough."

"Bullshit," Justin said.

Chapter Three — Class

ROGER SHIFTED HIS WEIGHT again. The plastic seat hurt his ass. He couldn't wait for the end of the lecture. His eyes returned to the chalkboard where the woman had written her name. "Dr. Deborah Grossman." The D in doctor was significantly darker and larger than the D of the professor's name. She clearly had feelings of inadequacy.

Roger glanced at his fellow classmates. He was one of only four students. The guy with the dark hair—was his name Aaron?—was probably another paid helper. Aaron looked just as bored as Roger felt. The other two were probably students, or interns, or whatever. What did they call them? Teaching assistants? Something like that.

The door groaned on its hinges and Dr. Deb came back in. She licked her fingers before handing out the copies of the instructions to the four of them.

"Sorry," she said. "The copier was broken and I had to go to the one upstairs. These are the procedures. Feel free to bring that copy with you on Sunday, but I want you to have those memorized. You'll be in dark, cramped places and your hands will be full. I want you to have a good sense of the procedures even when you're not looking at the paper."

The girl, Florida, was already hunched over her copy, running her finger down the sheet as she memorized it. Roger looked at his and squinted. The type was tiny. Half of the instructions were numbers for calibration. It would take him a week to memorize that, and he only had two days. He was going to have to fake it.

"I've showed you the Hoffman probe and the drop-stamp.

What haven't we gone over?"

The kid in the front shot up his hand. Roger couldn't remember the kid's name.

"Kevin?" Dr. Deb asked.

That was it—Kevin.

"Have you told us about sampling and containment procedures yet?" Kevin asked.

"No, but that's a good point. If you get a positive reading on any of your devices, you're going to stamp, log, and then call in. That's all you're going to do. I don't want any of you to try any of the sampling or containment operations. Are we clear about that?"

"Crystal," Roger said. Dr. Deb locked eyes with him. Roger blushed and looked down at his paper. He had no room for snark. This job didn't pay much, but he needed the money. His mouth had cost him enough paychecks and he was determined to not let it happen again.

"Good," Deb said. He could feel her eyes on him. He kept looking down at his paper. "I want to say one thing, and I want you to all take it to heart. You *will* witness something this Sunday that is outside the realm of your experience or understanding. Believe that. I don't want anyone surprised about what they encounter. *When* you encounter something, I want you to *stay put*. We're not here to be frightened or run away. If you have a problem with that, you can bow out now and I'll thank you and pay you for your time today. If you are serious about showing up on Sunday, please raise your hand now to indicate that I can count on you."

Roger looked up. Dr. Deb was staring right at him.

Kevin and Florida already had their hands up. Aaron frowned and raised his hand. Roger put his hand up slowly to join the others. These people were crazy, but he needed the money.

"Good," Dr. Deb said. "Florida, I want you to pair with Roger. Aaron, you're going to go with Kevin."

Kevin gave a little fist-pump and put his hand out to Aaron. Instead of shaking with him, Aaron just waved at the kid. Roger smiled at Florida, but she didn't even glance his direction.

"Okay," Dr. Deb said. "See you on Sunday." She gathered her bag and walked out.

Roger was still extracting himself from the chair while the others fled. He got to the doorway and saw the girl moving quickly down the hall towards the stairs.

"Excuse me!" Roger said. "Florida?"

She turned but didn't come back. Roger hurried after her. When he caught up with her, he was out of breath. "Hi," he said. He started to put out his hand but then retracted it. He didn't want to seem as needy as Kevin. "I'm terrible with numbers. I guess I have one of those learning things or whatever. Also, my eyesight is not great. I'll recopy these numbers to a bigger sheet unless you're already going to memorize them. I figure that if we're together, there's probably no need for me to get all worried about having all the numbers, you know?"

"We're supposed to double-check each other," she said, folding her arms.

"Yeah, I know. Trust me though, it's going to take forever if you want me to be worried about the numbers."

"We both have to know the calibrations. If you want to back out, I'm sure Dr. Grossman can find me another partner."

"No! No. That's okay. I'll manage it. I suppose I can copy them over to cards or something," he said. She had already turned to walk away. "Thanks, Georgia. See you on Sunday."

"It's Florida," she said over her shoulder.

"Okay, Virginia," he said to himself. The door to the stairwell closed behind her.

Chapter Four — Mission

"GO HOME," JUSTIN SAID, pointing emphatically. "Go on, get! We don't want you. Go home!"

Travis covered his mouth as he laughed.

"But I want to come with you guys," Ryan said.

The night had cooled off a little, but it was still too hot to be walking halfway across town. Justin's temper got worse with every new drop of sweat that formed on his forehead.

"You can come with us, but you have to keep up," Justin said.

"He's too high to keep up," Miguel said. "Give him a break."

"Do you believe in the gold?" Justin asked.

Miguel shrugged.

"No, seriously, do you believe in it or not?"

"Yeah," Miguel said.

"Then move faster. If we don't catch up with Joy, then we can't go find your gold."

"Technically, we can," Travis said. Justin turned to this new voice and raised his eyebrows. Travis buckled under scrutiny. "No —you're right. We need the equipment."

"Good. We all agree. Miguel, why don't you help Ryan keep up?"

"Yeah," Ryan said, inexplicably turning on Miguel. "That's true. Why don't you?" Ryan sounded upset at Miguel's shortcomings.

Miguel laughed until everyone joined him.

"Come on," Justin said. He took the lead walking down the dusty sidewalk. A wind was kicking up the sand. It wasn't enough breeze to cool anything down, but the sand gave the streetlights an orange glow. Justin imagined that hell would look like this at night. It would probably feel like this too.

At the next intersection, Travis tugged on his arm. Justin stopped.

"This way," Travis said.

"How come?"

Miguel and Ryan were following arm in arm. They caught up to the conversation.

Ryan, as befuddled as he was, came up with the explanation. "You can't just go *talk* to Joy. If you want to talk to Joy, you better have Kristin with you. And don't talk to Kristin without clearing it with Carlos first. Everyone knows that."

Justin nodded along. Ryan was right—everyone did know that. It was the damn heat that was making his brain malfunction. For the life of him, he couldn't understand how anyone could function in that heat.

"Got it," Justin said. Travis led the way. They went past the front of the store and down the side street to the alley. They walked right down the middle of the access road. Neighbors behind the grocery store would call the cops if they saw anyone slinking around the shadows. It had happened before.

When they got to the loading dock, Travis climbed up the bumper and banged on the metal door. It pushed open a second later. A pair of women came through and walked by Travis while pushing cigarettes into their mouths. He caught the door.

"¿Está Carlos?" Travis asked the women.

"Yeah," one woman said, lighting her cigarette. "Go on in. Nobody cares."

"Be right back," Travis said to the others.

Ryan wandered over to the women to talk to them. Travis slipped through the door and disappeared inside.

"This is convoluted," Miguel said to Justin.

"You have a better plan?" Justin asked.

"Can't we just go buy a bunch of flashlights and batteries?"

"With what? Have you got a bunch of money that I don't know about? We're going to need whatever we scrape up just to buy enough gas to fill up Jordan's truck."

"I didn't think of that. I guess I figured we could ride bikes out there, but it would be too far."

Justin nodded. "Yeah, and if we're going to be optimistic, you gotta figure we'll have some rocks to carry back, right?"

"We should get some backpacks or something too."

The door banged open. Travis came back out, followed by Carlos. He was slapping flour from his hands as he walked.

"What's up?" Carlos asked.

"We want to talk to Joy about that caving equipment," Justin said. "We figured we needed to talk to Kristin first, you know?"

"Yeah? What? You need me to talk to Kristin? Go talk to her yourself."

Justin looked to Travis. This wasn't going as he expected.

Travis took over. "You know where Kristin is?"

"Sure," Carlos said. "She's probably over at Downside like she is every Friday night. You know that."

Travis shrugged.

"What do you guys need caving stuff for? You know all she has is those crappy carbide lamps, right?"

"And helmets, and some ropes," Travis said.

Carlos nodded and tilted his head. "Why do you want that stuff?"

"We're going into Old Hang," Miguel said.

Carlos began to wipe his hands on his apron. He shook his head and frowned. "Is this that gold thing? Jordan was talking about that. Sounds like bullshit."

"That's what I said," Justin said. "But we're going anyway, just to check it out."

"What time you guys going over there? I've got another hour here and then I'm off until Sunday."

Justin, Travis, and Miguel exchanged glances. Nobody had an answer.

Miguel finally thought of a response. "We're going to try to borrow Jordan's truck. You going home after? We could meet you there."

"Cool," Carlos said. "I gotta get back." He turned and left them.

"You guys stay here and watch him," Justin said, pointing at Ryan. "Keep him out of trouble for ten minutes, okay?"

Travis nodded.

"Sure thing," Miguel said.

Justin pushed his way through the heavy door and stopped at a line that wound down the dark hall. For a second, he thought it was the line to get into the bar. It was all women—they were waiting for the ladies' room. He excused himself as he worked his way down the line.

At the archway, he blinked and scanned the crowd. Most of the people were either crowded at the bar or along the stage. The middle of the room only held scattered people. Justin realized that the person he was looking for was the woman on stage. She was singing some karaoke version of a song he vaguely recognized.

Returning to his search, Justin spotted Leslie, Kristin's roommate and partner in drinking. She was at the bar. Justin headed to her. He squeezed in next to her, between stools.

"Hey," Leslie said.

"How's it going?" Justin asked. He had to shout to be heard over Kristin's singing, amplified to drunk levels.

Leslie leaned in to yell to him. "Where's your cadre? Don't you boys usually move in packs?"

"We're on a mission. We want to borrow some of Joy's stuff. Her Dad's stuff, I guess."

"So why are you here?" She held up both her hands, nearly toppling her drink.

"Can't go to Joy's alone. Brit is an asshole."

"That's so true," Leslie said, slapping his arm. Some people had an inner beauty that shone through their exterior appearance. Leslie was the opposite. She was gorgeous, but had such a rotten disposition that she remained single. It didn't help that she always hung around Kristin, who was both pretty and nice. The contrast was drastic.

The bartender approached and claimed Justin's attention.

"What'll you have?"

"I'm good," Justin said.

"You have to order something."

"Water."

"Two drink minimum for dudes."

"I'm driving," Justin said. He held up his house key as a prop. The bartender shot him a disgusted look and disappeared.

"Hey!" Leslie yelled. "You were amazing!"

Justin turned around and smiled. Kristin approached, wiping imaginary sweat off her brow.

"Was it okay? You think?"

"Yeah," Leslie said. "You were great."

"Hey," Justin said, inserting himself into their conversation.

"Oh! Hey," Kristin said. She automatically looked past him to see who else was there. He might have been acting casual about it tonight, but everyone knew that Carlos was jealous. None of his friends approached Kristin without Carlos around. It was messed up, but she seemed to accept the arrangement.

"I left the guys outside so they wouldn't get in trouble in here. We're looking for your help to go talk to Joy."

"You mean those guys?" Kristin asked. She pointed over Justin's shoulder.

Down the bar, Justin spotted his friends. Ryan was waving his arms frantically and talking way too close to some guy who looked very annoyed. Miguel was leaning halfway over the bar, probably describing some infinitely complex cocktail to the patient bartender. Travis was engaged in a deep conversation with several women who were clumped around him.

"They look like they're doing fine," Kristin said.

Justin didn't even have time to comment before the situation exploded. The guy that Ryan was annoying suddenly took a swing at him. Meanwhile, Travis had said something to the women. They all began to push him towards the door.

"Shit," Justin said. He turned back to Kristin. "Can you come with us to Joy's house?"

She nodded and took one more sip of her drink.

Justin had to fight his way upstream against the crowd that

was forming. They seemed to want someone's blood and they were focused on Justin's friends.

"Wait up," Leslie said.

They were back on the street, walking the blocks between the bar and Joy's place.

She was trailing the group. There was one positive thing about Leslie tagging along—with her in the rear, Ryan didn't lag at all. Leslie had a crush on Ryan and he didn't want any part of it. With her behind the group, Ryan led the way.

"I should get her home," Kristin said. "Let's stop on the way."

Justin nodded.

"You know," Travis said. "We can go talk to Joy. You don't have to come along. Brit might not even be home, you know? Doesn't he usually work on his car on Friday night?"

"It's okay," Kristin said. "I don't mind. In fact, I was thinking about tagging along with you guys. I love exploring places, especially underground."

"No offense," Miguel said, "but you've been drinking. I don't think it would be the best idea for you to go stumbling around an old mine. No offense."

"What about him?" Kristin asked. She pointed to Ryan. He seemed okay at the moment, but it hadn't been long since he had been swatting at imaginary bats that he claimed were trying to lay eggs in his hair.

Justin nodded. He turned to Miguel. "She has a point. Maybe we should ditch Ryan at your place."

"No way," Miguel said. "We'd come back to find a Ryan-shaped spot on the floor once Vince was done with him."

"We know too many assholes," Justin said.

Kristin nodded.

Several paces ahead, Ryan turned around. "What's that?"

Kristin, Miguel, and Justin shared a laugh.

Travis had lagged behind. He caught up quickly when Leslie

started to advance on him. She had a sturdy, even pace that belied how drunk she was. It was dangerous to get too close to Leslie when she was drunk. She got grabby.

"Someday I'm going to buy a great big car and we're going to drive everywhere with the air conditioning on full-blast," Travis said.

"You might need to get a job first," Miguel said.

"Nope," Travis said. "I'm going to buy it with my cut of the gold."

"What gold?" Kristin asked.

"Don't worry about it," Justin said. "It's just a fantasy."

"You'll see," Miguel said.

Joy shut the door behind herself before she would even talk to them. Even with it closed, she would only whisper. "What's up?"

Kristin was their ambassador. "Can we borrow your father's equipment? The carbide lamps and helmets?"

Joy shrugged and considered the request. "What for?"

At the bottom of the stairs, Ryan shouted at a line of fire ants. Justin saw Joy glance down at him and pushed Travis towards the stairs. "Go shut him up," he whispered.

"Thanks," Joy said. "Brit has to work in the morning and he does *not* sleep well if there's any noise."

Kristin answered the question. "We're going to go exploring in Old Hang."

Joy smiled. "That's a fun place. Dad took me in there a few times. It's relatively safe. Go in the lowest entrance and *don't* climb anything. You have my permission if you agree to that, okay?"

Justin shrugged.

"Sure," Kristin said.

"Actually," Joy said, "it's a good time to go. You know they're going to collapse the entrances in a few weeks. There's a trail going in on Flattop, and they don't want kids to wander into the mine."

Justin hit Miguel's shoulder. "I told you they weren't going to mine that place again."

"No," Joy said. "They don't even mine gypsum that way anymore, I don't think. It's all open-pit mining now."

"He thought they were mining gold," Justin whispered, pointing his thumb at Miguel.

Joy laughed.

Miguel kept silent.

"How many of you are going?" Joy asked.

Justin counted. "Five, unless we can ditch Ryan."

Joy nodded. "Wait here."

She disappeared back through the door and shut it carefully behind herself. They waited for a few minutes on the landing of the apartment. Justin moved over to the railing and looked down at Travis. He and Ryan were squatting in the gravel yard, poking at something with a stick. The building had a row of bushes near the sidewalk. Their green looked extravagant compared to the dirt and rocks that decorated most of the nearby yards. He wondered how much water the building dedicated just to keeping those things alive. Barstow was deadly to outdoor plants. Only the heartiest survived.

The door whispered open again. Joy handed out a wooden crate full of helmets and supplies. She held up one finger and disappeared. When she came back, she handed out a second box. This one had bags and ropes. She handed the second box to Miguel and then shut the door behind herself. She slipped a key in the lock and set the bolt.

"I haven't been underground since Dad died. I'm coming too," Joy said.

Justin bit the side of his cheek and looked over to Miguel. "We're going to be pretty cramped in Jordan's truck as it is," he said.

"If the helmets and lamps are going, then I'm going," Joy said. "Besides, I've got this." She put her hand in her pocket and pulled out a set of keys. The logo on the keychain read, "Jeep."

Justin had seen the Jeep around. It had four doors and tons of seats. He looked at Miguel.

26

"Let's go," Miguel said.

Chapter Five — Excursion

FLORIDA GLANCED BACK OVER the seats. Everyone else on the bus was neatly paired with their partner. She drummed her fingers on the bar in front of her and let out a frustrated breath. When Dr. Grossman climbed the stairs and leaned in to address her, she knew what the doctor would say.

"You can come and wait at the entrance. You'll be able to monitor the radios from there and you'll be out of the sun," Dr. Grossman said.

"Can't I join one of the other teams?" Florida asked.

Dr. Grossman shook her head. "No, I'm sorry. We're doing pairs only. The partners are responsible for each other and we have to maintain that focus, given the nature of the mission."

Florida nodded. She understood, but it was rotten luck. No, it was worse that rotten luck, it was a rotten partner assignment. She had taken Dr. Grossman's class as an elective outside of her major, but now she needed the damn grade. Anything less than an eighty-six and her scholarship would go into review. Scholarships never survived review, and Grossman's students who didn't participate in field study never got higher than an eighty. Because Dr. Grossman had paired her with the one flake of the group, Florida was going to have to take out a loan to cover tuition. It was a rotten partner assignment.

The driver started the bus.

Dr. Grossman took her seat.

Florida gathered her things. She didn't have control over the partner assignments, but she certainly had control over her Sunday. If she couldn't participate in the fieldwork, then she wasn't going to waste her time spending all day at the entrance of a mine. Maybe she could spend the time thinking of a way to improve one of her other grades to compensate. It was a long shot, but that was better than no shot at all.

She stood up as the bus driver began to shut the door.

An arm shot through the gap, stopping the door from closing.

The driver opened it and the sweaty man stumbled up the steps.

Florida sat back down. Roger came to the edge of the seat and loomed over her.

"Can you scooch?"

Florida nodded and slid. She had already given up. His appearance wasn't a relief at all. It seemed more like an inconvenience.

The bus jerked forward and he flopped down. Roger smelled even worse than he looked.

"Sorry I'm late," Roger said across the aisle to Dr. Grossman. He turned to Florida. "Sorry."

She shrugged.

"Whoo! I'm glad I made it. Jesus, I'm thirsty. You didn't bring anything to drink, did you?"

She tilted her head. Of course she brought something to drink. They were all supposed to bring two bottles of water. They were going to be in the mine all day and they were responsible for their own drinks and lunch. Roger was empty-handed.

"Sorry. I don't have anything to spare," she said.

They bounced and jostled as the driver took the turn out onto the main road. From behind them, someone handed a bottle over the seat. Roger took it with a nod of thanks and stared at Florida as he took a sip. He handed the rest back to the owner. Florida blushed.

"Listen, Carolina, I think we got off on the wrong foot. Since we're going to be together all day, I think..."

"Florida," she said. "Say my name."

"Louisiana?"

She set her jaw. "You need the money, right? Am I right? Well I need the grade. But you get my name wrong one more time, and

I'm out. Guess what—if I refuse to be your partner, then you get to sit in the bus all day while the research continues without you. You sit on the bus, and Dr. Grossman isn't going to pay you one cent. So you say my name or you just wasted a Sunday." She narrowed her eyes and stared him down.

He folded his lips and looked at his hands. "Florida."

"That's right. Don't fuck it up."

He looked her in the eyes and seemed to study her. The scrutiny was hard to bear, but she didn't look away. He gave her a little nod.

"Nice to meet you, Florida," he said. He reached into his back pocket and pulled out the paper Dr. Grossman had given them. It had been folded and creased to oblivion. The numbers were barely readable. "I didn't have any luck memorizing these," he said. "I have what you might call a learning problem, especially with numbers."

She sighed and looked out the window. Civilization was already giving way to desert out there. They were leaving the oasis and traveling into the land of sand and heat.

"But I made these," Roger said. He reached in his pocket again and pulled out cards. The numbers were written large and the cards had been sealed with packing tape as a crude form of lamination. "I made you a set too, in case it's hard to read the paper in low light, you know?" He held out a set of cards.

She nodded and took them. The gesture seemed nice until she touched the cards and felt the clammy sweat on them. She did her best to hide her disgust. "Thank you."

She returned her attention to the window.

"Follow your flags. Report your positions. Execute with your instruments. Record your measurements. Any questions?"

Roger raised his hand. "Bathroom?"

Dr. Grossman rolled her eyes. "Again, leave nothing on the site. Come with me."

Roger left to follow Dr. Grossman. Florida wandered over to where a few of the pairs had clustered.

A skinny little guy had everyone's attention. "Of course, I'm the skeptic, but I will say that I read an account of a proximate-six inhabitation from last year's study."

"Six?" a young woman asked.

The skinny guy nodded.

"Austin was only a five-five. Are you sure it was a six?"

He nodded even more vigorously. "Yup. Pure six. They had everything—psychological alteration, physical evidention, a climbing Hoffman delta."

The others seemed shocked. The skinny guy kept nodding and smiling.

"Your numbers don't mean anything," a voice said from a little distance.

Florida turned and saw one of the other guys from her orientation group. It was Aaron. Next to him, his field partner Kevin was looking embarrassed to be with him.

"The numbers are what we're here for," the young woman said. The skinny guy smirked.

"I was in there last year. I saw the team that registered the six. Do you know where that team is now?"

"Where?" the skinny guy asked. He squared his shoulders to Aaron and practically dared him for the answer.

"The authorities don't know. Their parents don't know," Aaron said.

"Right," the skinny guy said.

"What was it like?" the young woman asked. "Did you experience anything?"

Aaron nodded slowly and looked directly at the young woman. "Yup," he said eventually.

One of the other people spoke up for the first time. "What do you mean that the numbers don't mean anything?"

Aaron looked off towards the entrance of the mine. It was just a black hole in the side of the hill. The edges were too straight and the corners too square for it to be natural. It was a man-made artifact of California's heritage.

"What's in there is a collector too, but it doesn't care anything about numbers," Aaron said.

Dr. Grossman came up over the hill, followed closely by Roger.

"Okay," she said, "let's collect our gear and head in. Nobody sets foot in there without their emergency pack and their helmet. Remember your radio protocol and stay safe. Any more questions?"

Florida glanced around the group. Several people looked preoccupied by concerns, but nobody asked any questions. Aaron was staring up at the sky, like he was trying to memorize the color.

"Let's go," Dr. Deb said.

Chapter Six — Entrance

TRAVIS WAS STUFFED INTO the back of the Jeep. He and Miguel shared the space with the boxes of equipment.

"Park behind those rocks," Justin said. "So nobody will see us."

Joy killed the engine and turned around. "That's not how this works," she said. "We park here, so if we have trouble, someone *will* see us."

"Oh," Justin said.

They all began to open the doors. The women had the best seats in the vehicle. Joy drove and Kristin rode in the passenger's seat. In the middle seats, Carlos, Justin, and Ryan were squished together. They spilled out to the sides as soon as the doors opened. It was harder for Travis and Miguel to exit. They had to wait for someone to open the rear hatch first.

"Who's staying with the vehicle?" Joy asked.

It was dark out. The only light was from the stars. It was mercifully cooler out in the desert and the sky was so clear that Travis thought he could almost read by the starlight.

"Nobody," Ryan said. "Why would we stay?"

"We only have six helmets," Joy said. "And you're drunk."

"I am not," Ryan said. He shook his head and dismissed the thought. "I'm high as fuck, but I am *not* drunk."

"That's true," Miguel said. "I can vouch for that."

"Regardless," Joy said. "You're not in any condition to go underground. You'll stay here with the Jeep while we go in."

Ryan folded his arms and widened his stance. For a second, he looked like he was gearing up to fight the injustice. Travis saw a smile play across Ryan's face and Ryan didn't end up objecting at all.

"The helmets are self-explanatory, but let me show you the headlamps. I'm going to do it in the dark, so you can all understand it's really pretty easy. You should be able to do it by feel."

She knelt. The process was simple. With pebbles of carbide in the chamber, the lamp would drip water on them to release acetylene gas. When the gas shot through the jet, the sparker would light it. Joy was rewarded with a bright yellow flame.

"We won't be in there long enough, but after the rocks run out you have to scrape out the paste into a plastic bag and pack it out. We don't leave anything in there. Everyone got it?" Joy asked.

The group answered back with a chorus of groaned yeses.

Quietly, someone said, "Yes, mom."

Everyone picked through the box to find helmets and lamps. They broke up into sets, filled lamps, and tested the fit of everything. Joy wore her helmet and her lamp blinded them as she moved around distributing flashlights and matches.

"Everyone gets three light sources. Three of us will have extra carbide and water, just in case. The others will have rope, just in case."

"Let me get the keys," Ryan said. "Just in case."

"No," Joy said. "I'm keeping the keys. Actually, I'll give the spare to Kristin. Here you go."

Travis couldn't figure out how to get the cap on his torch. Some water spilled into the carbide chamber while he was messing with it. The rocks hissed at him as he worked. Joy took it from him and put it together easily.

When Travis got his helmet on, he saw that the others were already halfway down the slope. He turned his head and his light swept over to Ryan, who put up his hand to block the light.

"You're going to stay here, right?" Travis asked.

"Yeah, yeah. Sure," Ryan said.

"Come on, man, don't fuck with us."

"Who said I would?"

"I can see it on your face. Listen—you don't have a light or a helmet or anything. Just stay here, okay?"

"You're right," Ryan said. He gave a sly smile and then pulled something from his pocket. He triggered a tiny flashlight and laughed.

"Stay here," Travis said again. "Stay."

He rushed to catch up with the others.

"Private Property. No Trespassing. Keep Out," Miguel read. "What do you suppose they mean?"

Justin smacked the sign with the skull and crossbones and made a kissing sound.

"Hey, guys," Kristin called. She was already down the opening tunnel. "Check these."

She pointed her lights at chains that hung from the ceiling supports. Miguel ran at one and wrapped himself around the chain. He swung back and forth and the beam above emitted a loud CRACK! Dust settled down as Miguel dropped to his feet and looked up at the shaking chain.

"Don't do that again," Carlos said.

"You shook the whole place," Justin said. He pointed deeper down the shaft. The next set of chains were swaying gently.

Travis looked back to the opening of the mine and wondered if there could be air blowing in to move the chains. He certainly didn't believe that Miguel had shook the whole mountain, and nothing else but wind would account for the swaying of the chains. Unless... "Hey—we don't get earthquakes here, do we?"

Miguel laughed at him.

Joy was moving away from the pack. "I think this room to our left was once a shelter of some kind. Yeah, there it is." She pointed towards the corner.

"What?" Justin asked. He moved to her side.

She walked across the space. The ceiling got noticeably lower towards the other side of the room. Travis would have to jump near the entrance, but on the far side he could reach up and brush the rock above. He didn't see what Joy was pointing at until he crossed all the way to the far corner, where she was. There was a passage that led behind the rocks. The way the walls blended together, it wasn't obvious at all.

Travis led the way.

He wound left and then right. The passage squeezed down to the size of a narrow hall, but on the other side, it opened back up again. It looked like a larger doorway had been filled with piled rocks to block it off.

Justin rushed by him to where there were olive-green cans stacked at the far end.

"Biscuits and water," Justin said.

Miguel caught up to him and picked up one of the cans. "I told you there was cool stuff in here."

"It ain't gold," Justin said.

Travis found a key and began to open one of the biscuit cans.

"Don't do that," Kristin said. "It's history."

"This is science, woman," Travis said. "I'm doing this in the name of science." He peeled back the green metal. It got harder as he went and his reward was small. The biscuit had shrunk away from the sides of the can. What was left was a dense, dark brick.

"Ugh," Travis said. He dropped the canned biscuit and the metal rang out against the rock floor. The sound echoed in the room.

"Hey," Joy said. "Try to not trash the place."

"Shhhh!" Kristin said. They all looked to her. Her face was lit up by five headlamps.

"What?" Joy asked.

"You didn't hear that?" Justin asked. He was standing closest to Kristin.

Travis shook his head.

"It sounded like heavy stone grinding on stone," Kristin said.

Miguel squirmed in his shoes. He started to shove his hands in his pockets. His eyebrows shot up with an idea. "Oh, shit! We're being sealed in." He was the first to the passage. Travis got back to the main room in time to see Miguel sprinting for the exit. The rest of the group caught up behind him.

"Don't run!" Joy said. "Everyone stay calm."

"Stay calm? What do you think is going to happen?" Justin asked. "This place shouldn't be any more dangerous than a parking lot, right?"

"There are tripping hazards," Joy said.

"Please," Justin said.

"Okay, fine," Joy said. "You guys want to run around like jackasses and get hurt? Fine. I'm not going to try to protect you from yourselves."

Miguel was standing near the skull and crossbones sign. "We're not sealed in."

"Really?" Travis asked. "You're sure?"

They collected into a rough circle near the entrance of the mine.

"Are you ready to admit that this was a joke?" Justin asked. "Are you ready to head out?"

"No," Miguel said. "We haven't even started yet." He shoved his hand down into his pocket. He pulled out a worn sheet of paper and unfolded it carefully. Once he had it out, he spun around until he oriented himself to the map. "We go this way for fifty paces. We should see a turn to the right and then we go another twenty. Then we start to look for a ladder."

"There's no ladder in there," Joy said.

"We'll see," Miguel said. With his map held out, Miguel led the way.

"See?"

Miguel pointed at the rough mine wall.

The first few footholds were simple iron spikes protruding from the wall. It wasn't until several feet above the ceiling of the shaft that there were actual rungs to the ladder. The metal was rusted and looked weak. Miguel put his map between his teeth, grabbed a spike at face level, and reached for the next one. His feet scrabbled against the wall until he found purchase. He climbed and accelerated when he got to the rungs.

Kristin went next. She was followed by Carlos. Justin waved for Joy to follow but she declined.

"I'll go last," she said.

Travis moved by both of them and made quick work of scaling the rungs. The walls closed in on him and he climbed through a fairly narrow shaft up to the next mine tunnel. When he got to the top, Miguel offered an arm and helped him reach the floor safely. He shone his light back down the shaft. It would be hairy getting down to that first rung.

This new shaft had a slope to it. Kristin and Carlos were already exploring the uphill side. Miguel left Justin to his own devices and turned his attention back to the map.

"It's this way," Travis said. He pointed downhill. The shaft took a bend. Travis's sense of direction said that the bend led deeper into the mountain.

"You're right. How did you know?"

Travis shrugged. "It makes sense. We're trying to go deeper, right? Also, there's this," he said, pointing at the wall. There was a big red arrow spray-painted on the wall.

Miguel laughed.

"Hey, guys, we're going this way," Miguel shouted.

Travis went first.

The tunnel was pretty uniform. The width and height of it didn't change much as they walked. The floor was smoother than the walls, which looked like they had been chipped away. Everything was a fairly uniform gray color, but now and then he saw streaks of white or red in the strata.

"What's gypsum used for?" Travis asked.

"I don't know," Miguel said. "If you see a branch up ahead, take a left."

Travis looked, but he didn't see anything except their straight tunnel. He didn't like looking in the distance. Their headlamps combined and split to produce a weird pulsing effect at the edge of his vision. It was like the tunnel was growing from the darkness—it didn't exist until they probed deeper. The illusion was unsettling.

When he looked again, he *did* see something. They were approaching a black section where his light didn't penetrate.

Travis slowed down and stopped. The black shape took up the entire width and height of their tunnel. He could see no detail, just a flat black wall.

Miguel ran into his back.

"Hey!" Miguel said. "Watch where you're going."

"You hit me."

"There's our turn," Miguel said. He pointed. Travis looked—the darkness was gone. Their lights showed a branch and a tunnel running off to the left. Carlos and Kristin passed them. Justin smacked the map out of Miguel's hand as he passed.

"Let's stop up ahead and take a break," Joy said. She took her pack from her shoulders as everyone drew to a stop. "Thirsty?" she asked. She pulled a bottle of wine from her pack.

"Hey," Justin said. "I'm finally starting to approve of your planning skills."

Joy gave him the finger.

Carlos pulled out a pocketknife and unfolded the corkscrew from the side. "I've never had a chance to use this before."

"Well you can put it away," Joy said. She unscrewed the top from the wine and took a sip. Carlos laughed and folded his tool away.

They sat in a rough circle and passed the wine. Travis put his back to the wall and kept an eye on the right branch of the tunnel. He couldn't shake the feeling that the darkness there was a little too dark. Maybe the wall he had seen had only been chased a few paces away.

"We're about halfway," Miguel said.

"You guys aren't serious about the idea that there's gold, are you?"

"Of course," Miguel said.

"He's crazy," Justin said. "Don't listen to him. I've never met anyone more willing to suspend logic for a good fairy tale."

"You'll see," Miguel said. "It won't take long, either." He stood up and peered down the tunnel. "There are rails up ahead. Like the kind you would run a cart on, you know? After that we only have a couple of turns and then you'll have to take back everything you said."

"Okay. I'm ready to prove you wrong," Justin said. He handed the wine back to Joy.

Travis reached for his bag. He was one of the carriers of the extra carbide and water. Carlos put his hand on the bag too.

"What are you doing?" Carlos asked.

"I thought we were ready to go," Travis said.

"Yeah, but that's the bag I'm carrying."

"No, man, I put it right here," Travis said as he looked around. He realized his mistake. He had put his bag down against the wall. Carlos was right. "Where's my bag?"

"It can't have gone far," Joy said. "Everyone come over this way. Let's get all the lights over here."

She waved them all back to the junction and had everyone set their bags in the center of the group. They counted several times, and each time they came up one short. They had started with three fuel carriers and three people carrying ropes and other gear. Now, they had only five bags between them no matter how many times they counted.

"Impossible," Joy said. "You must have left it back at the ladder or something. Did you take it off?"

"Never," Travis said.

"I saw him put it down," Kristin said.

"It didn't just walk off," Joy said.

"I'm sorry, Kristin, but you're probably mistaken. Travis, you must have dropped it along the way. We'll find it on our way out," Justin said.

"I'm pretty sure I had it," Travis said.

"He's right," Joy said. "We'll get it on the way out. The supplies are redundant anyway. I'm fine if we keep moving."

"I bet I know what happened," Travis said. He pointed his light back the way they had come.

"What?" Carlos asked.

"I'll tell you soon. Just everyone keep a close eye from here on out, okay?" Travis asked.

They all nodded.

Chapter Seven — Procedure

"I DON'T UNDERSTAND," ROGER said to Florida. "There has to be a more scientific way."

"Just pick," she said.

Until then, they had followed a more sensible process, in his opinion. When they got to a junction, they would take a tunnel that didn't have a flag. This junction had no flag. Florida said that it was up to them to choose.

"But wouldn't it make more sense to…"

She cut him off. "Just pick. Fine. I'll pick," she said.

She put her flag down in the center of the left passage and she stomped off into the dark. Roger stopped and considered the device. It had a weighted base so it would stay upright. Their color was bright green. With their trail of breadcrumbs, they were like Hansel and Gretel.

"If you see a gingerbread house down there, don't go in," Roger called.

"What?" she asked, turning around.

Roger caught up and they walked side by side. "Did you ever wonder about that Hansel and Gretel story?"

"What about it?"

"They wanted to get rid of the kids because there was a famine. But then the kids left a trail of breadcrumbs. Where did they get bread if there was a famine? And if you were starving, wouldn't you eat the bread instead of leaving it on the ground?"

"I thought they left a trail of pebbles," Florida said.

"No, it was bread because the birds ate it."

"I hate ginger," Florida said.

"Finally something we can agree on."

She put out a hand and stopped him.

"What? Did you hear something?" he asked.

"No," she said. "It's time to take a reading and leave a drop-stamp."

"Oh."

He pulled off his backpack. While Florida prepared the instrument, Roger got his cards ready.

"I'm seeing a seven point three, and a four," she said.

Roger did the conversion and set the dials on the drop-stamp. He used his tool to carve the holes in the wall of the shaft. After making sure everything lined up, he began to press the stamp into the wall.

"Wait," she said. "Let me check it too."

Roger nodded.

Florida made a small tweak to his settings and then waved him forward.

"Do you understand all this?" he asked.

"I understand the goal, but not necessarily all the theory behind it."

"Can you explain it to me again? Dr. Deb's lecture nearly put me to sleep."

"Sure," she said. "Some places have persistent mysterious creatures associated with them. You have the Loch Ness monster, Bigfoot, Chupacabra, and dozens of others you may have heard of. They call these 'cryptids,' which are rumored creatures that haven't been scientifically observed or documented. Some people believe that this mine is the home to one of those cryptids."

"But Dr. Deb seemed to suggest that this place had a ghost or something," Roger said.

"Yeah," Florida said, nodding. "That's one of the other explanations. Maybe the stories about this place were caused by some sort of paranormal entity. There's a third explanation that there is a psychoactive chemical in the air or maybe radiation. Maybe the stories come from an environmental source."

"So we're trying to figure out which one of those is true?"

"No," Florida said. "We're trying to document the experience without associating a specific cause. If we can make a database of observations, then theoretical causes can be mapped to that database and tested experimentally."

"Oh."

"Understand?"

"No."

Florida laughed. "It is pretty squirrelly, I admit. But that's why we're here. We're going to pin this down and make everything proper and scientific. We will shake all the magic out until we're left with cold, hard facts."

"And that's what these probes and drop-stamps are for?"

"Yeah, that's the part I'm not quite clear on. I know the steps we're supposed to follow, but I couldn't tell you what's going on inside those things."

"That all seems pretty reasonable," Roger said. "I don't know why she made it sound so ominous during the instruction, you know? It was almost like she was trying to scare people off."

"I'm sure Dr. Grossman felt some responsibility to make sure that everyone knew what they were getting into. It's not exactly the lowest-risk thing in the world."

"I don't know. The old mine seems to be in pretty good shape. We haven't seen any cave-ins, or supports that look like they'll give out any second."

"It's not that," Florida said. "Did you read the literature?"

"Pardon?"

"She gave us a series of investigative pieces to bring us up to speed. You read all that?"

"Was this on the first day? I missed the first day because I had another engagement."

"It was also mentioned on the waiver you signed."

"Let's say for argument's sake that I never read those kinds of things."

Florida sighed and turned the corners of her mouth down into a frown.

Her tone was flat and resigned. "So you're not aware of the deaths and disappearances?"

Roger furrowed his brow and shook his head slowly.

"You never heard any stories about Old Hang?"

"Old Hang? Isn't that a town or something? Didn't they used to hang people there? Or am I just confusing it because it has the word 'hang' in it?"

"You're confused. This place is responsible for dozens of disappearances and a ton of corpses. A lot of people come in and never come back out. I can't believe you're here without knowing any of this."

"If it's so damn scary, what are you doing here? What are any of these people doing here?"

"So far," Florida said, holding up her fingers and crossing them, "Dr. Grossman hasn't lost a single researcher. We've got good processes, radios, and plenty of light sources. If I make the call, someone follows our flags and help is here. I feel pretty confident that I'm safe."

"What do you expect to see?"

"Me? Nothing. I don't believe in any of that garbage. I think the fatalities here can be attributed to bad luck and superstition. It's like the opposite of the placebo effect. Convince people that they might die, and they're going to panic, do something stupid, and die."

"Huh," Roger said. He nodded. "I guess that makes sense."

Florida looked down at her watch. "We have four minutes to get to the next grid location. Let's step it up a bit."

"Sure," Roger said. When they arrived at a proper intersection, they had to choose a new direction and lay down one of their flags. Roger had some lingering questions about the procedure. For one, what if the mine had multiple ways to get to the same place? If they were choosing their path randomly, wouldn't there be a chance of them colliding with another team?

Second, why weren't they concerned with any of the vertical options? Every few minutes they came across something that looked like a tube leading either up or down from their tunnel. They must lead somewhere. The mine had different levels—maybe the tubes were shortcuts to different places.

He was thinking about this when they passed by one of the vertical tubes that led diagonally up from the corner of their tunnel. When he was directly in line with the tube, his light passed through it and showed him what was in the room above.

"Hey," he said. He tapped the back of his hand against Florida's shoulder. "Hey."

"What?"

"What is that?" He pointed up through the tube. She glanced and shrugged. "No, come right here. You have to see all the way." He motioned for her to take his place and then waited for her to find the right spot so she could see to the end of the tube.

"It looks like..." She squinted. "Is that?"

"A hangman's noose?"

"For future reference, you shouldn't impose your observation on me. Let me come up with my own."

"Sure, whatever, but do you see a hangman's noose up there?"

Florida's light bobbed as she nodded. "Give me a boost, would you?"

Roger climbed about a third of the way up before he looked down. The shaft was about twenty feet. If it had been truly vertical, they never would have made it up. If Florida hadn't been so impulsive—scrambling up the wall like a spider monkey while Roger stood there—he would have never tried the climb. But they were partners on this investigation and they were supposed to stay together.

His only foothold was an iron spike that protruded from the wall of the cylindrical shaft. He made it to the one that had broken off. As Florida climbed, one of the spikes had snapped and bounced down, almost hitting Roger in the face. She had caught a toe-hold. Roger used that same lip of rock to push himself up.

When he got to the top, he spread his arms across the floor of the upper tunnel and pushed. His arms were barely able to accomplish the task. He rolled to the floor, panting.

"How are we going to get back down?" he asked.

"I've got rope. Did you leave a flag?"

"Pardon?" He hadn't left one. It was one of his jobs, and he had spaced it. The climb had felt like a side-excursion, and it had never occurred to him to put down a marker for the turn.

"Let me have one," she said, holding out her hand.

"No, I'll go."

"We're not going anywhere." When Roger didn't move, she slipped around him and jerked open his pack. Florida took one of the flags out and straddled the hole. The shaft wasn't exactly vertical, but she played the bounce. She dropped the flag and it tumbled. The metal base rang as it hit the wall. Roger pulled himself over to the hole and arrived in time to see the flag land. It spun as it hit the floor below and rolled in tight circles. As it slowed to a stop, it tipped up and sat perfect. It even looked to point in the direction of the shaft.

"Well done," Roger said.

Florida wasn't even looking at the flag. She was examining the hangman's noose.

The tunnel they were in had a much higher ceiling, and more frequent supports to hold it up. Roger guessed it was at least twelve feet high. The hangman's noose hung from another vertical shaft that penetrated the center of the high ceiling. The rope hung in the dead center of that shaft. Florida moved underneath.

"I can't see where it's attached," she said. She added a flashlight to her headlamp. "It's too high up."

Roger stood. If he jumped, he figured he would just about be able to grab the loop. He didn't want to do that. Above the noose, the rope was light brown. But the working part of the noose was stained dark. Roger didn't want to touch whatever had left that stain.

"What's the point of a noose in a mine?" he asked.

"What's the point of this room at all?" she asked.

He spun and finally investigated the shape of the space. It didn't go far in either direction. The tunnel ended with rounded walls. The only ways in or out appeared to be the vertical shafts.

"Maybe they mined it and then shoved the ore down the hole?"

"With what equipment?" she asked.

"Maybe it used to be connected but cave-ins sealed it," he said. It was a stupid idea. The walls had clearly been carved from solid mountain. "Let's get back on track." Roger moved back to the hole in the floor that they'd come up through.

Florida had walked over to one of the walls. The rock changed color at eye-level. The lower half of the walls was the gray color they had grown accustomed to. The upper half was much whiter. Florida removed her drop-stamp tool and jammed it into the wall. The white rock crumbled away from the tool. Chunks of it fell away to the floor. Roger imagined a miniature avalanche, like she had removed the keystone and the walls would just crumble.

"It bet this is why the ceiling is so high," she said. She carved out another section of wall. A chunk the size of a football fell away. When it hit the floor it broke apart on its own. A wave of dust spread away from her feet.

"Hey, Alabama, back to work," Roger said.

"Huh? Yeah, of course. You know, we should record and stamp this room though. It's a dead end, but we should follow the process."

Roger thought about that for a second and then agreed. He pulled his pack to the side and started to get ready.

Florida walked away from the wall and more material tumbled after her. She didn't seem to notice, but Roger watched it carefully. He was convinced that the collapse would start a chain reaction until the whole room was falling in around them. It didn't. Only a few more chunks fell away.

But there was something there. Something had been exposed.

Roger stood slowly with his eyes locked on it. He was watching for movement. It was irrational, he knew, but this was an irrational place.

"What are you doing? Let's collect and stamp," Florida said. She finally keyed in on what he was looking at. They converged on the wall where she had started the cave-in.

It was lifeless, but still covered in fur. Roger moved around, considering the paw from different angles.

"It must be fossilized," Florida said. Her light moved back to the ceiling. "I bet this was a prehistoric lake bed or something."

Roger used his tool and touched the wall near the protruding paw. More of the crumbling stone fell away.

"I've never seen a fossil with fur," Florida said. "It must be incredibly well-preserved."

With the next piece to fall, something shiny caught Roger's light and reflected it back. He scraped at the metal with his tool.

Another bunch of rock tumbled away and broke at Roger's feet. The dog's head slumped out from its tomb. The tags on its collar clinked. Roger jumped back. Florida covered her mouth with her hand. They glanced at each other and converged back to the wall slowly.

Roger reached out with his tool and moved the tags.

The dog's cloudy, dead eyes stared at him.

"This rabies tag is from three years ago," he said.

Florida moved in close enough to confirm and then backed away again.

"I think those things are good for two years, so that means that this corpse is at most five years old."

"We mark this spot and then head back," Florida said. Roger looked at her, but she didn't meet his eyes. She ran her eyes all around the room. She eyed every inch of the wall with suspicion. "Dr. Grossman needs to know about this. Who knows what else is in these walls."

"Yeah," Roger said. "Even better—radio from here before we start back, yeah?"

Florida nodded. "Smart. And you know what? Fuck the procedure. She can do a drop-stamp herself when she gets here. You drop a flag and I'll call it in."

Roger nodded. He liked the way she thought. He flipped open his bag and pulled out one of their colored flags. He glanced around and then set it down near the hole. Florida put the radio to her mouth and began the call.

"Command, this is team J-6. Request an immediate rendezvous at our position. Over."

When she released the button, static erupted from the radio. "Command, do you read? Over."

More static.

Roger put up his hand. A gust of cool air wafted down from the hole in the ceiling. The hangman's noose began to sway in the breeze. Roger turned his nose upwards. He couldn't place the smell.

Florida's voice was lower when she called again. "Command, do you read? Over."

There was no reply.

"We've got too much rock between us and the closest repeater," Florida said. "Let's go back down and try from there."

Roger nodded. He didn't care about the radio anymore, but going back down seemed like a great idea. He motioned for Florida to go first. She lowered herself into the hole and found one of the spikes to support herself with. Roger wasn't sure what they were going to do at the bottom. They would probably have to drop to the tunnel floor. That was a problem for later. His first priority was getting away from that creepy, mummified dog and whatever else might be up here in the hangman's room.

As he lowered himself, his foot slipped off the spike. Roger barely caught himself on the lip. An image of tumbling down the shaft, plowing right through poor Florida, crashed through his mind. Roger paused to get ahold of himself.

His light flickered and went dead.

Roger blinked at the darkness. He couldn't believe the luck. He had spare batteries in his pack, and he'd been warned that the light would go out with little notice. That's why they carried so many backup light sources. But he couldn't fathom a worse time for his light to go out. He could only see by the residual light from Florida below.

Another breeze pushed past him from above. Roger looked up at the darkness and realized that the darkness wasn't complete. There was a yellow glow from the shaft in the ceiling. The hangman's noose cut a black figure against the glow.

Roger moved quickly. He found the next spike with his foot and dropped. The next spike was missing, but Roger didn't remember until he was already dropping. Only more incredible luck—good, this time—allowed him to catch himself on the next spike down. Dust and pebbles cascaded down on Florida.

"Hey," she said.

Roger stopped himself just before putting a foot down on her hand. "Keep going!" he whispered.

"The flag is gone," she said. He tried to see around her, but it was useless. The shaft wasn't big enough.

"Keep going," he said again. Mercifully, she started moving.

She dropped out of sight and barely made a sound when she hit. Roger wasn't nearly as graceful. He hung from the last spike and then fell. His body began to rotate in the air and he came down at an angle. After landing, he stumbled backwards into the wall.

Florida was scanning the floor with her light. Roger took off his helmet and began fumbling with the battery compartment. He flipped the batteries out and they sailed different directions. He didn't care. He found the replacements and nodded vigorously when the light came back on. He put his helmet back on and exhaled.

"Try the radio," he said.

"Who would take our flag?"

Roger glanced towards the shaft.

"Try the radio. Let's start heading back. You can call in while we walk."

"But where's our flag?"

"I'll drop another one," he said, struggling to keep his tone under control.

Florida nodded. She wandered as she pulled the device from her pack again.

Roger shifted carefully to the edge of the shaft and glanced up. The noose was still up there. He couldn't see the glow.

"Command, do you read? Over."

Roger put his hand over his lamp and waited for his eyes to adjust to the darkness. He didn't like the red light that filtered through his fingers. The noose was still up there, gently swaying, but now it was barely lit by light filtered through his blood. Florida turned back towards him and he couldn't see very far up the shaft at all.

"Command, this is team J-6. We'd like to request a rendezvous at our position. Over."

Roger moved away from the shaft. He pulled out a flag and dropped it near the wall. He thought about the breadcrumbs from Hansel and Gretel. He moved the flag farther away from the shaft. He didn't like the idea that something up there would have a trail to easily follow.

Florida laid her hand on his shoulder and he nearly screamed.

"I've got nothing," she said. "Not even static. I suppose that's good. We're getting signal at least, but they're not replying. Maybe they're having radio trouble."

Roger nodded.

"I'll try at the next stamp," she said.

She turned to move down the tunnel. Roger followed, but he didn't turn his back on the shaft. On the floor, the flag stood as a monument to their presence. The plastic flag fluttered in the breeze from the shaft.

Chapter Eight — Cave

THEY FELL INTO PAIRS as they walked. Justin and Miguel took the lead, arguing over the map. Kristin and Joy followed behind. In the back, Travis and Carlos pulled up the rear.

"How's the bakery?" Travis asked.

"It's fine," Carlos said. He ran his fingers along the wall. "I don't want to get stuck there too long though, you know? It's a placeholder job."

Travis nodded. "It's easier to find a job when you have a job, trust me."

"What do you keep looking at?" Carlos asked.

"Huh?"

Travis hadn't even realized he was doing it. He kept turning around to look where they'd been. He leaned in close to Carlos to answer in a whisper. "I think Ryan is following us. He took my bag. I bet he's going to try to scare us."

"If I know anything about Ryan, he's probably asleep in the back seat of the Jeep by now. That guy is such a lightweight. He does the same thing every weekend. He gets high and then passes out. I bet you just left your bag and then forgot it. You remember that time you gave away your harmonica and then you accused everyone of stealing it?"

"Yes," Travis said. His light shone down at his shuffling feet as he hung his head.

"You were mad for a week."

"I remember."

"When that girl came back into town and thanked you again, you should have seen the look on your face."

"I remember," Travis said.

Carlos laughed at him.

"You're probably right," Travis said. He turned around and walked backwards while he considered the passageway behind them one more time.

He plowed right into Joy's back.

Everyone was silent.

"What?" Travis asked.

"Shhh!" Justin said.

Miguel pointed towards the darkness where their lights failed to penetrate.

For a whole minute, nobody spoke. Travis stole several glances over his shoulder—now it was simply habit.

Justin threw up his hands. "It was right there. I guess it was a shadow."

"Hold on," Miguel said. "Everyone stay quiet." Miguel crouched down and inched forward. He held his hand out in front of him with his fingers curled down. "Come here!" he called. "Come on. It's okay." He continued to creep forward, keeping his body low.

Kristin cocked her head. "What was that sound?"

"Come on, pup. Don't be afraid."

Travis leaned forward and whispered to Justin. "Is there a dog down here?"

Justin didn't take his eyes off Miguel, but he whispered back. "I thought I saw one. It was probably just a shadow. Miguel might have seen it too."

Miguel stopped, turned his head to listen for a second, and then stood up. "Nothing." He turned back to join the group.

They formed a rough circle, facing each other. Their headlamps joined to create a safe-haven of light between them.

"Shouldn't we be to your special place by now?" Joy asked. "Are you sure you're reading that map right?"

"He's reading it right," Justin answered, "but I'm not sure we didn't miss something. The side-tunnel may be hard to spot."

"What side is it supposed to be on?" Joy asked.

"Izquierda," Miguel said.

"Left," Travis said.

"Thanks," Joy said.

"Is that it?" Kristin asked. She was pointing towards the darkness.

Justin followed the line of her finger and then began to walk into the darkness. Compared to the combined light of all their lamps, it looked like Justin was walking into a black abyss.

"I think she's right," Justin called.

Miguel began to follow.

"Wait!" Joy said. Miguel stopped and Justin turned back.

"What?"

"Where's your bag, Miguel? You were carrying ropes and tools. Where did you put your bag?"

He reached around to his own back, spinning as he felt for the missing pack.

Travis laughed a little at the sight. Miguel reminded him of a dog trying to chase its tail.

"Shut up," Miguel said. "Where is it? I had it a minute ago."

"You definitely had it when we all stood up. I counted. The only one missing was Travis's."

"Come on," Carlos said. "This is impossible. How do two bags disappear? What did you do with it?"

"Nothing!" Miguel said. "I swear. I've been walking ahead of you guys the whole time. Did you see me put it anywhere? Besides, I put my candy in that bag. The last thing I would do is lose it on purpose."

"Don't encourage him," Justin said. "He gets off on playing tricks. Let's keep going. When he doesn't get a response from us, he'll give up the game."

"It's not a game," Miguel said. He made a point of searching around the tunnel for his bag, but it would have been completely obvious if it had been anywhere near. The tunnel lacked any real hiding places.

Travis glanced back down the tunnel. If one of the lost bags hadn't been his own, he would have probably assumed it was one of Miguel's weird jokes. If Ryan was behind all this, he was operating at a completely new level. Ryan was generally too

57

clumsy to be very devious.

Joy had moved forward to join Justin.

"I've never seen this before," she said. "Incredible."

Based on Joy's surprise, Kristin and Carlos moved forward as well. Justin put his hand on Miguel's back. "Come on. We'll find your bag later." He led Miguel forward.

It was a cool optical illusion to watch Carlos disappear. One second, he was moving towards a crack in the wall. The next second, he had vanished. Shifting to the side, Travis understood. Part of the mine wall jutted out as the other part fell away. Seen from most angles, the walls overlapped and appeared to be continuous. But once his light hit it correctly, Travis saw the gap. Turning his body to the side, Travis was easily able to slip into the fissure.

The nature of the rock changed immediately. Instead of gray, chalky walls, the rock here was damp and red. The passage narrowed quickly. As Travis moved through it, he could feel the dampness of the rock. He put his hand down as he slipped around a bend and his fingers came away with red clay. The crack curved. Travis saw Miguel hunch over to match his body to the shape of the fissure. Travis did the same.

He glanced back towards the mine. The way their passageway narrowed, it almost looked like the rocks were squeezing together to crush them. Travis hurried to keep up with the others.

Miguel caught his arm.

"Watch yourself," Miguel said. He pointed down.

The crack in the rocks continued down. They were now traversing a ledge along the narrow passage. Below, the fissure continued. A misstep would mean falling into a tight squeeze. The danger only lasted a few yards. Travis saw where it opened back up and a hand reached out to pull him around the corner. They stood on a platform of red rock. The cavern opened up around them.

Travis turned his head, moving his light around quickly to take in the space.

"This room is bigger than my whole apartment," he said. He looked up to the ceiling where some of the sharp edges looked wet.

"It's cleaner, too," Justin said. That brought a laugh from the group. The walls played tricks with the sound of their laughter. The noise reverberated intensely for a second but dissipated rapidly. Travis thought it sounded like the cave was mocking them.

"So you've never been here before?" Kristin asked Joy.

"No," Joy said. She ran her hand along the jagged wall. "No, if my Dad had known about this cave, he would have been here every weekend. He wasn't that much into mines, but he loved caves. This would have been right up his alley."

Justin moved around the others so he could hover over Miguel's shoulder.

Miguel studied his map.

"We need to go..." Miguel spun and traced his finger on the paper. "That way. You should find another passage behind where that rock juts out."

Carlos moved in the direction that Miguel was pointing.

Justin started to follow. Travis didn't want to be at the back of the group anymore. He rushed to get around Kristin and Joy. He didn't make it far before his lamp began to spit and sputter. His headlamp dimmed before it went out.

"Hang on," Joy said. "You need more water. We'll probably all need water soon."

She reached up to take Travis's helmet, but he pulled back. Since his bag was gone, his helmet was his last possession. He already knew that without it he would feel naked and vulnerable. Still, he needed light. Travis took it off and handed it to her.

Joy dug in her bag and pulled out a bottle of water. She poured carefully, using his upside-down helmet to catch any spillage. When she had lit the flame again, she handed him back a recharged lamp. Travis felt better with it back on his head.

"Everybody want to hand me their lamps?" Joy asked.

From around the corner, they heard Carlos.

"¡Diablo!" he said.

Travis rushed to catch up. He came around the rock to find

Carlos crouching and Justin standing. Between them was a canvas bag.

"My bag!" Travis said.

Carlos teased up the flap with the end of his flashlight. He flipped it open.

"It's *a* bag, but not *your* bag," Carlos said.

Travis drew closer and looked as Carlos picked through the contents. He found matches, a lighter, some stubby candles, a flashlight, and a couple of paperback books. The covers of the books showed smoking guns, long legs, and fedoras. The bag was spotted with mildew.

"Someone else has trouble hanging onto gear," Justin said. Carlos stood up and Justin nudged the bag with his foot.

Joy appeared with her bottle of water. "Let me refill your lamps."

"We found this," Carlos said, pointing.

Miguel moved to the bag and began to paw through the contents.

"What's the date on those books?" Joy asked.

Miguel flipped through and called out years. "Seventy-six. Seventy-seven. Another seventy-seven." When he finished he looked at his fingers and wiped them on his shirt. "Everything in there is sticky."

"So we know it's no older than seventy-seven," Joy said. She shrugged. "I wish people wouldn't leave garbage in the cave."

"Give me the lighter," Travis said. "The matches, too. Can't hurt." He moved to the bag and picked out a couple of the longest candles as well. Travis stuffed things into his pockets as Joy filled the lamps of the rest of their group.

"We can do one more filling and then we have to turn back," she said. "We never use more than half of our budgeted water. The rest we save for an emergency."

"It's okay," Miguel said. "According to the map, we're almost there." He began to climb one of the rocks and headed towards an arched hole in the side wall.

"Where did he get that map?" Joy asked.

Travis turned back. "I'm not sure. I think he said it was from his uncle or his grandfather."

"I thought his whole family came here from Venezuela when he was a kid," Kristin said.

"I don't know. Maybe his uncle came earlier," Travis said.

Miguel and Justin were way off to the side. They were on a high ledge, a dozen yards to the right, working their way down the wall.

"Hey! Miguel!" Travis called. The way his voice echoed made him cringe. He resolved to keep his voice down.

Miguel didn't answer, he just waved dismissively and went back to his whispers with Justin. They were solving a problem and didn't want to be bothered.

"I think the way is over here," Carlos said. He had followed the rock around the next bend and come back with his arms folded. "I'll show you."

"I think we should all stay within sight of each other," Joy said. "The last thing we want to do is split up. It might not seem like a complicated cave, but you would be surprised at how different everything will look when we turn around and head back."

"This is the only way out," Carlos said. "I don't know what those guys think they are doing."

They all spun when Miguel whistled. The sharp noise ripped through the cave like an alarm. When he realized the source, Travis straightened back up.

"What?" Travis yelled.

"Come up here. We need help."

Carlos and Travis held out hands for Joy, but she pushed herself up to the ledge and moved right by them.

"My father always used to say, 'Take nothing but memories. Leave nothing but footprints.' I'm certain that rule includes physically moving one of the rocks," Joy said.

"Listen," Miguel said. "It's not like we'd be the first. You can see these scrapes over here. This rock was moved to this spot on purpose. It's on the map."

"Where did you get the map?" Joy asked.

"My *abuelito*," Miguel said.

"So your grandfather moved this rock?" Travis asked.

"No. He never came in here. He bargained it from a *Duende*." Miguel saw that they were confused. "You know, a *Duende*. What do you guys call it?"

"Call what?" Joy asked. She looked to Travis.

"Don't ask me. That's some Venezuelan shit," Travis said, shaking his head.

Miguel gestured. "You know—it's one of those little guys. It's like an elf at Christmas, but it's not. They don't work for Santa."

Carlos shook his head. "You've never been more foreign than you are right now."

Miguel laughed. "I don't know what to tell you. My *abuelito*— my grandfather—used to bargain sometimes with this little dwarf guy. The old people all thought he was mystical or something. He was probably just a dwarf. Anyway, that's where he got the map and the ore. It was probably a bunch of dwarfs in here who moved the rock. If they can do it, then so can we."

They all looked to Joy.

"There is precedent for moving rocks if it's to access a new area. I suppose that since we're not breaking anything, it might be okay."

Justin waved them over to the side of the rock. The thing was about waist-high on Travis. He crouched down to push on a lower part of the rock so others could push higher up.

"Let's get it rocking," Justin said. "No pun intended."

They grunted as they pushed. When the rock started to move, they fell into a rhythm. Travis could see that the rock hadn't just been shoved into position, the edges had been chinked with smaller rocks, and the resulting gaps had been filled with sand. Everything fell away as the rock really began to move.

"One more," Justin said, grunting. He was wrong, it took two more pushes.

A crack opened in the improvised mortar. Travis heard air

escape from the cave beyond. It seemed to exhale a giant sigh. For a second, it seemed like a yellow light was coming from behind the rock. Travis realized that it was just the glow of someone else's headlamp reflecting off the damp rocks.

When the rock finally went, it didn't stop. The edge they rolled it on was round, and the ledge sloped away. The rock kept moving and picked up speed.

They stood and watched it roll back to its flat side, but by then it was too late. The rock had already reached the edge of the ledge. It tumbled down to the path below, filling the cave with a terrible sound. The rock bounced and broke apart. The halves rolled opposite directions until they came to a stop.

"So much for footprints," Kristin said.

"Sorry, Dad," Joy said.

They turned their lights back to the hole that they had uncovered.

"What?" Miguel asked.

Travis was closest, kneeling where the rock had recently sat. He reached out to the place on the wall that the rock had uncovered.

"Don't touch it!" Justin yelled.

Travis looked back at him and rolled his eyes. "It's just chalk or something."

The rock had revealed a nearly round hole that was easily big enough to crawl through. At least it would have been, but the hole had almost been sealed from the other side. In contrast to the red rock, the circular hole was filled in with white powder, packed until it was rigid. Only through the very center could Travis peer through to the other side. The porthole was maybe the size of a grapefruit.

Before anyone else could object, Travis poked at the chalk accumulation, right near the center of the hole. It crumbled away easily from his finger.

He jerked his hand and hauled his finger back close to his body. He whipped around to the group and screamed. "It burns! My fucking finger is burning off! It's burning."

Joy fumbled for her bottle of water. She spun the cap off and rushed forward to pour it on Travis's hand. When she dropped to her knees next to him, Travis showed his hand and broke into a smile.

"Just kidding," he said.

"Jerk," Joy said. She splashed water at his face.

Travis laughed and wiped water from his brow. He frowned.

"Ow! Shit!" Travis ducked down and wiped furiously at his head with his hands. "Fuck, guys! What the fuck?"

"Very funny," Carlos said. "Quit screwing around."

"I'm serious," Travis said. He rose back up and Joy emitted a surprised shout. There was white smoke coming from Travis's forehead, just underneath the brow of his helmet.

"Shit," Joy said. She pulled a rag from her bag and lunged for Travis. He saw her coming and scrambled back.

"Get away from me what that shit. Damn it!" Travis flopped backwards and pulled himself away from her. He was flailing on the ground, kicking blindly to try to escape.

"Grab him before he falls," Joy shouted. "Hold him!"

Justin and Carlos rushed to obey. They pinned down Travis's arms, but he still kicked and thrashed. Kristin and Miguel moved to secure his legs. Joy went for his head.

"Hold still. Shit, this is pretty bad. Hold him still," Joy said. She dug in her bag and pulled out a different bottle. This one had a brown liquid. When she poured it on Travis's forehead, he screamed and bucked. The four of them barely managed to keep him down.

Joy blotted at his skin with her rag and moved his helmet to the side. Travis settled down and moaned.

"Are you okay? Does it still hurt?" Joy asked.

Kristin and Miguel let up their death-grip on his legs. Carlos and Justin hauled him up to a sitting position. When they let go, Travis took the rag from Joy and pressed it to his forehead.

"What was it?"

Joy glanced back at the hole and then took Travis's hand. She pointed her light at his fingers and then back up to his head. Travis squinted against the light.

"Let me see," Kristin said. "Carlos, you look."

"That's a chemical burn," Carlos said. Travis had a red spot on his forehead where the skin had been burned. The spot was about the size of a dime.

"Yeah," Joy said. "I think so too. I think that powder is like lye or something. I think it burned your face when it touched the water."

Travis coughed and then sneezed before he could speak again. "So why did you pour more water on then?"

"Oh," Joy said. She was still holding the bottle. She showed it to Travis. "It's soda. I figured the acid might neutralize."

"Maybe it just washed the powder away," Justin said. He took the bottle of soda from Joy and walked back towards the hole.

"How does it feel?" Kristin asked.

"It's okay now," Travis said. "It still hurts, but it's not terrible." He dabbed again with the rag.

"Didn't it hurt your finger too?" Kristin asked.

"No," Travis said, holding out his hand. "Why didn't it hurt my... Fuck!" He scooted forward on his butt.

"What?" Joy asked.

Travis looked down and smiled. "Nothing. I burned myself on the lamp." The headlamp on his helmet was still burning. Travis had grazed it. He picked up the helmet and set it gingerly down on his head, careful to wear it at an angle where it didn't get close to his forehead.

"We're going to have to be really careful," Justin said from over at the hole.

They looked over to him. He had used a chunk of rock to scrape away the compressed powder from the perimeter of the hole. There was a spot of it on the back of his hand. Justin wiped it carefully on his shirt.

"You've got to be kidding," Joy said. "I'm not going through there."

"Then this is where we split up," Miguel said. He hunched over and ducked through the hole.

Chapter Nine — Lost

"Do you see this?" she asked. Florida jabbed her finger at the wall.

"All I'm saying is that we can't be sure we took the right path."

Roger looked down each of the tunnels. They were at a four-way intersection of identical tunnels.

"Do you *see* this?"

"I mean, think about it," Roger said.

"Is there any chance you're going to answer me?" She thrust her finger at the wall again.

"Yes. Yes. I see it. Big deal. Why is that the point?"

"These holes were made by you with that tool. There used to be a drop-stamp here on the wall. That means that we came through here."

Roger tried to diffuse her frustration by staying slow and calm. "Hear me out, would you? Can I just finish a thought before you jump in? All I'm saying is this—when we came down the shaft, there was no flag to point us in the return direction. Because there was no flag, we could have gotten turned around and gone the wrong direction."

She was equally as slow, but her voice didn't sound calm. "If we had gone the wrong direction, then we wouldn't have found this spot where a drop-stamp used to be."

"Maybe those holes are from something else. Maybe a team from a previous year made them," he offered.

"This is the first year Dr. Grossman has used drop-stamps affixed to walls, and this rock oxidizes quickly. See this color difference when I chip away part of the wall?" she asked. She illustrated by jamming their tool into the side of the tunnel. "That color will change over time. From what Dr. Grossman said, it only takes a month for *this* color to fade to *that* color. And you would know this if you had paid even the slightest amount of attention."

Roger didn't reply right away. He wanted to master his anger first. "Please don't try to lay blame for us being lost at my feet. It wasn't my idea to climb up to see that noose."

"Stop changing the subject. We're talking about how to get unfucked and out of this mine."

"Easy," Roger said. "Clearly, we don't know which direction to go here. So we go back that way, try the other tunnel, and continue until we get to a junction. If there's no flag there either, then we know you were right. If there is a flag, then problem solved. Can we at least try that?"

"No," she said, shaking her head. "That's not procedure. The procedure says that if we get lost, we wait. We're supposed to camp out and simply wait. Radio checks every fifteen. We'll just relax here."

"Why didn't you say that before?" Roger asked. He unshouldered his pack and flopped it against the wall. Roger made his way carefully down to his butt. He was already starting to feel the exertion of the day down in his bones. He wasn't old, or particularly infirmed, but he wasn't accustomed to so much climbing and contorting.

Florida paced.

"That's how you relax?" Roger asked.

Florida mumbled something.

"Pardon?" Roger asked.

"I was just thinking out loud."

"Well think a tiny bit louder so we can both hear."

"I was thinking that they don't collect the stamps until the mission is complete. What if another team crossed trails with us and picked up our stamps? What if Dr. Grossman already crossed us off the attendance list?"

"That's crazy."

Florida gestured towards him. "I mean, *you* were late. Like *really* late. She might have already crossed us out on her sheet because the bus was about to pull out."

Roger sighed and let his head rest back against the rock. He tried to tune out her voice.

"We have a radio though. You would think that they would miss us because we didn't turn in our radio or our packs. It has to be too early for everyone to have left. I should have gotten a new battery for my watch. What was I thinking?"

"What indeed," Roger mumbled.

Roger looked down the tunnel, back towards the shaft to the hangman's room. He reached up and turned off his headlamp.

"Or maybe our drop-stamp and flag weren't picked up erroneously. What if someone did it on purpose? Maybe the point isn't about studying the mine at all. What if there is..."

"Do you see a glow down there?" he asked.

"What?"

Roger pointed, but she didn't see. She was looking the other direction and he wasn't wearing a headlamp.

"Look," he said. "Do you see a glow."

She turned and her light washed out the tunnel.

"I don't see anything."

"Of course you don't," he said. "Turn off your lamp."

"We're lost in a mine. I'm not turning off my lamp," she said.

"Then turn it away. Put your helmet on backwards. I don't care. Just tell me if you see a glow."

Florida didn't do it. Instead, he felt her light encircle him.

"What do you do for a living, Roger?"

"Pardon me?"

"Who do you work for?"

"At the moment, I work for Dr. Deb. Being lost in a mine is my sole source of income."

"Well, then what did you do before? How did you come to know about this experiment?" Florida asked.

"I answered an ad in the paper. Same as anyone else," Roger said.

"And what did they say was the purpose of the experiment?"

"What are you getting at, exactly? Aren't we both here doing the same work?" Roger asked.

"That's what I'm trying to figure out," she said.

Roger shook his head. "I don't think I'm following you."

Florida turned away and started pacing again. "This wouldn't be the first time. But what would they be trying to measure? Do they think I'll panic? Are they watching me right now? No. They can't be. This place is too big." Florida turned her light back to Roger. "But he's watching me."

"I get the sense that you're starting to go a little crazy," Roger said. He turned his light back on and stood up. "Here's what I'm going to do—fuck those flags. I'm just going to use my tool to carve arrows in the walls. Let's see someone move those."

He reached down for his bag.

"You're not leaving me," Florida said. "If anything, I'm leaving you. I'm going to decide which direction I'm going."

"What did you do with my bag?" Roger asked. Florida narrowed her eyes when he looked up at her.

"What are you doing?" she asked.

"Shut up for a minute," Roger said. He spun and pointed his light each direction. "This isn't funny anymore. I'm responsible for that bag. Dr. Deb made that abundantly clear. I can't afford to lose any pay to missing equipment. What did you do with it?"

When Roger approached Florida, she held out her own drop-stamp mounting tool like it was a weapon.

"I'm not doing this experiment anymore," Florida said. "Tell your boss that I drop out. If I don't get out of this damn mine in the next hour, I'm going to sue her and the university. She can count on it."

Florida picked one of the tunnels and ran.

Roger threw up his arms.

"Great."

Chapter Ten — Gold

SHE OBJECTED VEHEMENTLY, RIGHT until she ducked down and crawled through the hole. By the time Joy went through, she'd seen the mistakes of the others and she passed through without getting an atom of the caustic dust on herself. She stood up on the other side to see Carlos brushing some from Kristin's back.

"It's really not so bad," Travis said. "I was just freaked out."

Justin was holding his arm across his face, breathing in through his shirt sleeve.

"Which way?" Justin asked. His voice was muffled by fabric.

Miguel pointed.

Justin led the way, followed closely by Miguel with the map. The cave was different on this side of the hole. Instead of jagged edges and sharp corners, everything looked rounded. Sweeping curves defined the bowl-shaped room. There were no cracks to fall into. A big arch led to the next room. They walked through a dusting of fine sand.

"Hey," Kristin said. Her light was pointed to the wall on the right. "There's another one."

She was looking at another circle of white powder, compressed to the wall.

"It looks like a spider cocoon," Travis said.

"That's caterpillars," Carlos said. "Spiders have webs."

Travis climbed the sloped wall to get a closer look. "Haven't you seen when a spider will make a cocoon against the wall or something? It's the way some of them leave their eggs, I think."

"Gross," Kristin said. "Get away from it then."

"I think it's just another cave," Justin said. "Something about the air or whatever makes that powder collect at the exits."

"You think there's something wrong with the air?" Carlos asked.

Justin shrugged.

"People have been in here before," Miguel said. He pointed down at the sand in front of Justin. There were footprints leading off in the same direction they were walking. "Can't be too bad unless we find a bunch of skeletons, right?"

"Don't even say that," Kristin said.

"He's got a point," Justin said. When he started walking again, there was no hesitation from the others. They stayed clumped in a tight group and continued that way through the arch to the next room.

It was much like the first—a big round bubble in the rock.

"Hey!" Miguel said. He ducked around Justin and ran off to the side.

"Please be careful," Kristin said.

Travis looked back at Joy. She was taking everything in and not saying a word. When everyone else went after Miguel, Joy held her ground. It was a smart idea, but Travis couldn't help himself. He followed Carlos up the sloping rock.

They huddled around Miguel, who was tapping at the wall with a stray rock.

"Here," Justin said. He pulled something from his bag and handed it forward. "Use this."

Miguel glanced at the little hammer and then hit the wall again. His taps were focused on a quartz ribbon that ran through the wall. When he knocked off a piece they saw a brown vein through the white rock. Miguel increased his hammering. Little chips of quartz flew from the wall. Justin backed up and shielded his eyes from the debris.

"Here it is. Here it is!" Miguel said. He swung hard and flinched back when quartz flew. "I need a screwdriver or something. Anyone have something?"

"Here," Carlos said. He handed forward a knife.

Miguel wormed it into a crack.

"Hey, careful with my knife," Carlos said.

"I'll buy you a new one," Miguel said. He turned around with a triumphant grin. He held up a chunk of quartz lined with shiny gold highlights.

"Is it gold?" Carlos asked.

"What else would it be?" Miguel asked.

"I don't know. I'm not a geologist. How do we know for sure?"

"Just take it. We'll get it tested or something," Miguel said. He handed the rock to Carlos and turned back to his excavation.

As Miguel worked, Justin was scanning his light along the wall. Travis joined him.

"I don't see any other exposed quartz, do you?" Justin asked.

Travis's light waggled back and forth as he shook his head.

"It almost looks like the real source of that might be in another room or something."

"Or just underground," Travis said.

"Like maybe there's another passage behind that deposit of powder," he said. He pointed to a spot that was several paces to Miguel's left. Travis tried to imagine what Justin was envisioning. Did he expect that the line of quartz had to be exposed?

"Help me out, would you?" Justin asked. He was scanning the floor of the cave.

"What are you looking for?"

"Something to dig with."

Justin couldn't find a suitable rock. In this part of the cave, all the rocks were worn and rounded. Miguel was monopolizing Carlos's knife, so Justin had to settle for using the back of a flashlight. With his shirt pulled up over his mouth, he scraped at the wall of powder with the rounded edge of the flashlight's cylinder.

When his arms got tired, he handed-off the chore to Travis. They took turns, making very little progress before growing tired.

In Travis's hands, the flashlight bumped over something hard embedded in the powder.

"Is it a rock? We'll have to move more to the right maybe,"

Justin said.

Travis coughed and then pulled his shirt up over his mouth, imitating Justin. He bashed at the hard spot and more powder flaked away.

"Let me see some of that water," Travis said.

"Just a sec," Justin said. He had to go to Kristin to find someone with water. Travis kept working, exposing more of the hard place, until Justin returned. "Careful with it. It makes that stuff burn, right."

Travis got the mouth of the bottle very close to the hard spot. He poured a small amount of water over it to clean it off. He nodded and poured a little more. The water made the powder erode quickly. In the depression left in the powder wall, they could see the end of the impediment they had uncovered. It was spherical on the end of a shaft.

"What is it?" Justin asked.

Travis reached out and touched it with his fingernail, just to be sure.

"It's a leg bone. You know up near the top, where it goes into the hip?"

"Get out of here," Justin said.

Travis carefully looped his finger around the end of the bone and pulled. The powdery wall crumbled away as he liberated the bone. Flakes of compressed powder fell away. One section that fell revealed the gentle curve of several ribs. In another place, they saw the entombed tips of finger bones.

Justin backed up a step and nearly stumbled back down the sloping wall.

"What the fuck," Justin whispered.

"Didn't someone just say that we'd be okay unless we found a bunch of skeletons? I think we might not be okay," Travis said.

From back down the slope, Joy witnessed the discovery.

"Time to go," she announced.

Chapter Eleven — Clarity

ROGER BACKED UP UNTIL he was leaning against the wall. He listened to Florida's feet slapping down the tunnel. He reached up and turned off his light. In one direction, he could see her light getting more and more dim as she raced off in a panic. Down another passage, he saw the faint glow from the direction of the hangman's cave.

He didn't have a bag.

As her light dwindled, he reached up to turn his headlamp back on. His eyes raced back and forth as he tried to remember how long the battery in his headlamp was supposed to last. Normally, it wouldn't matter. They had packed plenty of spare batteries in the pack.

"Shit," he whispered. He started to run after Florida.

Roger stood at the intersection of tunnels and shut his light off. He had just seen her light a few seconds before. Now that he had to decide which way to go, her light was gone. Roger listened.

From one of the tunnels, he heard a drip of water fall into a pool. The sound echoed through the space and faded away. He heard a laugh and tilted his head to try to pin down the direction it had come from. It was impossible to tell. There was too much reverberation as the sound bounced.

"Shut up," he heard. Roger spun to his right in the dark. He heard some more conversation, but couldn't make out the words.

They were men's voices.

He took a step and then stopped. He could be heading towards one of the other teams. He didn't necessarily need to find Florida, he just needed to find *someone*. In fact, maybe it was best if he didn't find her. She had seemed a little reckless and unstable. Roger turned his light back on and continued down the passage.

He paused to listen after a few more steps. The voices were still there. There was a higher voice mixed in—maybe a woman. That meant more than two people. All the teams were pairs.

Roger picked up the pace. His light bounced as he jogged down the tunnel.

He came to another junction and paused. He cast his light down each choice, one at a time, and tried to catch his breath so he could hear.

He'd never thought much about mines before that day, but it didn't take a whole lot of reflection to realize that this mine didn't make much sense. It was a series of tunnels and shafts in a network through the mountain. Where was the actual *mine*? Why would someone make all those tunnels instead of just taking material away closer to the exit? It seemed less like a mine and more like the diggers had been looking for something that they couldn't find.

From the corner of his eye, Roger saw a spark of light. He turned and heard the woman's voice. She said something too quiet to hear and then, "Incredible!"

A man's voice answered her.

Roger ran towards the light.

As he sprinted down the tunnel, the light ahead turned, faded and then went out. Roger kept running until he reached the spot.

There was nothing.

The light had been there, accompanied by voices. Now, it was all gone.

"Hello!" he yelled. "Help!"

His voiced bounced back and sounded foreign. It sounded like someone was yelling back to him and mocking him.

"I'm lost!" he yelled. "Please help me!"

He waited. Nobody answered.

Chapter Twelve — Control

As FLORIDA RAN, HER thoughts settled down. She slipped into her breathing and let the world sort itself back into sense. Sometimes her brain felt like a cluttered room where she tossed all the information of her life. Running was the way she tidied everything up. Running was like housekeeping for her brain.

When she got to the intersection, she didn't ponder. She took a left. As long as she had a scheme and didn't miss any turns, she knew she couldn't get lost. She would always stick to the left wall. Either she would come back around to her starting position, or she would find her way out. Those were the only two eventualities she could imagine.

Until she saw the sun over her head, she wouldn't trust anyone. Strange things had happened—inexplicable things—and someone was to blame. Perhaps they were messing with her. Perhaps she was merely collateral damage to someone else's scheme. Maybe—it seemed unlikely—there was poison gas down here that was making her hallucinate. Whatever the truth was, she could sort it out when she was back under a blue sky.

Her tunnel took a right.

Florida followed it, pointing her finger at the left wall. The tunnel took a left. Florida jogged along, not even slowing when she saw the end of the tunnel up ahead. She ran a tight U and turned back the way she had come. It was no big deal. Florida ran faster to make up the time she'd wasted on that stretch.

Assuming that nothing sinister was going on in the mine, and assuming that the flag had been picked up by mistake and Dr. Grossman wasn't conducting some evil experiment, Florida wondered if she would get a decent grade for this lab.

Florida slowed and conducted a radio check.

She got back static.

She sped up again and saw the junction ahead. Florida veered to her right so she could keep her speed through the left turn.

"Shhh!" someone hissed.

Florida stopped. She held her breath and cursed the sound of her own heartbeat in her ears. Someone was mumbling in the dark, but she couldn't tell where it was coming from. She couldn't hold her breath any longer. When she let it out, the sound of released air filled the tunnel. Florida's head whipped around. She was convinced that the noise must be coming from somewhere else, but she was alone. By the time she caught her breath again, the mumbling had stopped.

She started jogging again. This time, she ran more cautiously and kept her ears trained for any noises.

Chapter Thirteen — Split

"I'M COMPLETELY SERIOUS," JOY said.

"Yes," Miguel said. "I am too, but could you just look at this?"

"I see it. Yes, it looks like gold—what's your point? We have to get out of here and notify the authorities that there are human remains in this cave. There's no debate."

"We're not arguing that," Justin said. "Of course that's what we'll do. All we're saying is that it looks like Miguel might have legitimately found gold over here."

Joy put her hands on her hips.

"She's right, guys," Travis said.

Justin shot him a look. "You of all people," Justin said. "You need money more than the rest of us put together. Why don't we take some time, carve out as much gold as we can carry, and then we'll go bring all the police in the world here?"

"I don't know why you're fighting me on this," Joy said. "That's a person. That person might have been murdered. What if it was someone you loved who was murdered and stashed here. There could be someone right now who is desperate to know what happened to their sister, or wife."

"You're absolutely right," Miguel said. "But what's a few hours going to do? Clearly they've been there a long time. If someone has been missing for years, maybe even decades, do you think that a few more hours is going to make a huge difference?"

"Yes. I do. And when the authorities come, they're going to see that you dug out that spot there. They're going to make you turn over the gold. Someone owns this mine."

"This isn't part of the mine," Justin said. "Look around. We're in a cave."

"It's not like someone doesn't own the mineral rights of this cave," Kristin said.

"But how are they going to know how much we took?" Miguel asked. "If we're careful and we hide the rocks that we chip away, how are they going to know anything."

"Guys," Carlos said, putting his hands out. "Why don't you all just shut the fuck up?" He waited until everyone was quiet. "Why do we have to make a decision at all? We split up—three go back and three dig. We split everything six ways."

Miguel raised his eyebrows and glanced around to see everyone's reaction.

"Sixty-forty," Justin said. "People who stay split sixty percent, and the people who leave split forty."

"What about Ryan?" Travis asked.

"Fuck Ryan," Carlos said.

"I think you guys are wildly overestimating how much money you're going to make off this gold," Joy said. "I don't even want a share. I'm leaving."

"Wait," Travis said. "We don't know how to refill the lamps."

"I know," Justin said.

"But what do we do with the stuff we scrape out?" Travis asked.

"I don't care," Joy said. "Good luck. We'll be back with the authorities soon. You probably don't want to be in here stealing when they get here." She turned and started to walk before she'd finished her declaration. Kristin tugged on Carlos's arm and they followed her towards the exit of the round room.

"It's not stealing," Miguel called after them.

"Are they going to be able to find their way out?" Kristin asked. She ducked through the hole rimmed with the caustic powder.

"It's pretty simple," Carlos said. "You just go through those two round rooms and then along the ledge, right?"

Joy didn't respond. She moved with confidence down the sloping rock. She glanced back to orient herself and then found the path they had taken along the ledge. When she saw the crack on their left, she knew they were on the right path. It was a little harder to navigate into the fissure from this direction. She'd seen this phenomenon before—something that seemed easy and natural from one direction could look harrowing on the return. In this case, it was the way she had to lean out over the crack to prop herself on the far wall in order to start down the ledge.

Once she had pushed off, it was okay.

"Oh shit!" she heard from behind.

She turned to see Carlos falling. He hadn't leaned out, opting to put all his weight on the ledge. The rock hadn't stood up to the pressure. A piece of the ledge crumbled under Carlos's feet and he had nearly slipped right down into the crack.

Joy put her hand on her chest and held her breath while Kristin hauled her boyfriend back up to safety. From her position, there was nothing she could do but watch. Fortunately, Kristin was strong and coordinated. She pulled Carlos up and they both advanced to safety.

"We should go back and warn them," Carlos said. "There's hardly anything to step on now."

Joy shook her head. "No. We keep moving."

"You can't be serious," Kristin said. "You can't be that mad. You can't be so mad that you'd let them risk their lives."

"They're risking their own lives," Joy said. "That was their decision. Besides, if that ledge is now a serious hazard, then we'd be risking ourselves to go warn them. If it's not a serious hazard, then they'll make it just fine. Either way, there's no sense in us trying to traverse it."

She turned and kept walking.

"What if they don't see it?" Kristin asked. "What if they stumble on it?"

"Then they're fools and they'll have to wait for us to get back with the authorities," Joy said. She turned sideways and hunched over to get through the fissure. It was tighter than she remembered, but still easily passable.

Joy could see where the crack led to the mine tunnel up ahead. She turned at the sound of grinding rock.

"What are you doing?" she asked.

She heard a muffled conversation and had to go back a few steps to hear what they were saying.

"His helmet is stuck," Kristin said.

She heard a grunt and the lights started moving again.

"Tight," Carlos said from behind Kristin.

Joy felt relief in her chest when she stepped through to the mine. With its hand-carved walls and regular floor, it was a more civilized place. Her father would have hated it. He was big on natural caves, and always talked about the caves he had grown up in back east.

Kristin pulled Carlos through.

"Why was it so much tighter?" Carlos asked. "Did we take a different route out than in?"

"No," Joy said. She shook her head. "Things just look different the opposite direction. There was a cave my father used to have trouble getting out of. He would go in just fine, but his shoulders would always get caught when he tried to come out. It's just different."

Kristin shrugged. "This way, right?" she asked, pointing.

"Yup," Joy said. She turned and strode up the tunnel. She didn't need Miguel's map—she kept a perfect picture of it in her head. This wasn't a skill she had ever needed to learn. It had always been a part of her. Joy could imagine a place and then spin it around in her head. She always knew just where to go.

"Hey," Carlos said. "When we bring the cops back here, we need to find that hole again. It's hard to see, you know?"

Joy stopped and turned around. "I'll be able to find it."

"Yeah, but why not leave something there. We could leave a piece of paper or something just to mark it."

"What was that sound?" Kristin asked.

Joy glanced at her, listened for a second, and then decided it was nothing.

She turned back to Carlos. "Yeah, okay. I've got a little hunk of rope." She dug in her bag and handed it to Carlos. "Put it on the floor, pointing towards the fissure."

He nodded and took the rope. Joy and Kristin watched as his light bobbed back down the tunnel.

"What did you hear?" Joy asked.

"Have you ever been in a plow truck?" Kristin asked.

"No. Why?"

"They make this noise when the plow hits pavement. It's disturbing at first, but after a while you start to like it. It sounded like that—metal on pavement."

"From where?" Joy asked.

"Hey, guys?" Carlos called.

They started to walk back towards his position.

"What is it?" Kristin asked.

"Wasn't it right here?" Carlos asked.

Joy ran her hand down the wall. Carlos was looking in the wrong spot. The fissure was farther down than where he was looking. Still, the walls were relatively uniform. It would be easy to misjudge the distance. And for something that they had all easily fit in, the fissure was strangely hard to spot from this direction. They might need to angle their lights differently. The thing was like a weird optical illusion.

Joy walked beyond Carlos and kept going. Her eyes might be fooled by the rock, but her hand would certainly feel the gap.

"You're too far," Kristin said. "Our footprints are here."

Joy turned. There were a bunch of marks on the floor, but she couldn't trust footprints on the mine floor. There wasn't enough dust to really make them distinct. Still, it did seem like she'd gone really far. Joy looked up and down the tunnel, trying to orient herself. She walked even farther down and then turned, carefully retracing her steps.

"Hey, Joy?" Kristin called.

Joy took her time returning. She examined every inch of the wall as she walked. When she got back to Kristin and Carlos, they waved her in close.

"Does it look like the mine is shorter in that direction?" Kristin asked, whispering and pointing with a short, jabbing motion.

Joy straightened up and furrowed her brow. "What are you talking about?"

"Point your light that way, and then down that way. Does it seem like your light goes the same distance both ways?" Kristin whispered. As she explained, Carlos nodded emphatically.

Joy slowly complied.

She turned back to Kristin, starting to get a little angry. "What are you talking about? Why aren't you focused on helping me find the fissure so we can mark it and go get help?"

Kristin tried to lean forward and Joy backed away. "It just seems weird. Why are the shadows so close?"

Joy grunted her frustration and stomped off. This time, she walked way up the tunnel and started a slow and careful scan. This whole thing was impossible. There was no way for the crack in the wall to disappear so thoroughly. All she could think is that she hadn't gone far enough.

Carlos and Kristin began to move towards her.

"Stop!" Joy shouted. "Right now, you two are the only fixed landmarks I have. Stay put."

They obliged. Kristin hugged her arms tight around herself. Carlos was whispering something to her. They were starting to lose their cool. Joy didn't want to be stuck shepherding two people who were starting to panic. She moved a little faster. Once she marked the fissure and got them moving again, they would be fine.

She walked until Carlos and Kristin were just a circle of light in the distance. She was deep into the area where Kristin had claimed the shadows were too close. Joy had seen it—the effect had been obvious—but it was nonsense. It must have just been a trick of the light or some change in the color of the walls. She was down here, where the shadow had seemed too deep, and there was nothing different about it.

She couldn't find the crack. She turned her light down into the shadows of the tunnel they hadn't explored yet. The darkness seemed very close. Her light didn't penetrate the way it should.

She would have blamed it on her lamp, but everything looked normal the other direction.

Joy began to doubt everything. Had they somehow gotten turned around? Was she looking on the wrong wall? She needed to reorient herself. She needed to anchor the map in her head.

Joy turned back towards Kristin and Carlos. They were just tiny points of light in the distance now. She realized how close to being alone she was. This was not good caving. She knew better than to wander off on her own. Her father had taught her better than that. Joy began to walk quickly back to her friends. She kept her panic in check and didn't allow herself to run.

She drew closer, but somehow the lights of Carlos and Kristin didn't get any brighter. It almost looked like the shadows were encroaching on the pair, muffling their lights.

Joy had a terrible thought. What if the shadows were actually descending on her? What if she was being swallowed by a fog of blackness.

Joy began to run.

In the distance, Kristin saw her and began to take steps towards her. She could almost see the inner debate going on in Kristin's head—she wanted to come to Joy, but Joy had ordered her to stay put.

Behind Kristin, Carlos turned away. Joy saw what he saw. His light didn't penetrate the darkness at all. Joy wanted to yell to him, but she didn't have the breath. She ran raster. Joy was only five paces away when Carlos reached a hand up to the darkness. His hand jerked back and he clamped it down on his own neck.

"Are you okay?" Kristin asked as Joy ran to her.

Joy dodged around Kristin and continued to Carlos. He was slumping to the ground.

"Carlos?" Kristin asked. "What happened?"

Joy looked down the tunnel. The darkness was receding.

Kristin caught Carlos's shoulders and held him up.

"Carlos? Carlos?" Kristin asked. She shook him gently from behind.

Joy put her back to the receding darkness and looked at Carlos's face.

His eyes slipped shut.

Chapter Fourteen — Mining

"HOLY SHIT!" MIGUEL SAID. "Look at this one!"

He cradled the piece of quartz in both hands and brought it back to Travis. They both shined their lights on it and stared as the gold vein sparkled.

"It's so beautiful," Travis said. He had never given gold a second thought before that day. But he had to admit it—there was inherent beauty in that metal. It softened the light and yet made it twinkle. It looked like the definition of wealth.

Travis stuffed it in the bag. They only had one bag between them, so Travis wasn't taking any chances. He had one strap tied to his wrist and his other arm looped through.

"Hey guys," Justin said. They both rushed over to him. He had found another streak of quartz to work behind a rock. Until that moment, he had nothing to report. "Guys?"

"What? We're right here," Miguel said.

"You're not going to believe this," Justin said. He turned his body so they could see. His light was focused on a giant hunk of gold. Travis reached forward to touch it. It was as big as his fist.

"You've got to be kidding," Miguel said. "How thick is it?"

"I don't know," Justin said. "Let's get it out of there. Quick."

The presence of the gold seemed to manufacture urgency. They still had the same amount of time until the others returned, but somehow the clock was moving faster now. They had to get this gold and hide it somewhere before the authorities showed up to take it away. Justin beat at the surrounding quartz with his rock. Chips flew every direction.

After a few seconds, Justin backed away.

"Someone take over. I've got something in my eye," he said. Justin scurried back and Miguel took up the rock. He took over the pounding at the same frantic pace.

Justin leaned back against the wall. "You remember when Dominic had that scheme about buying bicycles from the dump and then repainting them and fixing them up?"

"Yeah?" Travis asked.

"We all thought we were going to be rich. Do you remember that?"

"Yeah, until we found out that all those frames were junk. There's a reason they had been thrown away."

"Exactly," Justin said. "There's always that moment when everything falls through. Jordan going to Vegas and trying to count cards. He lost two-month's rent in one night. He kept figuring out what he was doing wrong and then he'd go back and lose even more. There's always that 'fuck you' that jumps up and knocks the beer out of your hand just when everything looks like it's going to work out."

"To be fair," Travis said, "those were shitty plans. Shitty plans fail. That's why they call them that."

"But this was a really shitty plan, too," Justin said.

Miguel paused for a second and turned around.

"No offense," Justin said, "but you have to admit. I mean, why was there a map that led precisely to where we would find gold? How come nobody ever came down here before? It's all a little hard to believe."

"You're just mad because you were wrong," Miguel said over his shoulder. His blows against the wall slowed down, but when Travis tried to take over, he waved him away.

"I get what you're saying," Travis said to Justin. "Maybe we just got lucky this time. Sometimes you just get lucky."

"This wasn't luck," Justin said. He pushed his helmet back and wiped his forehead. "We have a map. That's not luck. You got that map from your grandfather?"

"Yeah," Miguel said.

"And he got it from a dwarf?"

"A *Duende*," Miguel said. "He bartered for it."

"What did he trade, a monkey's paw?" Justin asked.

Travis laughed.

"I don't get it," Miguel said.

"Don't worry about it," Justin said.

"I think I've almost got it," Miguel said. He bashed the quartz with the rock. Travis went to look over his shoulder.

"I think we're going to have to find a way to melt this stuff down. Where do you sell gold?" Justin asked.

"What?" Travis asked.

With the sound of rock hitting crystal, Justin could barely hear himself talk. He waved at Travis to ignore him.

Justin wandered over to the powdery deposit on the wall that he had uncovered. While they worked on the gold, Travis had used the leg bone to uncover more of the skeleton. He was almost certain that it was human. The curve of the skull and the eye socket didn't look like any animal skull he'd ever seen. Of course he had only seen pictures of animal skeletons. He could be wrong. Regardless, Joy had been right to go after help.

The bones made his skin feel tight. He didn't want to be in their presence.

Justin swept his light around the room. There were other circles of powder packed into the walls. He wondered if they all contained bones. Once the idea entered his head, he had to investigate. One of the bones on the cave floor would be pretty good at scraping powder, but he didn't want to touch it. Instead, he found a flat rock that was the right shape. He walked to the next circle of white powder. He crouched in front of it and began at the center.

It didn't take long.

"Keep going!" Travis yelled. Justin glanced over his shoulder and saw Miguel's light bouncing as he wailed at the quartz.

Justin uncovered a hard lump in the powder. He scraped a circle around it and then dug into the powder. The thing in there wasn't white like the bones. This thing was gray and black. It had a sharp edge. It wasn't a bone. The edge was too straight.

Justin tried to worm his rock under the lip of the thing, but he didn't have enough exposed yet. He went back to work on the powder. He scraped a line into the surface of the powder and then worked at making it wider. With enough of it excavated, he saw a crack forming in the powder along the edge of the object. He tried prying again. This time, it popped out. The metal bounced on the rocks. Powder scattered.

Justin dried his hand on his shirt and then picked up the object between two fingers.

He walked it back to Miguel and Travis.

The bones could have been from any time. They could have been from before white people even settled the land. This piece of metal was made by a modern machine. Its presence in the cave made Justin uneasy.

They had switched positions. Travis was taking the last blows while Miguel cheered him on. Justin arrived to see the chunk of gold liberated from the quartz in the wall.

Miguel picked it up and turned it in the light from his headlamp. Travis worked on picking up the quarts fragments. They had dug a small hole in a patch of sand and they were hiding the quartz there. It wasn't a perfect plan, but they had felt the need to hide the evidence of their amateur mining.

"I found something," Justin said. They looked over to him. Justin held out the object, pinched between his fingers.

"Hey," Miguel said. He reached. His hand slowed as it got closer to the thing. "That's mine, I think."

He took it carefully from Justin's grip. Miguel used his fingernail to scrape a patch of powder from the side. In the metal handle of the knife, the initials, "M. P." were carved.

"Where did you get this?"

"It was embedded in that stuff. I found it over there," Justin said.

"That's impossible," Miguel said.

"I don't understand. What's the big deal?" Travis asked.

Miguel held up the knife. "This is *my* knife. It was in the bag that I lost."

"And it was buried in one of those powder deposits over there," Justin said.

"That can't be. Maybe it just looks like your knife," Travis said.

Miguel held it up in front of Travis's face. He pointed at the initials.

"There are a ton of people named Mike, and Matt, and Mark. Somebody else has the same initials as you. Big deal."

Miguel held out the knife for Travis to take. "Open it up. I put a dent in the blade when I was a kid. I accidentally shot it with a BB gun. Take a look."

"*You* look. I'm going to bury this quartz and then we can get out of here," Travis said. He scooped up some of the chips and began walking them towards their debris hole.

Miguel and Justin looked at each other.

"Let me see," Justin said. He took the knife from Miguel. His hands shook as he pulled the blade out and snapped it into place. He smiled and exhaled.

There was no dent.

"Turn it over," Miguel said.

Justin narrowed his eyes. He almost didn't want to know for sure. He flipped the blade and saw the circular indentation. It was the size of a BB.

"Yup," Miguel said. "That's it."

"We have to figure out what this means," Justin said.

Miguel nodded.

Travis returned. There were still scattered flakes of quartz on the cave floor. He scuffed these around with his foot to further obscure their digging.

"I think we're good," Travis said. He pulled the bag from his shoulders. He took the gold nugget from Miguel and dropped it in.

"There could be something in here with us," Justin said.

Travis shook his head. "Who cares? Forget about it. We're in the wind."

"No, man," Miguel said. "He's right. We have to figure out what this means. Something stole my bag, took the knife out, and packed it in one of those powder cocoons. That's some weird shit. What if the same thing did that to old boney over here?" He gestured towards the skeleton. "Then it could do that to one of us, right?"

"What's the difference?" Travis asked. "You could just freak out and it turns out that Ryan has been fucking with us all night. But what's the difference? Either way, we have to get out of here. You want to freak out and then what? You run into the dark and fall down a shaft?"

"Hey, man," Justin said. "Settle down, okay?"

"He's not wrong," Miguel said. He moved his light around the cave, chasing the darkness away with his headlamp. "Whatever is going on, I don't want to be around for it. We've got some gold. Let's get out and cash it in while we're young."

Justin moved his eyes between Travis and Miguel.

"Fine," Justin said.

"Careful," Miguel said. "You're going to get that stuff all over your neck."

Travis was trying to look behind himself while he crawled through the powder-encrusted hole. Justin had chipped away more of the powder before attempting the passage. Their hole had looked smaller when they found the exit.

"Someone is back there," Travis said. Miguel grabbed his arm and helped him the rest of the way through.

Justin was climbing down the slope to the path that led to the ledge.

"You guys need to keep up," Justin called.

"Stop running ahead," Travis yelled back. "This bag is heavy."

"Give it to me then," Justin said. "It's not that heavy."

Travis and Miguel scrambled down the slope. When they got to the bottom, their lights moved nervously up and down the long cave. The shadows were deep and they danced as the lights shifted around.

"Give me the bag," Justin said.

"I'm good," Travis said.

"Maybe we should add more water to our lamps. They seem like they're getting a little dim," Miguel said.

"Let's wait until we get back to the mine," Justin said.

Justin led the way. Their winding path reminded him of an old stream bed. It made sense, he supposed. The caves must have been formed by water erosion. The rocks swept through curves. He heard the sound of dripping water from off in the distance.

"You guys remember that earthquake a few years ago?" Miguel asked.

Justin whipped around and flashed his light across Miguel's face. "Shut up. There's not going to be an earthquake."

"No," Miguel said. "That's not what I was saying. I was just thinking that maybe the reason the miners never found that gold is because it wasn't there when the mine was open."

"These caves must be thousands of years old," Travis said.

"Right, but not that crack," Miguel said. "That crack that led from the mine to the caves could have opened up in that earthquake. Maybe the mine was close to the caves the whole time, but nobody knew. Then the earthquake comes and suddenly they're connected."

Justin shrugged. "It still doesn't explain why you have a map to gold that nobody took."

"We worked hard for that gold," Travis said. "Maybe they didn't know they had to look for quartz and then smash it out of the wall."

"First, *everyone* knows that. Second, Miguel had a piece of quartz with gold in it. Third, it was a map to gold. They knew gold was here but they didn't come get it? What sense does that make?"

"This is it," Miguel said.

"Are you sure?" Travis asked. He turned and looked back the way they had come. He made angles with his arms pointing at the far points of the cave.

"Look down," Miguel said.

Justin did. There was some sand scattered on the rocks. It was disturbed in a trail going to the right. The trail disappeared into a crack.

"Where's the ledge?" Justin asked.

Miguel moved around him. He approached carefully and dropped down to all fours as he got closer to the place where the floor fell away. Miguel hung his head over the edge and pointed his light into the crack. "There's a gap, but the ledge is there." He looked down again. "There's some rocks stuck down there. I think maybe part of the ledge broke off. Yeah, see here? There's a spot where the exposed rock looks fresh."

"Fresh?" Justin asked. "Rocks can look fresh?"

"Maybe we should set up a rope?" Miguel asked. "Help each other over."

"We don't have ropes," Travis said. "In the one pack we have left, all we have is carbide, water for the lamps, baggies, and a couple of flashlights."

"And gold," Justin said.

"Right," Travis said.

"Okay, so one of you guys hold my arm," Miguel said.

Justin came forward. He glanced at the ledge they were going to try to reach and then he found a place where he could grab the wall to anchor himself. He offered his other hand to Miguel. Using Justin's grip for safety, Miguel stretched his foot out as far as he could to step on the other side of the ledge. He was at the limits of his tendons and the fabric of his pants by the time he got his toe to the other side. With that foot secure, he braced himself on the opposite wall of the crack.

"Okay, let go," Miguel said.

"You sure?" Justin asked.

Miguel nodded. He pushed off with his trailing foot and pulled with his arms. Justin was certain that Miguel wasn't going to make it. His heart pounded until Miguel finally landed his second foot safely on the other side.

"You go next," Justin said to Travis.

"Fuck you," Travis said.

"I'm taller, and I can make it easier. You're going to need me to push you off from this side."

"Oh." Travis moved around Justin.

He tried to execute the same maneuver that Miguel had accomplished. It didn't work for him. Travis stretched his leg to its limit and Justin reached as far as he could to give him more slack.

"Just take my hand," Miguel said. "I can haul you up." He reached out from the other side. They brushed fingers a couple of times before they closed their grip. As soon as Travis tried to pull, Miguel realized that he was over balanced. He didn't have enough to pull on to get them both to safety.

"You're pulling me down," Miguel said between clenched teeth.

Travis relinquished his grip on the wall and dedicated both hands to holding onto Miguel.

Miguel grunted with the effort.

"I'll boost you," Justin said.

When Justin grabbed ahold of Travis's leg, Travis yelled, "Hey! Get off."

Justin shoved. With the extra momentum, Miguel was able to fall backwards, pulling Travis to the unbroken part of the ledge. Travis hauled Miguel back up to his feet.

"You stay there," Miguel said to Justin. "We'll go make sure help is coming. Maybe we can get some ropes from one of the other bags."

Justin shook his head. "No way. I'm going to jump."

"Don't jump," Travis said. "You'll just hit the corner. You don't have a straight shot."

"Then you guys can catch me," Justin said.

"No man," Miguel said. "Seriously. It's not worth it. Wait there, where you're safe."

"Safe? What makes you think I'm safe. I probably only have an hour of light left," Justin said. "If they've gone to get help, then you're not going to have any ropes until Joy gets back with the Jeep."

"She's smart," Travis said. "She probably left somebody behind with the gear in case we got out, you know?"

"I'm going to jump," Justin said.

"No!" Miguel said. "We're going. Don't jump. We won't catch you."

"You guys are assholes. At least give me a flashlight," Justin said. He waited and watched their lights turn towards each other. They whispered something between them before Travis turned so

Miguel could dig in the bag.

"Here," Miguel said. He tossed something and tracked it with his light. As the object came down, Miguel's light shone in Justin's eyes and he barely caught it. It was a candle.

"Heads up," Miguel said.

Justin looked up in time to see a small box of matches flipping through the air. He caught that with one hand.

"Thanks a lot," Justin said.

"The flashlight would probably only last an hour. A candle will go a lot longer," Miguel said. "Besides, we can't use a candle when we're walking, but you're staying in one place."

"Yeah," Justin said, frowning. "Thanks." He turned away from the crack and began to walk towards the middle of the cave.

Chapter Fifteen — Puzzle

ROGER LOOKED AT THE floor. He swept his light up to the wall and then across the ceiling. There was nothing to indicate anyone had been there. He had heard a woman's voice. Hell, he had heard a conversation and saw the lights. Then, nothing. Where could the people have gone?

It didn't make any sense.

Roger covered his mouth with his hand and spoke to himself as he thought.

"Hallucination. Dream. Ghosts," he mumbled. "Three possibilities. Four if I allow that someone could be fucking with me. But how?"

He pointed his light down the tunnel one way and then the other.

"Straight tunnels in a grid. If it were a mine, wouldn't they follow the ore? Wouldn't there be big sections carved away to dig up the good stuff? What were they doing here?"

He walked a few paces.

"Does it matter? I have to get out. I've got nothing."

He patted his pockets. That assessment wasn't exactly true. He began to pull things out. He had the cards he had made for the numbers. He had the original sheet of paper from Dr. Deb. He also had some matches, his house key, and his wallet. That had been a debate with himself at home—should he bring his wallet to a mine? Since he didn't have anything of real value in it, he had decided on yes.

At the moment, the cards and the paper seemed most useful. They were white and very visible against the rocks, and they were disposable.

He began to walk back towards the last intersection he had found.

Roger looked at his cards for a moment while he devised a plan. He would mark where he had come from with a tiny corner of paper. He would place it on the right wall, one foot in from the intersection. He nodded and considered the idea in reverse. To track backwards, he would simply examine the right wall of every option and then take the tunnel with the paper. It might not help him find his way out, but it would stop him from walking in circles.

First, he needed a starting point. While he thought, he peeled the tape from a card.

Roger considered the problem even longer. He thought about when he and Florida had left the hangman's room. He thought about when she'd run away and how he had chased her. After replaying it in his head several times, he thought he had a pretty good grip on how it had played out.

"She ran down that one tunnel, took a left, got to the next intersection and I lost her," he mumbled. "Then I heard the voices and saw the light. I went right and came down here."

He marked the corner of the tunnel and tried to backtrack his route.

It looked familiar, but then again, all the tunnels looked the same.

At the next intersection, he marked it and continued on.

Roger's eyes reported nothing, but the hair on the back of his neck made him pause. Against his better judgement, he reached up and shut off his headlamp. Roger blinked at the darkness and waited for his eyes to adjust. He gave up. There was nothing. He fumbled for the switch to turn his light back on. Just before his finger found the switch again, he stopped.

The glow was there. If he looked straight forward, he didn't see it. But if he turned his head slightly to the side, his peripheral vision picked up the yellow light. Roger crept forward in the dark towards the shaft. He stopped a few feet away, when the glow was obvious. He had found the shaft to the hangman's room.

He didn't want to turn on his light. He didn't want anything to draw more attention to himself.

Roger backed away. He traced his finger down the wall of the tunnel and stared at the yellow glow.

He stopped.

The light was changing. He blinked again.

It almost looked like a black smoke was coming down from the shaft, obscuring the light. His brain tried to make sense of what he was seeing. It tried to form the dark mass into the shape of a person, or a bat, or anything. If it was smoke, he couldn't smell it.

Roger backed up more.

After a few more paces, the smoke was blotting out the yellow light.

Roger's hand found the intersection. It was already marked, but he didn't want to take the turn in the dark. That was a sure way to get lost.

Roger took a breath in slowly and turned on his light.

The tunnel looked perfectly normal in the light from his headlamp. He was too far back to see the hole in the ceiling of the tunnel, but...

"That's perfectly normal, right?" he asked himself. A chill ran down his back. He glanced at his scrap of paper—yes, he had marked this tunnel. This tunnel was special though. It was the tunnel with the hangman's room. He tore another dot of paper and set it next to the first. The hangman's tunnel was double-marked. He would know it if he ever came back this direction. He was beginning to believe that coming back this direction was a very bad idea.

His light swung back upwards with his attention and he saw down the tunnel again. Something had happened. Roger was paralyzed at the sight. The tunnel was easily half as deep as it had been a second before. Either that, or his light was now refusing to penetrate the depths. Whatever the reason, Roger didn't want to stick around to see if the phenomenon would progress.

He oriented himself and turned. He walked quickly backwards, keeping his light focused on the last intersection. When he got to the next break in the wall, he found his dot and verified that this tunnel was marked as well. He saw the flaw in his plan. He could easily tell if he'd been in a tunnel, but he didn't know which was the next tunnel to explore.

"Fuck it," he said.

He had a pretty good idea of where he'd left off. He went straight across and turned his back so he could walk forward. It took all his willpower to not look over his shoulder. Roger broke into a jog. It didn't last long. He didn't have the stamina to keep it up.

Another intersection and he dropped another of his breadcrumbs.

"How did Hansel and Gretel get to the gingerbread house?" Roger whispered to himself. "Didn't some bird lead them there? Wait." He stopped. "Yeah, a bird. And there was a bird that helped them once they escaped, too. And birds ate the breadcrumbs. That story is lousy with birds."

He walked on.

A sound, like a distant release of air, stopped Roger in his tracks. He spun slowly, fearing what he might find in the tunnel behind him. It was just a normal tunnel. The rock walls looked the same as every other rock wall he'd seen. Still, there was something back there in the darkness. Even if he couldn't see it, he could feel the presence. Roger tried to shake it out of his head. He tried to not think about the mountain of dirt and rocks above his head, keeping him from seeing daylight. There was an exit here somewhere, and he was going to find it.

He was Hansel. Gretel had run away and he hadn't met the witch yet, but he was going to shove her in the oven and get away. That was the full extent of his plan.

Roger came to the next intersection. He left behind a breadcrumb and decided to continue straight. Eventually, if he kept heading one consistent direction, he would have to find *something*. That was the plan, at least.

There could be worse things. As far as he knew, he was still getting paid to walk around underground. For a second, he imagined himself stumbling around the tunnels in complete darkness. That might happen when the batteries in his light wore out. He had matches, but those would make a lousy light source.

The cave was too quiet. The sound of his feet shuffling across the rocks was a lonely sound. Roger started talking to himself again just so he wouldn't have to listen to his own feet.

"Hansel and Gretel survived because they were able to predict intentions. They knew their parents were going to abandon them in the woods, so they left a trail to get home." Roger ticked off the things he knew on his fingers. "They knew the witch was fattening them up, so Hansel let her feel a bone instead of his finger. Gretel predicted that the witch was going to push her in the oven, so she plays dumb until the witch checks it for herself. So all I need to do is perfectly predict the future so I can outsmart my captor."

Roger smiled to himself as he walked.

He glanced up at the ceiling. "My captor is a mountain. All I have to do is figure out what it wants."

Roger shot another look behind himself.

"What do you want, mountain? It's going to take some work to break my spirit, if that's what you're after. I've been through a lot."

It was an exaggeration. Roger knew people who had been through a lot worse than he had. Then again, he'd certainly met many people who were way more fortunate. Sometimes Roger thought that empathy was his greatest attribute. Other times he figured that it was the one thing holding him back. He would never force his way to the front of a line, or even really stick up for himself. There was always someone more deserving.

After all, he had a room with a bed. It didn't have air conditioning, but it had hot and cold water. In the winter he got enough heat from his neighbors to keep from freezing. It was a decent existence compared to Sioux Falls.

"And if you believe my parents," he mumbled, "Sioux Falls was Utopia compared to Russia. I'm not sure what's creepier—the silence, or me talking to myself."

Roger stopped again. His light picked up something in the distance on the floor of the mine. A deep, primal instinct told him it was a snake.

He spoke to himself as he crept forward.

"There's a part of my brain wired to recognize and react to that type of shape," he whispered. "Some survival mechanism from when people were little more than clever monkeys with a capacity for learning."

The stripes on the thing made Roger search his memory. Which colors was he supposed to be afraid of?

With one more step he relaxed and picked up speed.

He put on a British accent to narrate his approach. "It's not a deadly cave snake at all," he said. "It's merely a simple climbing rope."

Roger knelt in front of the rope and let his light stray down the length. It disappeared around a corner and into the darkness.

His accent drifted from proper British announcer to cockney, or at least his version of the accent copied from movies. "I suppose that might come in 'andy, that might." He reached for the rope. Roger jerked back from the rope when his fingers touched it. He got a small shock from the rope, like touching the toaster after scuffing across the carpet.

"Hmmm," Roger said. The next time he touched it he got nothing. He shrugged and picked up the rope. He stood, holding the rope like it might be attached to a bomb. As he walked, he coiled it. When he got to the intersection, he put down the coil so he could mark the corner. Roger tore a scrap from a card and moved to set it down on the right side of the tunnel. He froze.

There was already a scrap there.

Roger dropped into a crouch. He whipped his head around, sending his light down each tunnel.

He still had his cockney accent. "Somebody is fucking with us, they are."

He picked up the scrap. It was one of his. He saw a portion of a word written on the back. The scrap was a piece of one of the cards he had written as a cheat sheet for Dr. Deb's precious procedures. Roger set it back down and put his second scrap next to the first.

He turned his attention back to the rope. He half expected it to not be there when he looked again. It was there.

"So where did you come from?" he whispered.

The rope didn't answer.

"I guess we'll just have to see where you go."

Roger turned the corner and resumed coiling.

"Mysterious rope, lying in a mine, in a tunnel where I've already been." As he walked and coiled, he tried to imagine how it was possible that the tunnel was already marked. He could only come up with two possibilities. Either someone was messing with him, or the tunnels were curved enough that he had made a loop.

Neither option was very encouraging. If someone was messing with him, then they could be watching him right now. If the tunnels were curved, then he could loop forever.

Roger gave the rope a little tug. He wanted to get a sense of how long it was. It came freely. Roger started to reel it in faster. Something snagged and then popped free. Roger stopped and set it down when he saw the stains coming towards him on the rope. He stepped to the side and walked next to the rope, shining his light down the length.

The stains appeared closer together. Soon, the rope looked like it had been soaked in some dark fluid.

"Who am I kidding?" he whispered. There was no mystery to this—the dark fluid was blood. In the distance, he saw where the rope ended. He saw something tangled in the cord.

Roger backed away even more as he walked down the tunnel. The rope was stretched along one wall and he was near the other. Roger felt his neck tense up as he kept his light locked on the end of the rope. The thing wrapped up in the rope didn't make sense. It looked like a hand was coming right out of the floor.

Roger drew within a few feet of the thing before he really saw it for what it was. There were two fingers wrapped around the rope, gripping it. The fingers led down to the top part of a hand, but that was it. Beyond the first knuckle, there was no more hand. Roger scuffed the rope with his foot and the fingers tumbled over. Roger was looking at torn muscle and the ends of broken bones. He felt his stomach make a slow turn in his guts. Roger bent with an abdominal cramp, but he didn't take his eyes off those fingers.

He took in every detail. He saw black hair on the digits. The trimmed fingernails had a little dirt under them. The finger pads weren't calloused at all—they were either young, or hadn't been exposed to hard work. His body shook with revulsion, but he had to know. He had to be sure these were real fingers and not some trick played on him by the college students on this research trip.

Roger reached down with an extended finger.

He clenched his teeth and touched the flesh. The fingers were real.

Roger exhaled slowly. The stakes on this mystery had been raised.

Chapter Sixteen — Rescue

"ARE YOU SURE THIS is right?" Kristin asked.

"No," Joy said. "I'm not sure at all. It looks okay though, don't you think?"

Joy looked up at the big red arrow painted on the wall. At least she was certain that they had the right shaft. The big arrow was good confirmation.

They regarded Carlos. Kristin pulled him forward so she could check the way the ropes looped under his arms. It had been hard enough carrying him—nearly impossible. Kristin had taken his legs and Joy had lifted under his armpits. They had moved him a dozen shuffled paces at a time. They stopped every time they were out of breath. Finally, they had found the vertical shaft where they had climbed up into this section of the mine.

Now they just had to get Carlos down.

"There has to be another way," Kristin said. "You go out for help and I'll wait here with him."

Joy shook her head. "No. Nobody goes alone. That's rule number one. We can't leave him here alone and neither of us is going to try to get out alone. It's a recipe for disaster."

"We're already in a disaster," Kristin said. "I don't know why we can't wake him up, but it's not good."

"Agreed," Joy said. "But we can't compound the disaster. We get him down this shaft and then we only need to carry him to the exit. We've already proven we can do that."

Kristin put her head to Carlos's chest to hear his heart and breathing. She looked back up to Joy. "Okay. What's your plan?"

"We both stay up here. We lower him down until his feet touch down. Then you hold him here while I climb down and make sure he makes it to the floor in one piece. You climb down and we're out," Joy said.

"Okay," Kristin said.

They slid Carlos over to the hole and positioned his legs over the lip. With his body ready to go, Joy showed Kristin how to anchor the line. Joy then took up the slack and nudged Carlos into the drop. Kristin grunted with effort as she felt his full weight on the line.

They began to lower Carlos down.

"The rope is rubbing," Kristin said between clenched teeth.

"It's okay," Joy said. "This rope can take a beating."

It was impossible to lower him smoothly. The women let him drop a little and then struggled to arrest his fall. The result was barely-controlled chaos. They were both sweating and panting by the time they felt the tension ease on the line. Joy worked her way, hand over hand, to the edge of the shaft and looked down.

"His feet are touching," she said. "Can you hold him here while I climb down?"

Kristin's face was red with effort. "No."

"Okay," Joy said. "We'll go a little lower to take more weight off the line." She braced herself again and they played out another foot or two of line.

"You okay?" Joy asked.

"Yeah," Kristin said, grunting. "I can hold him here."

Joy let go of the line carefully, ready to engage again if Kristin couldn't maintain. She imagined Carlos crashing down to the rock, breaking open his skull. They couldn't afford an injury. If Carlos got injured, he would be impossible to move and they would have to violate the rule and split up. Joy didn't want to do that.

She turned her back on the shaft and reached her foot down to find the iron rung on the side of the shaft. Mentally, she was already three steps ahead. Once they were all down in the lower tunnel, it was only a couple of turns before they would find the exit. She would leave Kristin with Carlos while she and Ryan went to call for help.

Suddenly, the rope sang as it was pulled over the lip. Kristin's grip was firm, but she was being dragged towards the edge of the shaft. Joy saw how it was going to play out. Kristin would be pulled right into Joy and the two of them would tumble down the shaft and collide with Carlos on the mine floor. They would all three be injured.

"Let go," Joy said.

At this point, Carlos slumping to the rocks was the least of her concern.

Kristin didn't let go. She was leaning back, trying to dig in her heels, but she was still accelerating towards Joy.

Joy braced a foot against back of the shaft and put her arms out. She was ready to catch Kristin and keep her from knocking them both down the shaft. Joy caught Kristin's legs with her hands. Kristin stopped sliding forwards, but began to crumple. Joy saw the problem.

Kristin had looped the rope around her midsection, and it had tightened and caught. Kristin couldn't let go if she wanted to and the rope was pinching her in half.

Joy shone her light down the shaft to see if Carlos had fallen. He was no longer directly below the shaft. Joy leaned forward to grab the loose end of the rope. She put more pressure on Kristin, so Kristin tried to push her away.

"Just let me get this," Joy said.

Kristin barked out a cry as Joy leaned down.

She came up with the rope. She looped it around Kristin the other direction and then pulled on the snag that was pinching Kristin in half. The bind pulled free. Kristin's hands were jerked forward as the rope ran down the shaft. She let go.

Joy threw the loose end around Kristin. She feared that it would bind again.

As the rope accelerated, Joy began to wonder why. This was more than gravity. Something was pulling on that rope. She pushed away from Kristin and looked down the hole again. Maybe Carlos had regained consciousness and was confused? Maybe he was trying to run?

While there was still some slack above the hole, Joy didn't want to lose an opportunity. She took the end of the rope, crouched, and looped it around the rung of the ladder. She barely had time to loop it into a simple knot before the slack ran out.

The rung was jerked down by the rope. The rusty metal bent and Joy dropped with it. Her feet were on either side of the loose knot. Now she hoped that the rope would pull free, or else she would fall as it tore the rung from the stone.

It jerked again. Joy tried to prop herself up on the sides of the shaft. Her hands slipped and she dropped. She tried to climb and the rung gave out. One side snapped and Joy fell. The rope slipped off the end of the rung. Kristin caught her hand.

Joy was too heavy for her. Maybe if Kristin hadn't exhausted her strength, she would have been able to hold on. Joy slipped in stages. Kristin's grip gave her enough time for her foot to find the next run. When she pulled free from Kristin's grip, Joy's foot slipped and she began to fall again. Her hand caught the lip, but that grip didn't hold either. Joy fell and one of the rungs smashed her elbow and bounced her into the back wall of the shaft.

She looked up and saw Kristin's head appear at the top of the shaft as Joy's feet hit the floor. Her ankle turned and snapped. As she fell backwards, her helmet tumbled off and the flame snuffed out.

She was alone with her pain in the darkness.

Joy's arm was so numb that it felt like maybe her forearm and hand had been ripped off. Her foot was on fire. She saw Kristin's light disappear and then begin to leak down the shaft again. She heard Kristin's feet on the rungs.

Soon, Kristin dropped from the lowest rung and landed on the ground. She stepped over Joy and picked up her helmet. She re-lit Joy's lamp from her own and set it next to Joy.

Joy looked up at Kristin and puffed out her cheeks with a frightened exhale.

"Ankle?" Kristin asked. Her light pointed down towards Joy's foot and then back up. Joy nodded. She didn't like the fact that

Kristin already knew where she was hurt. That meant that the injury was bad enough to see.

"And elbow," Joy whispered.

Kristin's light was pointed down the tunnel. She looked back and forth. "Carlos is gone," Kristin said. "We're going to get you out of here and then figure out what happened to him, okay?"

Joy nodded. Her pain was trying to drive her towards selfishness. "Are you sure though? He could need help."

"He could, but you definitely do," Kristin said. "And I'm not qualified. Let's get you up. Don't put any weight on your right leg. And don't look at it, okay?"

Kristin knelt next to Joy's side and lifted her by the arm. Joy's other arm was useless anyway. It was still numb from hitting the rung on the way down. She didn't take Kristin's advice. As she sat up, Joy couldn't help but look down at her foot. It pointed the wrong way. Nausea swept through Joy as she looked at her own mangled foot. It was flopped over to the side and the toe was pointing up towards Kristin. It seemed like there must only be skin holding the foot on.

"I have to splint it," Joy said.

"I don't doubt that it's a good idea, but we're going to get out of here," Kristin said. "I'm sorry, but you can splint it when we're back outside."

Joy swallowed. She understood and was thankful that Kristin's panic was exhibited in the form of cold pragmatism.

Kristin lifted.

The pain swelled. Despite her headlamp, the world went black for Joy. She woke up to Kristin screaming in her ear.

"I'm *not* strong enough to carry you. *Wake up!*"

A shiver ran through Joy and she straightened her good leg. Along with the pain from her right foot, she also felt a disgusting pull of the dead weight at the bottom of her leg. Kristin took a step and dragged her forward. Joy had no choice but to hop and keep up. It was either that or she would fall on her face. They settled into a painful rhythm.

Joy didn't know who Kristin was talking to. It was probably herself.

"I love Carlos," Kristin whispered, "but he can be a real jerk. He should know there's no way I can go after him. Then we'd each be alone."

Joy's limp foot bounced off a rock and she stiffened up. Kristin had Joy's arm slung over her shoulder. Kristin dipped and jammed her shoulder under Joy's armpit.

"I mean, I'm not blaming him for the fact that he passed out, but it's just like him to leave me in the lurch during a situation," Kristin said.

Joy didn't understand Kristin's reasoning, but she wasn't about to argue with her. Joy needed to get out of the mine. Whatever the twisted logic behind Kristin's decision, Joy was going to support it.

"Left," Joy said.

"Yeah?"

"Yes," Joy said.

Kristin helped her angle to her left so they could take the turn. One more turn and they should be able to see to the exit. Joy imagined what it would be like to finally see the stars again. Out in the open she would be able to make sense of everything—she was sure of it.

They moved around the corner and a stiff breeze hit them in the face.

"Fresh air—can you believe it?" Kristin asked.

Joy shook her head and squinted. Kristin was wrong. There was nothing fresh about that air. Kristin slowed to a stop as she realized the same thing.

"You're the experienced cave person," Kristin said. "What does that mean?"

"I don't know," Joy said. "I've never smelled anything like it." It wasn't exactly the truth. She had smelled something similar, just not on that scale.

"That smells like an old bandaid," Kristin said.

"Yes," Joy said. She had imagined the smell of a wet, yellow scab that refused to dry out. But Kristin's description was apt.

Whatever was making that smell, they were walking right towards it.

Kristin must have sensed that Joy was slowing down. "We're almost there. Just a little farther, right?"

"Yeah," Joy grunted. She put her head down and focused on lifting her bad leg high enough to keep her foot off the ground. Joy's foot brushed a rock. A lightning bolt of pain shot up through her. She squeezed her eyes shut as Kristin dragged her forward another step.

Kristin stopped.

"What?" Joy asked. She looked up and blinked. She couldn't see Kristin anymore.

"Our lights went out," Kristin said. "At the same time."

"The wind must have blown out the flame," Joy said. "Use a flashlight."

"Okay," Kristin said. "You lean against the wall, okay?"

They began to shuffle to the right. When Joy found the wall with her hand, Kristin ducked under her arm so she could take off her pack.

"Ow! Shit," Kristin said.

Joy turned her head towards the sound and nearly lost her balance in the dark. She automatically put her foot down to catch herself. The pain actually helped her regain her balance.

"What?" Joy asked.

"Touch your headlamp," Kristin said.

Joy puzzled through what must have happened. "The nozzle stays hot even after the flame goes out. You have to be careful."

"Touch it," Kristin ordered.

Joy reached up in the dark. Her fingers found her helmet. She felt the side of the reflector and then reached her...

"Ow!" Joy said. She pulled off her helmet and listened. She heard the gentle jet of the flame. It was still lit. Above that, she heard Kristin clicking a flashlight on and off. A second later, she heard the flint of a lighter.

"Nothing works," Kristin said. "I can't even see the spark from

111

the lighter."

"There's light here," Joy said. "We simply can't see it."

"What does it mean?" Kristin asked.

"It means let's get the fuck out of here," Joy said. Using the wall as a crutch, she started to push her way forward. It didn't work very well. Her bad foot came down several times before Kristin slipped back under her shoulder to take some of the weight.

"I don't understand—is there something wrong with our eyes?" Kristin whispered.

"Shut up and move," Joy said. She didn't even want to think about the implications. They would have plenty of time to ponder what was happening when they got out.

Joy froze. There was something right next to her—she could sense it. Kristin didn't get the hint. She kept trying to walk. She dragged Joy's arm for another step before she stopped and turned.

Whatever it was, it was right next to Joy's face. She couldn't run, but the urge to try was almost overwhelming. In complete darkness, holding her breath so she wouldn't make a sound, Joy turned her head slowly to the left. The presence retreated. Joy pressed on Kristin's back, urging her forward. Joy leaned heavily on her friend's shoulder when she took a step. She managed to move quietly in the dark.

The presence flooded back in, looming next to her again. Joy didn't stop. Kristin never slowed. Joy sucked in a surprised breath when she felt a tickle on her left side. It started just above her waist and continued up towards her armpit. Joy clamped her arm to her side, but it didn't stop the sensation. It felt almost like a drip of sweat, but it was traveling the wrong direction. When it got to her armpit, the sensation took a hard turn and continued down her arm.

Joy let out a small, involuntary sob. The tickle wasn't hurting her, but it was the uncontrollable unknown of it that was so upsetting.

"What?" Kristin whispered. "What's wrong?"

They continued for two more limped paces.

Joy heard and felt the liquid. It sounded like someone had

dumped a bucket of water over her, but the liquid wasn't dumped *on* her, it came from *within* her. She knew it. Even though she didn't feel the pain of her skin peeling apart, she knew that she had been split up her side. The blood splashed out of her, soaking through her clothes in an instant and draining all the energy from her muscles. She was helpless to stay upright.

Kristin couldn't hold onto her as she collapsed to the floor of the dark cave. Her arm doubled back under her and Joy felt her own hand being forced into the cleft in her own skin. Her eyelids fluttered as the muscles of her face ran out of oxygen.

Kristin's concerned face faded into focus. Kristin was blind. Her eyes were dancing around, trying to puzzle out what was wrong with Joy.

Just before consciousness faded out, Joy saw the horror in Kristin's face. Kristin's hands had found the blood soaking through Joy's clothes. Joy reached up to touch Kristin. She wanted to tell her it was okay. She wanted to tell her not to bother running. Joy barely had control of her own arm. The hand felt numb and worthless. She ended up smacking Kristin on the side her face, leaving a bloody handprint on her cheek.

The world faded away.

Chapter Seventeen — Ledge

TRAVIS SPUN AROUND. "ARE you sure?"

"Of course," Miguel said. "Let me go first."

"Oh, sure," Travis said. "Let me just snap my fingers and magically teleport to the other side of you. How the hell am I supposed to let you go first? There's barely enough room for me to scratch my balls."

Miguel didn't answer. He angled his head to try to shine his light around Travis.

They had been following the crack and everything had seemed normal. Travis felt bad about leaving Justin behind, but it seemed like the best course of action. It wouldn't make sense to have him try to leap over the gap and fall until he got wedged between the rocks. That was a horrible thought. It made Travis cringe just to think about it. But then, for no reason, their crack began to squeeze down into nothing. They had walked easily through it before, but now it petered out.

"This has to be the right way," Miguel said. "There's no other way to go. And I know we've been through here before. Look at this." He pointed to a rock at about eye-level. There was a piece of orange plastic on the sharp protrusion. "You remember when Kristin scraped her helmet?"

"No. I don't," Travis said. "That could have been from me a second ago."

"You're taller than this," Miguel said, pointing at the rock.

"Whatever," Travis said. "All I know is that I'm a hell of a lot smaller than Carlos, and there's no way he fit through this crack right here. I can barely get my hand through it. If you want to give it a try, then back up until we get to a spot where you can get past me."

Miguel was pointing his light up.

"What about up there?" he asked.

"What about it?"

"Why don't we climb?"

"I thought we were trying to get out of this place. Why the hell would we start climbing? We didn't climb down to get in here. Is there a reason why you're trying to invent a brand new path?" Travis asked.

Miguel reached up and shut off Travis's light. Before Travis could say anything, Miguel shut off his own lamp, plunging them into darkness.

"I keep seeing that," Miguel said.

Travis didn't know what he was talking about. He tilted his head around until he figured it out. Above them, there was a yellow glow coming from somewhere between the rocks. The light was faint, but it was unmistakable as Travis's eyes adjusted to the darkness.

Travis reached up and turned his light on again.

"Back up and we'll go back to that wide place," Travis said. "You can go first."

Miguel turned on his own light. "No, stay right there."

There was one benefit of the fact that their fissure had closed down—it was easy to reach the walls on either side of them. Miguel put his left foot up on a little ledge that was above knee-height. He grabbed onto protrusions and lifted himself up. His other foot found a hold. Working back and forth, Miguel climbed until his feet were over Travis's head. The passage narrowed up there, but there was more room than where the path went. Miguel was making good progress. He put his back to one of the walls and braced himself with his feet.

"It's easy," Miguel said. "I can see another passage up here."

"But where does it go?" Travis asked.

"It goes in the right direction. I think we'll be able to drop back into our fissure if we keep going this way."

"You're not making any sense," Travis said. "I don't like it. We should go back and wait with Justin. Joy will be back with help soon."

"If we wait, then maybe the cops will want to search our bags as part of their investigation," Miguel called down from above. "Maybe they search us, find the gold, and decide that it doesn't belong to us. Then the whole trip was wasted."

"You call it a waste, and I call it survival," Travis said. "I would trade the gold right now if it meant we got out of this damn place."

"Then go back," Miguel said. "Who's stopping you? I'll still give you a half-share of the take."

Travis watched as Miguel's light turned away. He began to climb again. It had been stupid to let Miguel take the backpack. He wasn't trustworthy.

Travis looked back the way they had come. At the end of that path, there was a big hole he would have to jump if he wanted to get back to Justin's position. They would be forced to wait with nothing more than two headlamps and a stubby candle. Everything else was in the bag on Miguel's back. In the end, it was the light that drew Travis. Miguel had light in the pack, and there was light coming from somewhere above. Travis didn't want to be alone in the dark.

"Come over to here," Miguel said.

Travis didn't see a way over there. The walls split apart in one direction. They were too far apart to allow him to brace between them, as he had been doing. Back the other direction, they squeezed together too tight for him to fit.

"How did you get over there?" Travis asked. Miguel climbed fast. Travis hadn't been able to catch up and see every handhold.

"You have to push off that wall and transition to the other one completely. Then just climb over."

"That's crazy," Travis said. He scanned the wall between himself and the ledge where Miguel was perched. It scooped down and only had a couple of cracks that would serve as a place to grab on. He imagined himself losing his grip and sliding back down into the fissure the hard way.

"It's easier than it looks," Miguel said.

"It would have to be," Travis said. "It looks fucking impossible." He was going to have to do something pretty soon. His arms and legs were both getting very tired. He couldn't afford to hang between the walls for too long.

Travis lost his grip with his sweaty hand. He couldn't reach the spot again. He was going to fall. In his desperation, he kicked off from the wall and tried to propel himself to the other side. He didn't have enough momentum. Pulling at the rock wasn't helping —it was only serving to mess up his grip. When his sweaty hand finally found the wall, he wrapped his fingers around a sharp hunk of rock. He felt the edge cutting into his flesh, but he didn't care. He kicked his free leg at the wall trying to find a foothold. His anchor-foot slipped.

For one terrible second, Travis was holding himself up by his hands alone. His grip wasn't up to the task. Just in time, his feet found a crack to support his weight.

"That's it. Now just shimmy over here," Miguel said.

"Fuck. Off," Travis said. He shifted one hand and then the other. He moved his feet the same direction. At this pace, he estimated that it would only take a week or two for him to reach Miguel.

"Now just move up to that big crack at your left knee," Miguel said.

"Will you shut the hell up?" Travis asked. "You're not helping." He did move his foot up. The crack was a good call—his foot fit in there naturally. Travis didn't have much maneuverability in his head. He was too close to the wall to point his light around easily. When Miguel turned away, Travis lost most of the light that was guiding him.

"Hey!" Travis shouted. "Look back this way."

"Yeah, sorry," Miguel said. "Listen. You might want to hurry up, I think."

"What?"

"Just a little. It's going to be fine," Miguel said.

"Tell me what you're talking about," Travis said. He inched his hand over to a new spot and then retracted it. The rock was too smooth and he couldn't grip it.

"It's probably nothing," Miguel said. The light disappeared and then swept back right away. "Don't sweat it. Just hurry."

"Those are two different things," Travis said. "I can either hurry, or not sweat it. You're going to have to decide." Sweat rolled down the side of his face as he probed for the next foothold. He wished that Miguel would offer him more advice on where to go, but he still had just enough pride that he wouldn't ask.

"Maybe you should hurry," Miguel said.

Travis stretched for a better grip. When he swung his leg out to the next crack, he lost his other foot hold. When his trailing hand slipped, he was fully committed. Travis swung on his handhold. His foot popped out of the crack before he could put any weight on it. Travis wedged it in again before trying. His hand felt like one giant cramp and his fingers began to give up.

He got both hands to his handhold and wedged his other foot against the wall. When he looked back towards Miguel, he was holding his hand out.

"It's too far," Travis said.

"There's something coming," Miguel whispered. "I don't like the sound of it, okay?"

"Shit," Travis said under his breath. He pulled with his hands and pushed off with his feet. He launched himself towards the ledge where Miguel was reaching out. His momentum carried him right into Miguel. They both fell backwards to the rock.

Miguel was sitting at the lip of a bigger tunnel. Travis extinguished his light before peeking up over the edge. The glow coming from the tunnel was unmistakable. For a second he wondered how long they had been underground. He wondered if it could be sunlight he was seeing.

He heard a big expulsion of air.

Travis sunk back down below the edge of the lip.

"Did you hear it?" Miguel asked.

Travis nodded.

"When I was a kid, my parents took me down to San Diego to

see the elephants. They sounded like that when they would blow dust on their backs," Travis said.

Miguel nodded.

"So where do we go?" Travis asked.

Miguel shrugged.

Travis's eyes grew wide. He grabbed the front of Miguel's shirt. "Why did you tell me to come up here if there's nowhere to go?"

"There's nothing back that way, right? I figured we had to go this way."

"Towards whatever *that* is?" Travis asked. He let go of Miguel's shirt.

"Maybe it's just mine equipment still running," Miguel said.

"You're crazy."

Travis ignited his headlamp again and looked down over the edge of the ledge. The wall beneath them was smooth. They would have to climb laterally, back over to the crack before they could start down. Travis wasn't sure he could even make the first reach.

Travis took a slow breath and turned back to the lip. He lifted his head over the edge and watched the yellow light. His headlamp was dim in comparison. As he watched, the light swelled and then faded.

"Okay," Travis whispered. "Let's go see what it is."

"Maybe one of us should hang back with the bag, just in case," Miguel said.

"Go fuck yourself," Travis said. "Come on."

Chapter Eighteen — Grounded

FLORIDA DOUBLED OVER AND propped her hands against her knees. Her light bobbed as she panted. She removed her pack, withdrew her water, and took a small sip. She held the bottle up in front of her light. It was about three-quarter's full. She put it safely back in the bag and pointed her light in there. She assessed her supplies.

Light wouldn't be a problem—at least for a while. Flares, flashlights, and batteries had been carefully packed by one of Dr. Grossman's assistants. Florida had added her lunch to the stash. One day. If she could get out in one day, she would be fine. Two would be a stretch.

Florida turned off the radio. She counted to ten and turned it back on.

"Command, this is team J-6. Request radio check. Over."

Static.

She turned the radio off again. Best to save the batteries until she had a reason to suspect there might be a signal.

Florida shouldered her pack and started walking again. She thought more clearly when she was in motion. Following the left wall had been a good first idea, but it didn't hold up to scrutiny. She imagined a mine that was shaped like a wheel with spokes that radiated out to a big ring. If they had entered on one of the spokes, She could have accidentally chosen the outside ring to follow. If that was the case, she would be circling forever.

She needed a map. She needed landmarks.

The mine just couldn't be that big. She had been jogging forever and she had seen no indication of the other students or her lab partner. Even if this was a big conspiracy to screw with her, they would have a difficult time completely disguising their presence from a woman running through their maze. That explanation didn't make sense anyway. Dr. Grossman would never get clearance to torture students as part of an experiment. And this was definitely torture.

If she assumed that she was on the outer loop of a big circle, then would a right turn work? She pictured it in her head and saw herself circling a pie-shaped wedge formed by two spokes and an arc. Florida shook away the thought. Following a wall wouldn't help.

The radio would give her a rough position. Regardless of whether or not they answered her, when she was within a certain distance of the base-station her radio was silent after a call instead of giving off static. She could use that to at least make one landmark. The vertical shaft to the round room was another potential landmark. She would have to put a mental pin in that one. Florida wasn't eager to return to the last place she'd seen Roger. He seemed to be up to something, and she wanted no part of his games.

Without breaking her stride, Florida pulled out her radio and held it to her chest. She turned the volume to its lowest setting and clicked the button on the side.

Static.

She kept walking. After twenty more paces, she cycled the button again.

Static.

Just after the radio shut off, she heard something else. It was a musical sound. Little notes tickled the edge of her perception. Florida walked another twenty paces and tried again.

Static.

Then, after a moment, she heard the sound again. It was laughter. Florida looked at the radio while she walked. As she counted out the twenty steps, she mustered her courage. She clicked the button on the radio.

Static.

Laughter.

"Hello?" she called out. The laughter stopped abruptly. The hair on the back of her neck stood at attention, but Florida forced herself to continue walking. Twenty more paces and another click of the radio. She listened.

Static.

Laughter.

But it was weaker. The laughter sounded farther away and it ended more quickly. After another twenty paces, her next click brought even less laughter. She couldn't stand it. She turned around and looked back the way she had come. After rushing back to her previous position, she tried again. It seemed louder, but she wasn't sure. She retraced her steps and found the spot where it was loudest. There was a definite change in volume.

Again, doubt crept in. How could she be sure that the change in volume was due to her location, and not just some random fluctuation? Florida let out an exasperated sigh. She turned to repeat the experiment. It was the only way to be sure.

Chapter Nineteen — Darkness

Justin listened.

As his eyes gave up on resolving anything in the darkness, his ears opened to the cave around him. With the rock in his hand, he tapped the big slab he was sitting on. The sound echoed. He tried to imagine how the echoes mapped to the walls around him.

He wondered about animals who become trapped in caves. If he could stay alive, would he eventually be able to navigate by clicks, like a bat? Did people have that capability, or was it some different kind of circuitry that connect a bat's ears to its brain?

His blindness was a function of his frugality. He had a headlamp, and he had a candle and some matches. If he wanted to, he could light up the room.

But he had been the type of kid who would ration his Halloween candy until well after Thanksgiving, and he was the kind of adult who would rather wait in the darkness than use up his limited supply of light.

If it were just Miguel and Travis out there, he would be worried. But Joy was responsible. She was a few years older than the rest of them and she had her shit together. She was in a terrible relationship with that bully, Brit, but from what Justin heard, she was on her way to breaking that off.

Justin envied her. She knew what she wanted and she moved towards it. Everyone had said she was crazy when she quit Del Taco. She had been on the fast track to managing the whole store. But a few months later she had become a real executive. She had avoided the ceiling of Del Taco and had landed a position with Chassman and Sons. They had offices everywhere. After she worked there a year, she would be able to transfer to a bigger branch and move out of Barstow forever. They all wanted it, but she had found a way to do it safely and strategically.

Justin wondered if he could follow her example. He was no good at math, and he couldn't stand a job where he had to wear a tie. Chassman was out. Justin didn't have any interest in grocery supply anyway.

His dad had trucked cattle his whole life, and somehow been able to pay for a decent house. Those days were over. Justin could barely afford a shitty apartment. How did they expect people to live?

"I'm going crazy," Justin whispered.

He wasn't doing any good just sitting there, thinking about how terrible his life was. He was young and capable. These were supposed to be his wild and fun years. This was the time before he settled down that he was supposed to be out making memories. Aside from being alone in the dark, this was a pretty decent memory. He had gone into a cave with a bunch of friends and found gold. That was a story for the grandkids. Now he just needed to stay alive in order to have those grandkids.

Justin dumped his matches into his hand with extreme care. He counted them as he put them back into the box—seventeen.

He didn't know how long the candle would last, or how much fuel was left in his headlamp. He didn't know how far underground he was, or how long it would take the others to get back. Regardless of what happened, they always had Ryan. He was their ace in the hole. Even if everything went bad, Ryan was on the outside and he knew where they were.

"Shit," Justin whispered.

Ryan didn't have the keys. Joy had kept her keys and given the spare to Kristin. Oh well—if daylight came, Ryan would probably walk to the highway and flag someone down. He would be hungry and thirsty, and then he would get help.

Justin stood up.

He unclamped his headlamp and turned on the valve to let the water drip. He shook the canister until he could hear the gas escaping from the jet. With a flick of the flint wheel, the lantern was going again.

He took two of his matches and made an X where he had been sitting.

He looked up and down the length of cave. The cavern looked like it had been an underground river. The walls were carved down into long flat steps. At the lowest part of the passage, their group had walked through the sandy deposits. Justin knelt and ran his fingers through that sand. He didn't know which way the water had run. It looked roughly the same either direction.

But, if he had to guess, he would say that upstream was the same direction as the fissure. The ledge had collapsed, but maybe it wasn't the only way to get from the cave to the mine. Maybe there was another fissure farther upstream.

There was only one way to find out.

Justin started walking.

He made a couple of agreements with himself. He made up his own safety rules.

First, he would turn back if his headlamp gave out. The candle should be enough light to get him back to safety, as long as he was careful not to let it go out too often. Second, and related to the first, he would only follow the dry riverbed if it was safe and easy to do so. As soon as he reached a place that required climbing, or traversing a pit, or fighting deadly snakes, or outrunning a pack of wild dragons, he would stop and turn around. This walk was all about alleviating boredom and killing time. He was not going to put himself in jeopardy just because he was bored.

The underground riverbed wound left and then right.

Justin felt the wind on his face. His headlamp flickered.

After a deep grinding that shook the floor—it sounded like stone on stone—the wind disappeared.

Justin stopped and moved his light around the space. It had sounded like a heavy stone being slid into place. That visual made sense with the wind being blocked at the same time. He imagined that a giant stone was now covering an exit that led out into the night. He'd heard the sound before, right after they came into the mine. It sounded more sinister this time—probably because he was alone. Where was Miguel to freak out and run away when he needed him? Making fun of Miguel always made him feel a little more calm.

Justin took a deep breath and looked up the sloping rocks. He had a sense of where the wind had come from.

"Here goes rule number two," he mumbled.

Justin grabbed the shoulder-high rock in front of him and jacked himself up. He swung a leg up and looked back to orient himself before he went higher. The ceiling of the cave followed the contour of the wall, so it closed in on him as he climbed. He still had plenty of room to move around. He wasn't really in jeopardy as far as he could figure.

He came to a place where the rock that was the ceiling curved upwards. The wall got pretty steep as well. He was standing on a ledge in a long horizontal channel that was a few feet wide. Justin glanced down to make sure he still knew how to get back. He couldn't shut off his curiosity. Just above his head, it looked like the cave opened up again. He had to know if it was true.

Justin made short work of the climb. It really wasn't difficult. He dusted off his pants and stood up in this new space. It was bigger. In fact, it was almost as big as the mine shafts he had started this adventure in. It was clearly not hand-dug though. The contours had been shaped by flowing water, just like the caves below.

"Speaking of which," he said. He looked down and scuffed an arrow on the rock with his shoe. His effort left a pretty good indicator. With that, he would know where it was safe to drop back down to the cave below.

The cave was flat and easy. It ran like a planned tunnel in both directions. Justin walked along it, just to see if he could tell where it went. He turned several times to make sure he could still see his scuff mark on the ground.

When he turned back around, he jolted with a minor shock. There was a face looking back at him.

Justin exhaled a relieved laugh. He reached forward and touched the painting. It was done with just one pigment, but it had been expertly applied to indicate shadows and highlights. The woman depicted was beautiful. She had a bold, straight nose and sad eyes. The hair framed her face perfectly. It wasn't the only drawing. Justin took another few steps and found a man's facing looking back at him. He kept walking and found an old man and then a girl. He cast his light down the cave wall—people stretched forever. He looked for some clue about the age of the drawings. They didn't wear any jewelry and the drawings never included the neck or any clothing. They could have been made last week or a thousand years before.

Did the native people of California ever create realistic cave art?

He didn't know.

Justin stopped in front of a young woman who looked very sad and frightened. Her mouth was open in what must have been a moan or a scream. The emotion was so clear on her face. It gave him the creeps to look into her eyes. Justin backed away from the cave painting.

"I'm going to add this to the list of crazy things about this cave," he whispered. Justin glanced up the length of the cave. It extended as far as his light penetrated. He had no idea how many paintings he would find. After looking at the sad and frightened lady, he had no interest in seeing more of those faces. There was a cold spot growing inside his chest.

He wandered back to the first woman.

She didn't look nearly as miserable. But her eyes—they were so sad. Maybe his perception had been colored, but he didn't even like looking at her anymore. None of the faces looked even a little happy. Justin wondered if this was the fault of the artist, or if the models had all shown that same emotion.

He turned his light back up the cave when he heard the

grinding sound again. Cool air blew in his face. His nose twitched at the odor. It wasn't overwhelming—in fact, he could just barely smell it. It reminded him of walking by a puddle of vomit that has mostly dried.

"Fuck this," Justin whispered. He backed away from the wall of paintings. He didn't want to turn his back on the breeze. It seemed like that breeze might be bringing something his way. If it was, he wanted to see it coming. Justin backed all the way until he found his arrow, scuffed into the face of the rock. He felt vulnerable climbing back down through the gap, but he stopped to brush away the evidence of his arrow. If the artist of those sad portraits was still around, he didn't want them following him back down into the cave.

Justin stole glances over his shoulder to see where he was going. The breeze was still blowing in his face. He heard the grinding sound again and the air stopped.

Justin stopped too.

His light moved around the cave as he thought. An image popped into his head. He imagined an enormous corpse, buried under the desert soil. The cave was a petrified tube leading into the corpse's lung. But the thing was waking up and starting to breath again.

The thought made him shiver. He was a tiny explorer, the size of bacteria compared to this giant creature. Something that size wouldn't even know of his existence. It would live and die without a thought for the miniature invader.

Justin imagined that somewhere there was an enormous skull, the size of an apartment building, buried under a mountain. He imagined that the thing's once-dead eyes were opening to the darkness.

Chapter Twenty — Together

ROGER HELD THE ROPE out to his side as he walked. He didn't like when it brushed against his leg. When he heard the sound up ahead, he reached up and turned off his light. Whatever else was in this mine, Roger wanted a chance to observe it before it knew of his presence.

He crept as quietly as he could.

He stopped when he heard static. After the click, he heard laughter. The sound was foreign in this place. It made goosebumps rise on his arms. Roger inched towards the corner and poked his head around. He saw her in the distance. She was crouching down, doing something on the floor.

He must have made a sound—she whipped around and pointed her light right at him.

"Don't run," he said. "Please?"

She stood slowly, tucking something under her arm and brushing off her hands.

"What do you want?" Florida asked.

"Probably the same as you," he said. "I want to get out of here while I'm still young."

He came around the corner with his hands raised like a bank robber. A thought flitted across his mind—how did he become the bad guy in this scenario? He brushed it off. It was what it was. She had the bag with the radio and the extra batteries, so she was in control.

"What's that in your hand?" she asked.

Roger looked. He had forgotten. "Dead rope."

"What?"

"It's a rope," he said. "I assume it belongs to a dead guy. If not dead, then the guy is missing a couple of fingers."

"What are you talking about?" she asked.

"I have no idea," he said. He inched forward and she held her ground. "What are you doing?"

"Mapping," she said.

"That's good. That's what I'm doing, too. I've marked all the passages I've explored. I think I'm getting a sense of this place. It's like a giant loop."

She tilted her head and regarded him. "It's not a loop."

"Pardon?"

"I mean, it's a loop, but not in two dimensions."

"Oh!" he said. He had no idea what she was talking about, but he had a real problem with admitting ignorance. He had the feeling that if he had nothing to offer to the conversation that she might run off again. Roger could never hope to keep up with her.

"You have no idea what I'm talking about, do you?"

"No," he said. He walked forward and looked at the thing she had carved on the floor of the mine. It was a circle with a set of lines inside. "What does that mean?"

"It's my system," she said. "I think I'm close to finding the center point."

"What does that mean?"

"The center will have the exit," she said. "I haven't figured out how we got into this section, but I think I'll know when we find the exit. It should be obvious."

"That's the part I figured out," he said.

"Oh?"

"Yeah," Roger said. "We got into this section because this place is magic."

Florida frowned.

Florida counted under her breath as she walked. Roger didn't bother talking. He figured out quickly that she wouldn't answer or even listen to him when she was pacing out the steps to her next measurement.

She stopped and held up her hand for him to be quiet. He hadn't said anything.

Florida clicked the button on the radio, listened to the static. Once that stopped, Roger heard the strange laughter again. Florida knelt and began scraping the floor with the drop-stamp mounting tool.

"What the hell was that?" he whispered.

"I don't know," she said. "But it's useful."

He tried to figure out the sense of her lines, but it remained a mystery. She didn't seem at all inclined to explain her system.

"Tell me about that rope," she said as she stood up. "Where did you find it?"

"Well," he said. He scratched his head up under his helmet and looked at the coil. "I'm not sure how to describe where I found it. It was a while ago. I marked all the tunnels since then, and the spot was the only one with a double mark."

"You said it belonged to a dead person?"

"That's a bit of an assumption on my part," he said. "I think some unfortunate person had looped it around his fingers and then it got pulled off. See this bloody end? There were a couple of fingers and part of a hand tangled in here. The flesh looked torn."

Florida scrunched up her body at the thought and then shook it off.

"From what I saw, all the packs that Dr. Grossman gave out were identical," Florida said. "And that rope doesn't look anything like the rope we had in our packs. I have to assume it's from a different expedition."

"You think there are two groups in here studying the mines today?" Roger asked.

"Maybe. Maybe not *today*," she said.

"What the hell does that mean?"

"You heard the laughter after I used the radio, right?"

Roger nodded.

"Do you see anyone around who was laughing?"

He shook his head.

"Where do you think the laughers are?"

"I don't know. It's a disquieting sound though."

"Exactly. Your disquiet could be an instinctive response to something that shouldn't be here. It makes you uneasy because it's not of our time."

"Time-traveling laughter?"

"Maybe ghosts," Florida suggested.

"You can't be serious."

"I'm not going to reject the idea just because it seems preposterous," she said.

She turned and started walking again. Roger followed her and listened to her count. She stopped again and clicked the radio.

Static.

Nothing.

He waited for the laughter. It didn't come. Florida nodded and bent to mark the floor. Roger waited for her to finish with her strange lines.

"So where were your ghosts?"

"We're out of range," she said. "One more set and I'll be able to triangulate the center."

"I hope you're right."

"Okay," Florida said. "This is the last spot."

Roger had been following her around for a dozen readings. He still had no idea what she was doing, but she seemed confident that she had it figured out.

"So this is the center?" he asked.

"No. This tells us where the center will be. We go this way and then take our next right. Then the tunnel we want will be on our left."

Roger shrugged. He was content to follow. He could tell that his headlamp was becoming weaker. If he had to, he would wrestle away her bag and take the batteries from her. She hadn't yet offered to give him any.

As she turned the corner, Florida turned on the radio and clicked the button. This time, she didn't pause. The radio gave static. When she clicked it again, the static was intermittent. He saw a tunnel coming up on their left. Florida clicked it once more before they turned. There was no static following the click. Florida looked at Roger with a triumphant smile.

"That's good?" he asked.

"That's very good," she said. So quiet that it was almost impossible to hear, she added, "I think."

"There was no laughter?" he asked. It wasn't really the question he meant to ask. Roger revised it. "Was there supposed to be no laughter?"

"I think we're getting farther away from the spirits and closer to reality," she said. "The center should be right up here."

Roger couldn't believe what he was seeing. Right in the middle of the tunnel, he saw their flag sitting below the hole in the ceiling. It was the flag they had dropped when they went up to the hangman's room. It felt like he was waking up from a bad dream. Roger raised his finger to point to the flag and he shook his head with disbelief. The rope was gone. It had disappeared from his hand without him noticing.

"Holy shit," he whispered.

Florida's grin was infectious. She nodded and sped up.

He caught up with her as she stood below the vertical shaft. She was looking up towards the hangman's room. Roger slowed. Even with his light on he could see the yellow glow coming from up there. He felt a dull ache in his stomach. That glow seemed sick, like the light itself might be contagious. He wondered what the glow of uranium looked like. He wondered if he was seeing it now.

"Give me a boost?" she asked.

"I don't think we should go up there," Roger said. "I don't like the looks of it."

"The rest of this place is just a maze," she said. "There's no way in or out. If we don't go up there we're just going to wander around here forever."

"But we've been up there," he said. "We saw the paws sticking

135

out from the walls. We saw the noose and felt the wind. Why would we go back up there?"

"Somehow that's the way that leads out. Our flag is here, see?"

"That's the one I dropped because our first one was missing," he said. "Remember? I dropped another one while you tried the radio."

"I don't remember that," she said. "We put down a flag, went up the shaft, and it was gone when we came back down."

"Right," Roger said. "So I dropped a second one. I know because I moved it out of the way so it wouldn't be visible from the shaft. I didn't want anything to follow us."

"Whatever," she said. She pointed. "*That's* the way out. Now give me a boost."

"This is a lousy idea," Roger said.

The ache in his stomach grew as he climbed. The breeze wasn't as strong as before, but it was still there. He could see the hangman's noose swaying every time he glanced up. It looked like it was waiting for them.

Florida was scanning her light across the walls when he finally pushed himself up through the hole in the floor. He sat there for a second with his legs dangling—unwilling to commit to the room. He imagined hands reaching up from below and dragging him back down the shaft. That thought was enough to make him pull up his legs.

"Where did we chip away the wall?" Florida asked.

Roger spun slowly, scanning with his headlamp. The walls were all undisturbed.

"I'm not sure," he said.

Florida shrugged off her bag from one shoulder and dug through it. She pulled out her rope. After playing out a length, she wound the rest into a ball and knotted it. She backed towards the wall of the chamber and tossed the ball of rope underhanded, while holding onto the loose end. It took a few tries. The ball arced through the noose. Florida walked the loose end to the center of the room and stood on her tiptoes to release the ball. She made a knot in the rope so she had a loop connected to the hangman's noose. She tugged on it and tested her weight.

"What are you doing?" Roger asked.

"I'm going to climb."

"Why?"

"I think it's the way out. Don't you understand?"

"No," he said. "One thing I can say for sure—we didn't come down through that hole. Why would you possibly think that the way out is through that hole?"

"Well, for one, there's a light up there. It could be sunlight. Also, that's the only direction we haven't tried. It could be as simple as climbing up there and then we're out."

"I don't think I can climb a rope like that," Roger said.

"You only have to get as high as that shaft and then you can use the walls," Florida said. "Hold this." She handed him the ends of the loop. "I don't know how it's attached up there, so hold this tight. I'm going to test it."

Roger took up the slack while Florida grabbed the rope at shoulder-height. She jumped and tucked her legs, jerking the rope. It held steady. She gave him a nod and then began climbing. Florida moved very fast at first, pulling with one arm to reach a higher grip with the other hand. Her strength faded fast and she locked the rope with her feet so she could push with her legs. Roger held the sides of the loop together so she wouldn't be working one side against the other. As her feet passed the height of his head, Florida began to grunt. She had looked like a gymnast at first. Now she looked like a tired kid trying to win a schoolyard dare.

She paused when her hands got to the hangman's noose.

"Don't stop!" Roger shouted. Stopping was the predecessor to giving up.

With another burst of speed, Florida grabbed the old rope and inched her way up. Roger's loop went slack as she transferred her weight to the rope. She slipped her foot into the noose and stood. It tightened on her foot but stopped constricting before it really latched onto her.

"What do you see?"

"Same as down there," she said. "The shaft goes up for a while. This rope is warm."

"Warm?"

Florida adjusted her grip and she started to spin with the rope. Roger took up the slack, but it didn't stop her. She put out a hand to touch the wall and stopped herself.

"The shaft is warm too," she said. Florida reached over her shoulder and withdrew a short section of rope. She tied a loop into the end and then a fancy knot around the hangman's rope. When she was done, she slid the thing down as far as it would go.

"What are you doing?" Roger asked.

"I'll yell down when I'm ready. See if you can get up to the noose once I'm off the rope," she said.

Florida slipped her foot into the little loop she had made. She lifted her knee to her chest, dragging the slipknot up the hangman's noose. She tested her weight on the foot carefully and then used the leg to lift herself up. It held. She had made a knot that slipped up the rope but gripped when she put her weight on it. It was ingenious. The only thing that would have made it better is if she had shown Roger how to do it before she left. He stood there with the loop of rope and looked up at his predicament.

The noose wasn't actually that high. If there hadn't been a hole in the middle of the floor, with a shaft leading back down to the mine proper, he might have tried leaping for it. Then again, his vertical leap was never that good even when he had been a much younger gentleman. He took the two ends of the rope and began fiddling with an idea. Florida was making good progress. He had to lean under the shaft to see her climbing. It looked like she was propping herself against the walls to hold herself up. She was certainly industrious.

Roger had a plan. He was only a foot off the floor, but he thought it would work. One end of the rope was looped over his shoulder. The other was tied in his best idea of how a slipknot would work. At first, the end kept coming loose, but he finally figured out that a knot in the loose end of the rope would keep it in place. He put one rope in the crook of his elbow for balance and pulled on the one draped over his shoulder.

His foot had no other choice—it had to elevate. Roger pulled until his leg was bent at a right angle. Now the hard part—he tried to straighten his leg without falling over backwards. As he rose in the air. He started to swing back and forth. Above him, the noose picked up the opposite swing.

"Hey!" Florida yelled from above. "Cut it out."

"Sorry," Roger said. He tried to play out some slack in his shoulder rope, but nothing happened. His plan didn't include a contingency for lowering himself. It was a simple pulley made of ropes and it only moved in one direction. He couldn't even fall to the floor—the shaft was below him. With no way down, he hugged the ropes to his chest and prayed that the vibration would settle down.

"You're not climbing are you?" Florida yelled. "You're supposed to wait until I'm off the rope. I don't trust this thing with our combined weight."

"Okay," Roger said. He had forgotten about waiting. Their combined weight was indeed on the rope. At least it seemed to be holding.

He spoke too soon.

With a creak from above, he dropped an inch. Something up there was giving way. Roger's heartbeat broke into a gallop. He breathed fast, glancing down. With his gentle swing, his situation went from reasonable to precarious.

A new wave came down the rope and he started swinging from side to side. He tried to counter the movement by shifting his weight, but he only made it worse.

"Okay," Florida called. "Come on up."

The rope creaked again and Roger stiffened himself, waiting. It didn't drop again, but he could sense that it wanted to. The rope had a personality, and it was not a pleasant one.

With a shallow, cautious breath, Roger pulled on the rope looped over his shoulder. The fibers dug into his muscles as he used his own body as a pulley. His foot rose grudgingly and he was ready to straighten out again. His hands were already cramping. His thigh was hot from exertion.

Above him, the rope swung again. This time it was pulled all the way to the side of the shaft. Roger's stomach fell as he swung back and forth. The noose above him promised a place to rest his climbing leg. If he could reach it, he could take a break. He hauled down the shoulder rope and made his next attempt to ascend.

Every part of his body was exhausted, and he was only halfway there.

The old rope creaked and he dropped a few inches before jerking to a halt.

Roger climbed frantically. His fingers reached the noose—not that it did any good. He needed to get his feet up to it.

As Roger's shoulders crested the noose, his makeshift pulley started to break down. He had to brace the loose end with one foot while he raised the slipknot with the other. Lifting himself an inch was a struggle. The fibers of the hangman's rope bit into his raw hands.

The rope creaked again, but this time it actually jerked upwards.

Roger lost his grip on Florida's rope and he clutched the hangman's rope with both hands. Without tension, the rope connected to his foot went slack and his fingers began to slip. Roger pedaled his feet in the air trying to get a foot up to the noose. It was too high.

The hangman's rope pulled upwards again and his hands banged against the shaft wall. The skin on his knuckles was scraped away, but Roger got a foot up to press against the shaft. Using that, he pushed his body back against the opposite wall.

"Stop!" he screamed. "Whatever you're doing, stop it for a second."

"Okay," Florida called. She sounded perfectly calm.

Sweat poured down Roger's face as he tried to find the noose with his foot. Florida's rope was still hanging from his foot. The loose end slapped against the floor below him.

His toe found the noose. Roger tested the foothold and then moved his other foot to join the first. When he stretched out his legs and stood up in the noose, the relief was instantaneous. Roger tilted back his head and released a huge sigh. He shook out his arms one by one and looked at the rope burns on his palms. He was going to make it.

"Okay," he called. "If you can, pull me up some more."

"No problem."

Florida worked whatever magic she hand conjured and the hangman's noose resumed its creaky ascent. Roger was the merry cargo.

His foot snagged.

Roger felt the hangman's rope stretch. He looked down to see what the problem was.

"Hold on," he called.

He couldn't get a good angle to shine his light. Something was pulling on his foot. Florida stopped pulling, but the tension increased on his foot. He saw the problem—the rope he had used to climb up to the noose was caught on something, and it was still looped around his foot.

Roger's eyes darted left and right as he searched his memory— what could the rope have caught on? There was little down there except a round chamber and a shaft leading down to the mine. The only thing might be the spikes that were driven into the side of the shaft. They had climbed them to get to the hangman's cave. But those would be directly below. The rope appeared to be pulled to the side.

Regardless, all he had to do was free his foot of the loop and he could continue upwards. The price would be the spare rope, but there was no helping it.

Roger took his trapped foot from the noose and tried to shake the loop from it. Florida's rope was caught on his shoe. He tried to raise his foot to relieve the tension.

His whole body was jerked down. His knee popped and it felt like his hip was being pulled from its socket.

Roger screamed.

"What is it?" Florida yelled.

"I'm caught!" he screamed. His foot was jerked from side to side as the rope whipped back and forth.

The hangman's noose began to rise again. The old rope creaked and dust filtered down from above. Roger couldn't keep his other knee locked under the pressure. The noose was raising his foot up, but his body wasn't going with it. He was going to be torn in two by the opposing forces.

After a moment of slack on the line, Florida's rope jerked down again. Roger felt his skin and muscles flare with heat. He was being stretched to the point of breaking. He had to let go of the hangman's rope. The fall might kill him, but at least it wouldn't rip him in half.

Roger readied himself for the fall. He pushed the hangman's rope away from himself.

His snared shoe popped off.

With the pressure relieved, the hangman's rope jerked upwards. The energy drained from Roger's body and he barely held on as he began to ascend again. His dangling leg was numb.

Florida pulled him over the edge and Roger flopped on his back. His hip and knee throbbed. The air was cool on his bare foot.

He raised his head enough to look down at his foot. It wasn't completely bare. He was still wearing a sock. It was red with spreading blood.

"Away from the edge," he groaned. Florida helped pull him away from the shaft. He saw the crank mechanism she had used to lift him. It was made of wood and riveted together with straps of iron.

"What happened?" she asked. She moved down to his foot and shone her light on it. Mercifully, she didn't touch his tender flesh.

"Someone grabbed the rope. Someone down in that cave. They tried to pull my leg off."

Florida's eyes grew wide she leaned her head carefully over the shaft.

"I see the rope. I don't see anyone down there."

"Trust me," Roger said.

"Maybe it just got caught on something? A rock maybe?"

"No. It played me like a tuna."

"Where's your shoe?"

He gestured towards the hole.

Roger blinked and tried to make sense of the ceiling. It was the source of the glow. The light was fuzzy, like a blacklight.

Florida noticed the direction of his attention and she looked up at the ceiling.

"The ceiling is some kind of crystal. I think the glow might be sunlight coming through."

"From where?" he asked.

"From the sky?"

"Isn't there a mountain of dirt above us?"

"I guess not," she said.

"Can we break through the crystal and see if it's sunlight?" Roger asked. He took in a sharp breath when he sat up. His entire leg began to throb. Roger pulled his pants leg to move his foot closer He peeled his sock back enough to see the scrape. It wasn't bad. The blood flow was already slowing down. Flexing his leg took some of the pressure off his hip somehow. It didn't feel quite as bad.

"I don't think so," Florida said. The crystal ceiling was at the limit of her reach, but she pressed the sharp tool into it. She banged on the hard crystal to no effect. Roger didn't like looking at it. The fuzziness made his eyes ache.

Roger looked around instead. This place looked more like he expected a mine should look. The tunnels branched off in several directions at random intervals. He saw one small room at the end of a tunnel, like they had found something of value there and dug to excavate it. It was different than the grid below.

"Now what? This certainly isn't the way we came in," he said.

"Right," she said. "I think the shafts below were for extraction. This is the real meat of the mine. We'll have to go up to get out."

"Up where?"

Florida shrugged.

"I think you're going to have to go alone if you want to make decent time," Roger said. He rolled to his knees and pressed himself upwards. He limped on his sock and felt his joints settling back into place. It wasn't as bad as he expected.

"That's fine," Florida said. "I'll be back with help."

"Oh. Well thanks for all the concern," he said. "Yeah. I'll be fine alone here."

"Do you want to stay together or do you want me to get help?" She asked, turning back to face him.

"You just walk," he said. "If I'm slowing you down then feel free to ditch me."

"Fine."

"Fine."

She chose a tunnel that appeared to have some length. Roger hobbled after her.

Chapter Twenty-One — Alone

KRISTIN COULDN'T BREATHE. EVERY time she tried to inhale, her breath hitched and caught. Light leaked back into her eyes slowly, and the scene it revealed was horrible. Joy was lying on the floor of the mine next to her. Joy's face appeared calm, but her body was ripped open. Joy's arm had been flayed, but the worst was her ribcage. The bones were broken apart and her shirt torn. Kristin could see Joy's exposed organs.

She turned away and squeezed her eyes shut. It couldn't be real. This couldn't be happening.

"Stop," she whispered. She opened her eyes and reassessed. Yes, Joy was there, and she was dead. Denying it wouldn't help anyone. Kristin needed to act.

She abandoned Joy's hand and pulled away from her body. Kristin held still and darted her eyes every direction, looking for the assailant. She saw nothing but the mine shaft. She whipped around and looked behind herself. Her headlamp revealed nothing. The walls and ceiling seemed to press in. Her heart beat faster as she thought about how she was underground in a tunnel carved into rock. It could collapse at any second.

These thoughts were crazy.

Kristin oriented herself. She knew where the exit should be. She turned her back on Joy and started walking. Her legs were barely under her control. She jerked forward like a marionette. Every few steps, she glanced over her shoulder to make sure that Joy was still there, split open like a side of beef.

Kristin ran.

When she saw the blue of the night sky, she could hardly

believe it. Hope welled up in her chest, but she forced it back down. Believing that she might take a breath in the open air was a jinx. She refused to jinx herself out of that gift.

When she burst through the entrance of the mine, Kristin threw her arms and head up to the sky. She sprinted to her left. She tripped on a rock, but kept pumping her legs until she regained her balance. She saw the dark Jeep sitting there on the access trail.

"Ryan!" she screamed.

He didn't answer.

She ran right for the driver's door and clawed at it with one hand while jamming the other into her pants pocket for the key. In her panic, neither of her hands completed their tasks. She stopped. She pulled the handle, swung open the door and then took a breath before reaching for the key. She was back under control. Her helmet banged on the Jeep's frame as she climbed in.

Kristin had never driven a manual transmission before, but she knew the concept. She found neutral and got it started. With the lights on, she started to believe that everything might be okay. Again, she chased away the jinx back to the corners of her mind.

In the rearview mirror, a shape appeared.

Kristin screamed and her foot came off the clutch. The Jeep bucked and then stalled.

"You scared the fuck out of me," she said.

"And you me," Ryan said. "Where is everybody?"

"I don't know," Kristin said. "Carlos disappeared and then..." Her tears burst forth like a stinging cloud. Kristin willed them back. "Someone killed Joy in the dark. She died in my arms. Her blood was everywhere. We have to get help."

"What?" Ryan asked. He squeezed between the seats and landed in the passenger's seat. "What the fuck? Where is everyone else?"

"We split up. They're staying. Listen, can you drive this thing? We have to get help."

"Where's Joy?"

"She's in the mine," Kristin said. "Are you going to help me or not? I'm not going to stick around here waiting for something to happen to me."

"Yeah, of course. You're sure there's nothing we should be doing to get the others out before we leave, right?"

"Yes, I'm sure."

"Because I don't want to have everyone saying that we should have helped our friends before we went off trying to find help, you know?"

"I know what you're saying, but I'm sure."

Ryan nodded. "Switch places with me."

Kristin crawled over the seat and flopped down in the back. Ryan worked his way carefully over the gearshift. She let out her breath as he started the car again. Ryan put it in reverse.

"Hold on," he said.

The Jeep lurched backwards.

Chapter Twenty-Two — Glow

THE CEILING WAS HIGH and arched. The glow was coming from up there. The jagged crystals were translucent and light was seeping through them. The brightness was fairly consistent, but every now and then the light would either swell or fade and then return back to where it started.

Travis glanced at Miguel.

Miguel shrugged back.

"How should I know?" Miguel whispered.

Travis patted the air, telling him to be quiet.

Miguel adjusted the straps of the backpack. The lump of ore pressed into his back. It felt reassuring. At least they were making progress. And the light seemed like a good sign. It felt like they were getting closer to civilization.

They reached a branch.

Travis started to head to the right. Miguel put a hand on his shoulder.

Miguel pointed to the left. Travis shook his head.

"Stay with the light," Miguel whispered.

Travis got close to his ear to whisper his response. "We don't know what that light is coming from. It could be some secret military stuff or something."

"Are you crazy?"

"Are you?"

"If we go that way," Miguel said, pointing, "we have to fire up our lights again. How long do you think this carbide is going to last?"

"It's reacting all the time either way," Travis said. "Whether or not we burn the gas, it's still giving it off."

Miguel shook his head. "We turned off the water."

"It's still wet. Trust me, these torches are on a timer."

"I still think we should stay with the light. It must be man-made. I'd rather stick to the part of the cave where people have left a mark, you know?" Miguel asked.

Travis was about to respond when another burst of air chuffed out from somewhere deeper in the cave. A second later, a blast of warm wind came from the tunnel with the glowing crystal ceiling. The air smelled vaguely of garbage, or compost, or a dumpster that has sat too long in the sun.

Miguel pointed to the darker passage of the cave. "Go that way."

Travis rolled his eyes and nodded.

They picked up speed as they walked into the darkness. As soon as they moved around the first turn, they had to spark their headlamps again. Travis was right, even with the water off there seemed to be enough gas for a flickering flame. Miguel turned on his water drip again to even out his headlamp. They picked up speed as they got away from the glow. Being under that crystal ceiling, they had moved slowly, almost reverently. It was like they thought they needed to tread carefully, lest they wake something up.

When Miguel had been a boy, they had moved around their apartment the same way on Saturday mornings. Nobody wanted to be the one who accidentally woke up their father. Miguel watched Travis climb up over a rock that blocked their passage. As soon as he was up and over, Miguel followed.

Travis pointed at something as he walked by. For a second, Miguel didn't recognize the brown lump on the wall. He moved closer and then jerked back when he saw the eyes. The bat tucked his head back into his wing and ignored Miguel.

"We must be close to the surface, right?" Miguel asked.

"I guess," Travis said. "Maybe we should wake him up and see where he flies. We could follow him out."

Miguel shook his head.

They both turned when they heard another expulsion of air

behind them. It sounded like it was off in the distance, and they felt no wind. Miguel's heart felt a little lighter—they were moving away from the unknown. But they were also moving away from someplace that felt living, almost inhabited, and walking through a dark, inert cave. He was conflicted.

Their cave took a downhill turn. Travis put a hand out to support himself on the wall. Miguel leaned back. The backpack helped him balance himself as they descended.

Travis stopped at a lip. Miguel drew alongside him.

Their cave opened up to an enormous room. Miguel stumbled back a step at the sight. The floor of their tunnel fell away at a steep angle. They were at least halfway up the wall of the huge room. Miguel didn't like the way his light petered out before it reached the other side. He could see a few stalactites near the center, and he could see the white sediment on the cave floor below, but the other side was lost in darkness.

"It's got to be a hundred yards across," Travis whispered.

"More," Miguel said. "I don't believe it." His breath came in short gulps.

"We have to turn back," Travis said. "We'll try the other glowing tunnel."

"No," Miguel said. "I think that's the wrong idea. Bigger is better."

Travis just looked at him.

Miguel tried to explain and realized that his gut reaction was hard to put logic behind. "These caves are formed by erosion, right? Rivers and stuff get bigger downstream. If we head downstream, we're bound to find a way out. If we continue upstream, we're just going to find a trickle of a cave that we can't get through."

"I don't think it works that way at all," Travis said. "Besides, this wall is smooth. If we drop out of this tunnel, there's no going back. Is that what you want?"

"There's already no going back," Miguel said. "We can't make it down from that ledge in one piece. The only other option is where that wind is coming from. I've come around to your side—I don't want to know what's making that wind."

Travis moved his light around the big room. Miguel followed Travis's beam and added his own light to the features of the giant room below. There were a few stalagmites that rose up from the floor of the cave, but it looked mostly flat and was covered by that white sediment. It looked almost like a dry lakebed. They could see cracks in the white floor. The walls sloped down from the ceiling, making the bottom of the cave a giant bowl. Off to the right, just at the limits of their headlamps, they could see what looked like a huge passage that led off from the enormous room. It was impossible to tell unless they got closer.

"I don't even know," Travis said. "We could slide down this edge. It looks easy enough. But, like I said, there's no coming back."

"I'm okay with that," Miguel said. "We'll find a better way out. There has to be a way."

"I'm not so sure that's true."

It was easier than it looked. Miguel went first. He sat on the lip of their tunnel and then scooted forward. He rode down the smooth rock like a slide. As it curved towards the floor, his acceleration was kept in check by friction and he slowed to a stop before he even got to the white sediment.

He turned and watched Travis.

Travis slowed to a stop even higher. They stood up on the unstable angle and began to walk the circumference of the bowl. Based on the caustic powder they had encountered earlier, they kept their distance from the white sediment. But walking sideways along the slope was incredibly tiring. Miguel's ankles burned.

"This sucks," Miguel said. He stopped.

"It's okay," Travis said, but he immediately turned his feet uphill to the relieve the strain of holding his feet on the tilted slope.

"I'm going to see if I can walk on the flat part," Miguel said.

He inched his way down the slope. It felt better immediately as the bowl-shaped wall got closer to horizontal. When he got to the edge of the white, he touched the toe of his shoe to the chalk. It was firm. He raised his foot and looked at the sole—his shoe seemed no worse for wear.

Miguel coughed into his hand and tried his whole foot. The white chalk was solid.

"It's fine," he said.

He stepped onto the edge.

They continued walking, and Miguel began to pull away from Travis. Stubbornly sticking to the sloped wall, Travis struggled to stay upright.

"You're going to have to come down eventually," Miguel called back to him. "The wall gets vertical a little farther down." Miguel coughed again. He tried to keep his footfalls clean. He didn't want to accidentally scuff up any of the dust, in case it was irritating his lungs.

"I'll deal with that when the time comes," Travis said.

Miguel looked back. Travis was hunched over, retying his shoe.

While he walked, he turned his light to cast it across the bowl of the room. His light still didn't reach the other side. It was creepy to think of what might be over there, on the other side of that haze. Miguel slowed down. The far side hadn't looked hazy when they were up on the lip of the tunnel. He distinctly remembered that his light had disappeared into black. For some reason, down here, looking across was like trying to see down the length of a long road on a hot summer day. Everything shimmered into a haze.

Miguel kept moving.

His own shoe was a little loose. Walking sideways like that had done a number on his laces too.

He had to wait up for Travis anyway. Miguel bent over to tie his shoe.

He was only halfway through retying his laces when the world began to sparkle. Bursts of light fired off in his eyes. His balance floated away on a dream. Miguel started coughing and couldn't catch his breath.

Travis kept to the slope out of equal parts stubbornness and caution.

Nobody else had been burned by the powder. They didn't understand how much it had hurt. In fact, they barely seemed to care. Travis was going to steer clear of the stuff if at all possible. Of course, he didn't know if it was even the same white powder, but better safe than sorry.

He could tell something was wrong with Miguel even before he keeled over.

His friend had slowed to a stop while he was looking out over the floor of the vast cave. He had seemed distracted, or even hypnotized by what he saw. Travis was about to ask him what the problem was when Miguel went down.

Travis rushed down the slope to go help him.

He noticed the smell immediately. Something in the air burned his nostrils and made him think of his old car. The battery had exploded one hot day, spewing acid all over the inside of the hood. That's what it smelled like down near Miguel.

He started coughing as he grabbed Miguel by the arms. There was something bad down in the bowl—he knew that for sure. He had to drag Miguel up. Travis pulled.

"Get up!" he yelled.

Miguel's body convulsed and spasmed as he gasped for air.

Travis's feet slipped on the powdery rock as he tried to drag his friend up the slope. He couldn't get traction. Meanwhile, as Miguel's body contracted, every little motion seemed to propel him back down. Travis spotted a stalagmite a few paces away. He dragged Miguel laterally towards it. When he reached it, Travis braced himself against the spire of rock and pulled at Miguel's shirt and the straps of his backpack. He clawed and pushed at his friend's body to shove him up the gentle slope.

Miguel's convulsions graduated to a full-on seizure. He bounced and flopped. Foam leaked from the corners of his mouth. Travis pushed.

The air smelled fine here. Travis couldn't detect anything like the choking smell from below.

Miguel stopped thrashing. His breath still tore through his throat in a wheeze, but at least he was breathing with a rhythm now.

"Miguel," Travis said. He leaned over him and nearly lost him down the slope again. He propped Miguel up, so his own feet were braced against the stalagmite. "Miguel!"

His friend moaned. He began coughing again. Travis rolled him a little to the side so whatever he coughed up would go out instead of back down into his lungs. Travis patted him on the back.

"Are you okay, man?" he asked.

Miguel coughed harder. Travis heard the liquid rattling around in his chest.

"Spit it out," Travis yelled.

With an enormous, hunching effort, Miguel shook as he tried to clear his lungs. Finally, the blockage began to come up. Miguel spat and chewed and coughed. Travis backed away involuntarily as he saw the stringy blood start to fly. The rock below Miguel was stained with dark blood. Miguel's coughing transitioned to vomiting. The stuff that came up with his retching was even blacker. Wave after wave of chunky blood flowed from Miguel's mouth and nose. The smell alone, let alone the sight, was enough to make Travis's stomach turn.

"Oh, shit," was the only thing Travis could think to say. He repeated it.

After a minute Miguel shook and then became still. Travis checked his wrist. Miguel's heart had stopped.

Chapter Twenty-Three — Evidence

JUSTIN SQUATTED NEXT TO the mildewed bag and picked through the contents. He pulled out the old paperbacks and flipped through them. Some of the paper was disintegrating, but he found half of one book that seemed like it might be flammable. He set it aside and shook the bag. There was another pocket. He found a silver-barreled flashlight that didn't even slightly work. After unscrewing the red cap, he saw the problem. The batteries were bloated and oozing greenish acid.

He turned the bag upside down and shook.

"Great," he said. "Half a book."

Justin took the dry half of the book, put it back in the bag, and put the moldy strap over his shoulder. As he walked away, his headlamp began to sputter. It wasn't the first time. He took it from his helmet and shook it. The flame came back to strength.

As he turned around, he noticed something. The other book, the paperback that Carlos had pulled from the bag earlier, was a good five paces away. He tried to remember back to when they'd found the bag. Had Carlos thrown the book? Had he carried it away from the bag? Justin didn't think so, but then again he hadn't really been paying attention. It wasn't just the book though. When he'd returned to the spot where he had sat in the dark, he had expected to find his X made of matches. Both the matches were there, but they were separated by several feet.

The cave looked like an old, dried-up riverbed. It acted like the river was still there, slowly scattering things left in the ghost currents.

Justin devised an experiment. He took the stack of old books and set them at different elevations of the cave. They were in a line, perpendicular to what he imagined was the direction of flow. With that set up, he continued on his mission.

It wasn't difficult to find the portal back to the circular room. When they had dug out the caustic white powder, it had scattered everywhere. Justin followed the path and ducked through the hole. He retraced his steps back to where they had dug out the gold ore.

Justin wasn't interested in the vein of quartz. He turned his attention to the pods of white chalk embedded in the wall. In one, they had found the skeleton. In another, they had excavated Miguel's knife. Justin wanted to know what was in the others.

He found the flat rock they had used for scraping and dug it in where they had found Miguel's knife. Justin was about to give up and move onto the next round, chalky deposit when he hit something. He scraped frantically to expose the thing.

It was a buckle. Laced through the buckle was a green strap. The chalky powder flew as Justin beat at the wall. When enough of the strap was exposed, he started pulling. Soon, he freed the canteen from the wall. He unscrewed the cap and shone his light on the water inside.

Justin had his headlamp removed in an instant. Careful to not disturb the flame, he filled the torch's reservoir with fresh water. The flame perked up somewhat. It was good enough for the moment.

Justin recapped the canteen and stuffed it into the moldy bag. He almost set it down but thought better of it. He put the strap over his shoulder and kept the bag close while he returned to scraping the wall.

He didn't find anything else in the deposit. It ended when Justin uncovered the rock behind the chalk. He scraped the rest of the chalk away from the wall and stepped back to look at the result. There had been an alcove in the wall a couple feet across and a foot deep. Something had filled it with the white chalk,

Miguel's knife, and the canteen. He swung his light around the rest of the room. There were a bunch more chalk deposits and even more depressions that hadn't been filled. He moved to the next one with chalk.

The bag was heavier on his shoulder.

The most disturbing things he had found were two more skeletons and a carcass that still had meat on it. He didn't know for sure, but one of the skeletons looked like it was from a dog. Another might have been a gopher. The carcass with meat was the biggest thing. From the ears, he guessed it might have been a donkey at one time.

Combined with the human skeleton they had found earlier, he deduced that something in the cave had claimed four lives. Justin didn't care. Maybe the carcasses had died of natural causes.

He had more pressing problems. Fortunately, one of those problems didn't weigh as heavy as it had before he started digging. His bag now held one of the lost jars of carbide. With it, he could refill his headlamp a few more times. He had also added a rope to his collection. It wasn't one of Joy's super-strong ropes, it was an older thing made of some kind of fiber. It seemed to be in good shape.

His last find had been the most interesting. It was a steel box. The latches were corroded shut. He had beaten them with a rock to get the box open. Inside, he had found a journal. Justin hiked back through the round caves so he could get back to the dry riverbed cave. For some reason, he felt more comfortable there.

Justin worked by candlelight to scrape out the carbide chamber of his headlamp. It might have had another twenty minutes of fuel left, but he felt eager to prove that he could refuel the thing and make it work again. It turned out to be pretty easy. The expended carbide came out like a paste. He imagined Joy's disapproving look as he dumped the sulfurous mess on a rock. He put fresh carbide in and screwed the headlamp back together. The effect was undeniable. His light was bright and fresh.

Justin used it to examine the journal he'd found.

The ink was dark and clear, but he still had a hard time reading it. The looping script looked unfamiliar—almost like another language. Justin read carefully.

Chapter Twenty-Four — Journal

IF YOU HAVE A heart beating in your chest, I pray you'll convey this diary to my loving wife. You'll find her located as such:

Gertrude Smith
  The Elms
  Rural Free Delivery #1
  Springfield, Massachusetts

Our cave-in came as no surprise and was greeted with little fanfare. George Sinclair warned us that the east tunnel number fourteen was dangerously unstable. We sent carts through that gap on a fast rail with little concern. Hugh Sutton even joked that he would ride the cart ringing a bell if we would collect a dollar for the spectacle. When the ceiling finally did press down, we simply shifted our tailings to number seventeen and thought nothing more of it.

Bert was the one who discovered the collapse of number seventeen.

His news sent some of the men into an uproar, but we knew there was no worry. We could climb the raise and join the early crew for a late breakfast. I led the advance to ascend the winze. It was blocked. My report brought some real panic for the first time. Only the greenest men had a strong reaction. It was my opinion that we could sit tight and wait for the diggers to find us. Mr. Russell was in favor of continuing our work. I talked him out of it. It would serve no purpose to pile up carts on number fourteen if seventeen was the one they chose to rescue us through. We had no way of knowing. Furthermore, I knew we would use less air if we sat still.

The men filled the silence with jokes at first. Bert told a story of when he was a boy. A melancholy mood spread through us and I called on Hugh Sutton to play us a tune on his mouth organ to cheer up the boys.

Hugh Sutton was nowhere to be found. We searched the shafts and looked behind every rock. It was a short journey. Our cave-ins had left very few hiding places and Hugh Sutton was nowhere to be found. Conjecture spread that Hugh had found a way out and would arrive back to save us shortly. The mood rose and stayed high for nearly an hour. When it was clear that Hugh Sutton had been missing too long, the men became anxious. Even some of the old hands began to panic somewhat. I confess that only the need for leadership helped me keep fear out of my voice. I ordered everyone to settle down and stay quiet.

Mr. Russell was moving rocks on number fourteen. Bert joined me back at the carts. He said that a rumor was circulating about Seventy-Eight. That was the last year the mine had operated under its previous owners, and it had shut down amidst controversy. Precipitating the closure was the unexplained loss of many men. Since then, Mr. Montgomery's commission had explained it all. Most of the missing men had run off with stolen fortune from a chance hit on gold. In the town, old miners whispered a different tale. The mine was haunted and it woke up every so often to add to its legion of ghosts. Bert told me that our men were debating that version of history as we spoke.

He was right.

Furthermore, the men had settled on a course of action to alleviate the problem. They said that the mine wouldn't be sated until it had taken the head man into its rocky guts. They were going to offer Mr. Russell's blood to the mountain and hoped it was enough.

Bert is a good man, but I didn't believe him. I knew all those men personally. Some were green, but none were unstable enough to drop into such insanity so quickly. I convened the group and told them to hold steady. I told them that help was surely on the way. All we had to do was keep our heads and stick together.

I should have made a count of heads before I began my entreaty. As it turned out, another of us was missing. A young man named Yancy Bell had vanished without a trace. Upon this discovery, the rest turned on Mr. Russell and beat his life quiet with their tools.

I'm ashamed to say that there was nothing I could say to stop them.

Being the second-highest ranking man there, I'm afraid that if I was seen to be against them, I would have been next on their list. Mr. Russell's body was left in the dark at the back of the deepest shaft. We retreated to the junction and waited. Men linked arms to guard against another disappearance. Nobody moved alone.

We snuffed all but two of the lanterns to conserve our air. We've been sitting here in the near dark for what must be hours. Bert has Mr. Russell's pocket watch, but didn't think to wind it before it stopped.

Two more men have disappeared. They went down to number seventeen to relieve themselves and never returned. As a group, we've scoured every inch of our prison and found no trace. Mr. Russell's body has gone missing as well.

Some of the men looked angrily to me, as if I might have some complicity in the disaster. Bert, being the new second-in-command, stayed strong with me and we argued them down. We heard the sounds of rescue coming from fourteen. Our spirits rose for a while. Someone brought the idea that the sound might simply be another cave-in. I have no opinion.

We've all agreed not to discuss our hunger.

What possible good could come of such a discussion is not

apparent to me. I'm pleased that my compatriots are of a like mind.

We found John Harlow, but it was too late. His torso was protruding out of the darkness, but the lanterns would not illuminate his lower half. Bert suggested that the shadows were attempting to swallow him whole. We pulled on his hands and begged him to struggle. John's eyes fell shut and he didn't respond to us as he was consumed. I let go of his fingers before the shadow could swallow me as well. I suppose our mysterious disappearances have been explained. The darkness has ingested the missing men.

No explanation has been forthcoming.

Robert Clyde discovered a crack in the wall. While it's true that no man knows every inch of this section, we all know enough about mining to recognize that this crack is unnatural. It was not made by human hand or one of our clever tools. This is a crack of the mountain itself, and I'll swear that it was not present before the cave-in trapped us here.

Bert believes that the darkness that swallowed John Harlow came from, and retreated into, this crack. He may be right.

Robert Clyde thought this crack might be a way out.

Perhaps he is correct.

So far, he has no other volunteers willing to explore the crack alongside him.

Bert has killed Charles Ulrich.

Unless Robert Clyde returns from the crack, we have only six men remaining of our crew. Our cave-in trapped twenty-four men. With two murders and one elopement, the other fifteen disappearances remain unexplained. The theories grow more wild with each passing hour.

Ulrich wanted another sacrifice, but not to appease the ghosts of the mine. I'm reticent to speak ill of the dead, but Charles Ulrich wanted to murder Kyle Henry and consume his flesh. Kyle has not moved in some number of hours. His eyes are closed and he will not respond to our ministrations. When Charles made move to end Kyle's life, Bert took steps to restrain Charles. Their scuffle turned into a fight. I don't blame Bert for what he has done. I would have done it myself if I had summoned the energy. Some of the men dragged Charles to the deep part of the mine and offered him to the darkness. I've heard no report on the status of his remains.

Robert Clyde's crack has disappeared. He attempted to explore the crack for a way out and we never saw him again. Now, that crack has disappeared. Bert found another crack near the raise. The discovery divided our group. Three of us believe that the correct course of action is to stand pat. The other men, led by Bert, want to explore the crack. They now believe that Robert Clyde is happily above ground, though there's no evidence to support such a claim.

I suppose that there is no evidence to the contrary. Still, the crack leads down into an unknown abyss and we have no lanterns to spare. There is precious little fuel left and we may soon have only one lantern for all of us. If Bert's group leaves, we men who stay will be left in the dark.

A foul breath of sulfur came up from Bert's crack just as the men set to investigate. I thought for sure that the toxic odor would dissuade them, but the opposite was true. Convinced that the smell was organic, they decided that the smell proved that the crack would lead them to life.

They wrestled the last of the fuel from us.

We're going to extinguish the lantern now and only relight it if we hear the approach of a rescue. Darkness awaits.

When I heard the scrape of boots, I called to my men to light the lantern. Nobody responded. I struck the match myself and wished I had left their terrible deeds to the dark. I won't give their names here. They deserve no memorial.

The light swelled and exposed the grunting fools as they desecrated the remains of Charles Ulrich. I've never seen the like. As soon as the light had revealed the men, darkness flooded back in to consume them. I was not ashamed to cheer for their demise.

I'm alone in this wretched cave.

Chapter Twenty-Five — Voices

FLORIDA PUT UP HER hand to tell Roger to stop.

He slid his bare foot forward and rested. After a second, he understood—she had heard a voice.

"Spit it out!" the voice yelled. It echoed through their tunnels. After a few seconds, he heard the voice again. It was barely audible. "Oh shit. Oh shit. Oh shit."

They waited to see what else it might say.

There was no other sound.

"Hello!" Florida called. Roger listened to the reverberations fade away and strained to hear a response. "Hello?" she yelled again.

Roger limped forward.

"I've heard voices before. They never answer," he said.

Florida narrowed her eyes. "There has to be some explanation."

"Yeah, there is—this whole cave is fucked."

Florida thought about it for a second and then nodded. She marched on. She didn't take any care to wait for Roger. Her position was clear—she was going to get out as quickly as she could. If he kept up, he was welcome to tag along. Otherwise, he was on his own. Roger was starting to grow accustomed to the pain. His hip and knee were a little sore, and the cut on his ankle stung. He had lived through worse.

Florida slowed down.

Roger maneuvered to the side and saw why. Their tunnel was ending. The wall curved down and there was a dark hole in the floor.

"Careful," Florida said. "The rock could be thin here."

She edged towards the hole. From what he could see, the space below was enormous. His light picked up one of the walls below as it curved away. Florida had a better angle. She moved to the side and projected her headlamp down through. Florida dropped to her knees and moved down closer. Her hands were right at the edge.

Roger was just about to say something when she waved him forward.

"Look!" she said.

Roger crawled forward, trying to spread out his weight. He finally found a good angle to see where she was pointing her light.

The cave beneath them was shaped like an enormous, flattened bubble and they were peering through the roof. Their light barely reached the far side, where a couple of shapes looked black against the reddish rock.

One of the shapes was projecting its own light. It was a person —so far away that they looked tiny—and they were walking around the perimeter of the giant room.

"Hey!" Florida yelled. "Hey!"

Roger joined his voice to hers. His message was more direct. "Help us! Please help us!"

There was no thought of trying to get down there. Below the hole it was at least a thirty foot drop to the floor, if not more. It was impossible to judge the distance. Also, the floor was covered with something white. It could have just been a mineral deposit, but it was impossible to tell from their height.

The figure on the opposite side of the cave didn't respond to their yells. He kept walking.

Florida turned to Roger. "Why doesn't he hear us?"

Roger shook his head. "We can see his light. He should at least see ours."

When Roger looked back to the figure, he couldn't see him anymore. He shifted his light around, trying to pick up the moving shape again.

"I lost him," Roger said. He looked to Florida.

"I can't believe it," she said. "Where did he go?"

They moved their lights around the cave for several minutes, but they saw nothing. Roger yelled a few more times, and they listened for a response. Even the other shape—the dark, unmoving one—had disappeared.

"Where could he have gone?" Florida asked.

"Let's turn out our lights. Then we'll see his light."

They tried it and the cave below them was lost in darkness. Their little tunnel was still illuminated by the ghostly glow from the crystals in the ceiling, but none of that light reached the depths of the cave.

"Unreal," Florida said.

They turned on their lights again and resumed scanning.

"Can we string together enough rope to get down there?" Roger asked.

Florida shook her head. "No. Besides, what would we anchor to?"

"Yeah," Roger said. "Well, there are other holes. See the wall over there? Maybe one of these other caves leads to a better way."

Florida pushed up away from the hole. "I'm not so sure we should focus on getting down there."

"But that guy—there was someone there. He might know the way out."

"Or he could be as lost as we are. And I don't like that he couldn't hear us, and I really don't like that we didn't see where he went. Maybe he tripped and fell into a pit or something." She shook her head. "If we had seen more than one person, or a search party, then I would be all for it. But one solo guy? That's not necessarily a positive thing."

"You're crazy," Roger said. "If we have a chance to find another person, we should jump at it."

"We can debate this again when the opportunity arises," she said. She brushed off her hands and stood.

When Roger pushed himself up, part of the rock crumbled and fell down into the hole. He watched the pebbles tumble away and hit the white floor below. A cloud of powder erupted from the impact. Roger inched backwards and then stood to catch up with Florida before she left him.

Chapter Twenty-Six — Doubt

RYAN SHIFTED INTO FIRST gear and turned off the key.

"What are you doing?" Kristin shouted.

Ryan hit a switch and the interior light came on. Kristin squinted.

"Where's the blood?" Ryan asked.

"What?"

"You said that someone killed Joy in the dark. You said there was blood everywhere and that she died in your arms. How come you don't have any blood on you?"

Kristin looked down. She flipped her hands over and looked at both sides. She felt her shirt.

"I don't know, I guess I didn't get any on me. We have to get help. Please!"

"She died in your arms and there was blood everywhere," Ryan said. He opened the door and got out. "I think there would be a little blood on you." He began to walk in front of the Jeep. The headlights were still on. Ryan cut a shadow in the light that was pointed towards the mine.

Kristin rolled down the window.

"Listen—if you don't believe me then you stay here and I'll go get help." She got out and walked up to him. "Give me the keys."

"No way," Ryan said. He stuffed the Jeep's spare key down in his pocket. "Those are my little insurance policy. Why don't you tell me what kind of work you guys are planning to play on me?"

"Work? What are you talking about?"

Ryan circled the Jeep the opposite direction. He opened the rear door and pulled out Kristin's helmet. He brought it back to the headlights so he could figure out how to light the flame.

"What are you doing?" Kristin asked.

"I'm going to ruin the practical joke by sneaking in on them," he said. "Can't fool me if I'm fooling them."

"You can't go in there," Kristin said. "There's something terrible happening in there. I'm not going to let you stop me from getting help for Joy and Carlos."

Ryan fired up the light and loosened the helmet so it would fit his head. He put his hand in front of the acetylene flame and smiled when it burned his fingers.

"I'll be right back," he said. "Where are they hiding?"

"Just think about this," Kristin said. "If it were a joke, why would I want you to drive *away* from those guys. I would be trying to lure you in. This isn't a joke. We'll go right to a phone and call the cops, or an ambulance."

"Right, that's exactly what I'm going to do. I know how those guys think. They're not going to get me that easily." Ryan turned towards the cave and started walking.

Kristin stood next to the Jeep, stunned as Ryan walked away. She couldn't let him go. She needed the key.

"Just give me the key, Ryan," she said.

He made a dismissive wave over his shoulder.

Kristin felt cold desperation settling into her chest. She had been so close to salvation, and now the key was walking right back into danger.

She couldn't let him go.

Kristin searched around for something appropriate. Her eyes landed on a rock that was about the size of a brick. With no more warning, she picked it up and ran at Ryan. She prayed that the helmet would do its job. She brought the rock down on the back of his head.

He tripped and then splayed out on the ground. The headlamp went out as he hit. Kristin fell on him and jammed her hand into his pocket.

He moaned as she pulled out the key.

"Sorry," she said. She ran back to the Jeep.

Kristin hauled the wheel to the side and then reached over to lock the doors. Her eyes tried to find Ryan in the dark, but he was just a dark shape on the ground. The Jeep's headlights didn't extend to where he had collapsed.

She kept a firm foot on the gas and let out the clutch slowly. The Jeep started forward smoothly, but it picked up speed too quick. Kristin wasn't ready for it. The vehicle started to buck and she slammed down on the clutch. She rolled back to the narrow access road.

As her speed began to wane, Kristin tried the clutch again. This time was even worse. When the clutch began to engage, the jerking motion made her foot slip off the pedal. She lurched forward and stomped on the accelerator. The engine whined and the Jeep sounded strained. When she pulled her foot from the gas, the vehicle began to buck again.

Ryan appeared at the window. He banged.

"Stop!" he shouted.

Kristin gave it gas again. The road took a sharp left. Kristin didn't. The front wheels spilled over the edge of the road and hit a patch of loose rocks on the sharp descent. She forgot about the clutch and the gas and slammed both feet down on the brake pedal.

The Jeep stalled.

The steering wheel stiffened in her grip.

The Jeep began to tip.

Before she could straighten the wheel or let up on the brakes, the Jeep was on two wheels. It slammed down on the passenger's door and began to slide. Kristin hadn't buckled in. She was tossed to the side.

The Jeep slid to a stop.

Kristin was pressed against the passenger's door and was looking at a sideways world lit up by the headlights. She heard Ryan's feet as he jumped on top of the vehicle and ripped open the driver's door. He stood above her and reached down into the vehicle.

"Grab my hand," he said.

She slapped his hand away.

"This is your fault," she said.

"*My* fault? You just crushed me with a rock and then flipped Joy's Jeep. How the fuck is it my fault?"

Kristin pushed herself up.

Chapter Twenty-Seven — Hike

TRAVIS FELT NUMB EVERY time he looked back to Miguel. He wanted to go back and verify that there was no pulse. He wanted to shake him and listen for breathing. He knew it was no use. It was easier to not think about it as soon as he got far enough away that his light didn't reach Miguel's form.

Travis inched his way towards the outlet of the giant bowl. The walls were nearly vertical. There was no way to leave the big room in that direction without descending to the white floor. He couldn't be sure, but it seemed safe to assume that the white floor was responsible for Miguel's death. It was some kind of poison.

Travis looked around for another solution. Up the wall, he saw a few more holes like the one they had dropped through. Those were too high up to reach. He made a run at one. As soon as he lost his footing, he slipped back down the rock and barely caught himself before he slid right into the white part of the floor. He wasn't going to try that again.

"Shit," he whispered.

There was a spot of Miguel's blood on the strap of the backpack. His eyes kept returning to it.

"Okay. Fuck," he said. He couldn't go forward and he couldn't go up. The only direction left was to follow the curve of the room back to where he'd left Miguel. He could only hope that there was some other exit around the other side of the room.

Travis turned and started walking. As soon as the dark shape of Miguel appeared in the reaches of his light, Travis crossed his arms. He didn't want to look at Miguel's eyes—he was sure they would be open. He swung high up the sloped wall. He climbed until his feet slipped with each step and ached from the angle. He gave Miguel a wide berth and tried to not look at his friend's face.

Travis slipped and came down on his ass. He slid a few feet closer to Miguel. When he came to a stop, he sat there. His light was trained on Miguel's helmet.

Travis sat in silence.

"I'm sorry, man," Travis said to the body. "I'm sorry there was nothing I could do to help you. This whole trip was a stupid idea."

Thinking about the beginning of the evening reminded Travis of the map. He rooted around in the bag until he found it. He took his first good look at the document. The paper was grade school notebook paper. The lines were drawn in pencil and ballpoint pen. The annotations were "Muerte," and "Peligro." It seemed less like a map and more like a written warning to stay away from the mine.

Travis shook his head and stowed the map. He pulled out the biggest chunk of ore they had found. It really did look like gold embedded in the rock. Travis was amazed at how shiny it looked. It wasn't hard to imagine how the element had become so valued. Anything that was so beautiful in its natural state would surely be refined and coveted.

He spun the rock and admired the sparkle of the quartz crystal as well.

"It really is beautiful," he whispered to Miguel.

One part of the quartz sparkled more than the rest. It seemed to pick up the light from his headlamp, twist it and split it, and send it back to his eyes in a million little stars. Travis pulled Miguel's knife from the bag and used the blade to chip off part of the crystal. He wanted to see if the illusion would be diminished or enhanced.

Travis stared at the rock for a full minute, trying to figure out what he was looking at. Embedded in the quartz and rock, he was looking at faceted stone. He chipped away a little more of the quartz and the stone fell out. It landed in the palm of his hand.

"What?" he whispered. He took the little stone between two fingers and held it up to the light. The cut was simple, but it looked like a gemstone. Travis tilted his head and puzzled over the thing.

"They don't just grow like this. Someone has to cut them," he said to himself. It was too symmetrical and too perfect to be an accident. Travis looked back to the chunk of ore. He spun the thing, looking at the stripes of gold in the rock. It took a second, but he found another unnatural feature in the ore. There was a graceful curve embedded in one of the gold stripes. Travis angled the stone and his light caught the edges of one cursive word.

"Eternity."

"How did a goddamn ring get into a rock in the wall of a cave?" he asked the stone.

Travis looked up at Miguel. He scrambled backwards, nearly dropping the diamond and the ore.

Miguel had moved.

Chapter Twenty-Eight — Deduction

JUSTIN FLIPPED THROUGH THE rest of the diary, looking for more information. He had read all the text. The binding creaked as he closed it and stuffed it into his bag. He kicked the metal box and the sound echoed through the cave.

He stood up and shouldered the pack. Justin walked along the dry riverbed and thought about this new information.

As he paced, he whispered to himself. "Darkness swallows people. Bones end up in those powder pods. How do they get there?"

He had forgotten about his experiment with the paperback books until his light picked one up on the trail ahead. Justin had arranged them in a line at different elevations in the cave. They weren't in a line anymore. The one at his feet was several feet down-cave from the others. The higher the elevation, the less each book had moved.

"Some kind of force moves things through the cave," he said. "Like a giant, glacial digestive system."

He looked down at the sand beneath his feet. Suddenly, he wasn't thrilled to be standing there. He climbed the rocks at his side until he was standing on the ledge with the book that had moved the smallest distance. The cave seemed different with his fresh perspective. His notion of an enormous digestive system didn't match the horror portrayed in the journal.

The darkness swallowed them whole. Cracks appeared and then closed on their own.

Justin stopped. His eyes grew wide.

He was in one of the cracks. What if it closed and he was

trapped? Justin didn't waste any more time. He began to run towards where Miguel and Travis had left him.

Justin pulled up short when he got to where the ledge ended. His desperation cast a new light on the passage. The ledge had rounded a corner where it broke away. That's what made it so difficult to try to leap across. He could barely see the spot where he would need to reach. But jumping wasn't the only way across the gap. The walls weren't that far apart. Justin began to wonder if he could put his hands on one and stretch his legs over to the other.

He would have to try the technique in a safe place, just to try.

Justin retreated to the dry riverbed. He found a spot where rocks were similarly spaced. He put his hands on one and tested his foot against the other. He fell immediately to the sandy floor. Remembering his theory about the digestive nature of the cave, he jumped up and brushed himself off immediately. He thought about his failure for a second and thought he knew the answer. He had been trying to hold his body in a straight line. Architecturally, an arch was much stronger. He found rocks closer together and tested his theory.

It wasn't easy to walk his hands and feet along opposite walls, but it was possible. He broke off his practice with the idea to save his strength for the real test.

Back at the fissure, Justin examined the walls. He looked for a spot where the gap was manageable. He would have to climb down, below the ledge, to find a place where he could execute his plan.

Justin puffed out his cheeks with a sigh.

This was a bad idea. The only sane thing to do was to stay put and wait for help. With the supplies he had found, he had carbide and water, which meant he had light. And he could drink the water to stay hydrated. That should give him more than enough time to wait for help.

On the other hand, there was a chance that help wasn't coming. If his fissure was like the one from the journal, it might close at any second, trapping him inside. Or, the darkness might come and swallow him whole, like the people from the story.

Justin's eyes darted back and forth—what if the story was fiction? What if someone had made it up just to mess with explorers?

He shook his head.

"It was too well hidden," he whispered. "Can't be fake."

Yes, he could wait. He could also explore the hall of painted faces more thoroughly. The place had creeped him out, so he had given up on it, but it might also offer a way out. But the crack was known. That's how he had gotten in.

Justin decided.

He lowered himself to the ledge and hung his feet over.

This had to go perfectly on the first try.

Justin put his feet against the left wall. After a big inhale, he shifted his weight and braced his hands against the opposite wall. He began to shuffle.

Sweat dripped down his nose. Every time he turned his head to see where to put his hand, he burned his arm with the lamp. The helmet threatened to fall off when he looked down. Justin grunted and slid his hand. His abdomen pulled and strained. It felt like the muscles were tearing apart, and he was only a third of the way across.

Justin glanced back. He debated turning back.

The mental image of the trapped miners kept him going.

It was easier to move his feet. He could shift his weight between his heel and toe so he didn't ever lose contact with the wall. His hands were harder. For those he had to temporarily take all the burden with one arm while the other moved.

Justin's arms vibrated with the effort.

He shifted his weight and one foot slipped. Stretching out his toe, he finally caught an edge. He was at the far end of the gap, but he didn't know how to make the transition. The ledge was above the level of his shoulder, and the fissure was too wide to climb higher.

Justin had no choice. There wasn't enough strength in his body to attempt the climb back. He was well beyond the point of no return. With one big push, Justin thrust his hands away from the wall and twisted to his left. He caught the lip. For a second, it seemed like the climb would be easy.

His feet slipped.

Justin's body swung down and he lost his grip. Four fingers were all that kept him from falling down into the squeeze.

Flailing his feet, one caught a point of rock and he was stable for a moment. He swung his other hand back up over the lip. His muscles were almost useless. Justin began the slow process of inching his way up to the lip. He moved his feet with extraordinary care. He was panting by the time he got his elbows up over the edge. When he finally pulled his torso onto the ledge, he rolled to his side. The lamp sputtered as he turned it upwards.

Justin smiled and then laughed as the light flickered.

He sat up and looked at the gap.

It was wider than when he had started.

"Impossible," he whispered.

It was completely impossible, but it was also true. He was sure of it. This wasn't just a perspective shift because he was on the other side of the gap—it was at least fifty-percent farther to the opposite edge than when he had started.

"No going back," he said.

He rolled his shoulders, self-massaged his arm muscles, and stood. He set off down the crevice.

Justin walked with his head down. He followed the footprints in the dust. He stopped when he came to a place where lots of scuffed footprints covered the whole floor of the passage. Justin looked up. There was no reason to stop there—the passage continued on around a corner.

Justin kept walking.

After two more corners, his passage squeezed down into nothing.

Kneeling, he could still find traces of the footprints, but they moved into a space where the walls closed together, making passage impossible. Distrusting his eyes, he felt the walls. He felt where they came together and blocked his escape.

He sank down and leaned against one of the walls, trying to think through the problem.

Justin was tired and thirsty. He found his canteen and poured a little water into his open mouth. It was slightly gritty and tasted a bit of sulfur, but it quenched his thirst. Justin let his eyes drift shut.

After a second, his eyes flew back open. He'd had the distinct sensation that he was falling. He spun and looked at the wall behind him.

"Did you move?" he whispered to the wall.

Justin got back up. He retraced his steps to the place where he'd found the confused footprints and looked around. It only took him a second to deduce what had happened. Someone had climbed. He saw burn marks on the walls from the headlamps. He saw scuffed footprints on rocks above his eye-level. That was the direction that Miguel and Travis had gone, he was almost sure of it.

But, if his theory was correct, their path might not be reproducible. The walls of this crevice weren't behaving.

Justin moved back to the spot where the fissure squeezed down. Using a few of his matches, he marked the narrowest part of the passage that he could reach. He laid the matches end to end across the width of it and then settled back down with his back against the wall. He turned down the drip of his headlamp and let it burn low.

Justin waited.

Chapter Twenty-Nine — Choices

"I MEAN, THIS IS it, right?" Roger asked.

"Not necessarily," Florida said.

He turned away from the hole.

"Are you suggesting we go back down the hangman's noose?"

"We could," she said. "That's all I'm saying. We could go back that way instead of committing ourselves to this path."

"There's something down there, remember?" he asked. He lifted his foot for illustration.

"Your shoe?"

"My shoe and whatever was pulling on that rope. I have no interest in finding out what that was. I swear to you that it wasn't a snag."

"You were panicked—it's understandable. I was cranking the noose higher, your foot was caught. It's nothing to be ashamed of."

"I'm not ashamed. I'm telling you, there was something bad down there. I'm not going back that way. We've explored every inch of these crystal tunnels, and I think it's safe to say that there are only two ways out. We can go into this giant room and try to track down that guy we saw, or we can go back through the hangman's cave and stare into the face of evil."

"Don't be so dramatic," Florida said.

"I'll send help for you if I find it," he said. He didn't give her a chance to object. Roger pushed forward and let himself drop through the hole. It wasn't far down to the sloping wall of the enormous room. They had found many holes into the room, but this one had only a short drop to where the wall began to slope away.

He landed on bent legs and threw himself to the rock to increase his friction. Even on his back, he slid several yards before he came to a stop. He glanced back up to the cave where he'd dropped in. He saw a glow there, but couldn't tell if it was from the crystals or from Florida's light. Glancing around, he saw the glow from several of the other holes. It was an unsettling sight.

Roger scooted down the sloping wall until he got to a place level enough to stand easily. He was starting to figure out Florida. She didn't respond to cajoling or requests. His best bet was to keep moving forward and wait for her to join him. If she didn't, then so be it. He had fresh batteries from her pack, and that was the best he could hope for.

He swept his light around to orient himself.

The place he was looking for was off to the right.

Roger slowed as he approached.

He heard Florida come up behind him, but he didn't turn.

"Thanks for waiting for me," she said.

"I've never seen a dead body before."

"What?"

She moved around him and walked forward on the tips of her toes. Roger envied her two shoes and uninjured hips.

"I thought it was just a shirt on the ground," she said.

"No," Roger said. "Look there." He pointed with his toe.

Where the shirtsleeve ended, he could see the arm bones disappearing into the rock. Florida, perhaps unconvinced, walked right up to the shirt. She tried to lift it from the back, but parts of the fabric were actually embedded in the stone floor. Instead of lifting, the shirt ripped. She continued the tear and revealed the twisted spine and ribcage. The flesh was gone and all that was left was a half-exposed skeleton.

Florida knelt.

"I don't believe it. This is solid rock. I would have assumed it had been here for thousands of years, but this shirt is modern enough," she said.

"If I had to guess, this isn't rock, but some kind of supercooled liquid. Like glass, you know? Is it wrong that I'm less upset about the body and more upset that his shoes aren't exposed?" Roger asked.

"Yes," she said. She turned her light back and looked at the giant room. "That man we saw—this is what he was looking at."

Roger nodded. "I think so. I wonder why he didn't hear us."

"He went this way," she said, pointing.

She led the way.

Where their sloping wall ended, they stood at the edge of the white sediment that made up the floor of the giant room.

"You think it's safe?" Florida asked. She turned her head and sneezed.

"Nothing about this place is safe," he said. "We're not going that way unless we can walk on this shit." He pointed to the tunnel that led to the right. The vertical walls came right up from the white floor. He put out his socked foot and touched it to the white power a little puff swirled around his toes.

"Fuck!" he shouted. Roger limped backwards away from the white floor. He fell to the sloping rock and pushed himself up and away. Florida followed, looking puzzled as Roger tore off his sock. Once it was off, he used the sock to wipe at the sole of his bare foot. "Look at this," he said. He held up the sock. In the center of the bloodstain, the threads of the sock were gone. They had been eaten away and they were still smoking. He tossed the sock down.

"Whoa," Florida said. She sneezed again and wiped her nose on her arm. "Oh shit." There was a streak of blood on her shirt. She tilted her head back and pinched her nose.

"Shit," Roger said. "It's the powder. It's some kind of acid or something. We have to get away from it. It must be in the air, too."

Florida nodded. They climbed as high as they could up the sloping wall. Roger leaned back against the rock to take the weight off his foot.

"Those rocks over there. We can climb them and maybe get close enough to jump to one of the holes," Roger said.

"Then back down the hangman's rope," she said. "It's the only way."

Roger sighed and nodded. He looked at the bottom of his foot. He had a spot where the skin looked irritated, but it wasn't any worse than a minor burn. He set it down on the rock. He glanced back in the direction of the corpse that was embedded in the rock. The thought of it made him push back up to his feet.

"Hey," Florida said. She nudged him with her elbow. When he looked over, she was pointing to across the bowl. There was a shape moving there.

"Hello!" Roger shouted.

Florida put her hand on Roger's arm. "Save your breath."

"Huh? Why?"

She didn't explain. She just nodded towards the shape. Roger couldn't tell if it was the same person they had seen earlier. The person was too far away both times. He assumed it was a man, but it was honestly just a guess. The shape was climbing up the wall on the far side of the impassable tunnel. He must have walked all the way around the perimeter of the bowl.

Roger blinked and shook his head slightly. The person was gone. Then, before he had a chance to express his confusion, the shape was back again. But it had backed up several feet and was repeating the same move.

"What the fuck?" Roger whispered.

"I don't know," Florida said. "I'm not sure that's a real person. It looks more like a movie of a person or something."

"What does that mean?"

"I don't know. Let's go—it's a long way around to where he is."

She turned and started hiking along the steep slope.

"Wait, we're following him?"

"Yup," she said over her shoulder.

"What about climbing back up so we can go down the hangman's rope?"

"We'll never make it," she said. "We're going to follow him." She pointed across the cave.

Chapter Thirty — Entrance

"STOP!" KRISTIN SCREAMED. SHE stood ten paces from the mouth of the mine. It was as close as she was going to get. When Kristin had been a kid, her father had raised Alaskan Malamutes. The dogs were an absurd choice in the summer. They spent every day panting and leaving little drips of spit on the carpet. It didn't matter how cold her father turned the air conditioning—the Malamutes did nothing but slobber and shed. Her father could make them lie down, rollover, and present their paws to be wiped off before they came in the house.

Kristin couldn't even make one of the dogs sit for a treat.

Her father always said that you don't *ask* a dog to do something, you *tell* them. She heard it, eventually. There was a tone of voice he used that demanded obedience. She had never learned the trick until just that moment. When she yelled, "Stop!" to Ryan, it had been an undeniable *command*.

He was standing right at the mouth of the mine, and he jerked to a stop. He turned around to face her.

Kristin put her hands on her hips and summoned the tone again. "Listen to me, Ryan." She shook her head and lowered her voice so he would have to really listen. "Joy is dead. She's not going to care that I wrecked her Jeep, because she is somewhere on the floor of that mine, split open right now. Carlos is missing, and I don't have any idea where the others are. I'm going to walk back to the road and hopefully flag down a car. All I'm asking is that you don't go in that mine. Stay out here and wait. Maybe the others will get lucky. Trust me, it's not safe to go in there."

"You're serious," he said.

It wasn't a question, but she nodded. She felt pride and hope welling up. She had convinced him. He took a slow step towards her and then seemed to finally commit to the decision. He nodded with her and advanced.

"I'll stay here in case they come out."

"Good," she said.

There was a noise from the mine. Ryan turned and cocked his head.

She saw the darkness emerge from the cave entrance and snuff his light. Before she could scream, the black cloud had enveloped Ryan. As quick as it had emerged, it was gone. Kristin's arms dropped to her sides as her jaw fell open. She blinked.

Kristin turned and ran for the road.

Ryan heard the thing approach. It sounded like an enormous sigh.

The darkness grew from the center of the mine and it ate the ground, the rock, and the sky. The inky black swallowed his light and left his eyes useless. The air was forced from his lungs as he was jerked forward.

The sensation of movement only lasted a second. After that, he felt like he was floating in the ocean. The water was warm around him and all he could hear was the gentle sound of surf caressing the beach.

This wasn't the ocean though. He was in the mine. Kristin had been right to be afraid. If he'd listened sooner, he would have been fine. There was no sense in dwelling in that thought—he had to do something.

Ryan stretched his arms out, convinced he would find the walls of the mine. He felt nothing. He spun around in his weightless environment. His eyes detected no light.

A sensation—a light tickle—began on the backs of his legs. The feeling spread up to his back and then down his arms.

The tickle flared with heat and turned to pain. Ryan tried to scream. He heard nothing coming from his lips. The sound of his own racing heartbeat filled his ears and blocked out the sound of the gentle surf.

The pain wrapped around him from back to front. He felt like he was sinking down into lava. Something flowed into his ears. He heard the sound of a machine gun going off in each ear and then silence. His lungs began to burn with each inhale. He coughed and felt the heat penetrating deep into his chest.

Suddenly, the darkness exploded into a million stars. He was looking into the depths of space. The stars exploded and left him looking at an unbroken, unfocused field of red. His sense of smell went next. Ryan smelled lilacs and roses and then hot ammonia. After that, he smelled nothing.

His skin flared with one more white-hot sensation.

Ryan knew no more.

Chapter Thirty-One — Exit

He stared at the body for several minutes before he got the nerve to move closer. It was the arm that had moved. The cuff of Miguel's shirt had moved to the side. Travis watched Miguel's back as he advanced. He was watching for any sign of respiration—there was none.

"Miguel?" Travis asked. He didn't like the way his voice echoed in the giant room. It was a lonely sound.

He scooted forward until his foot was within reach of Miguel's hand. With the tip of his shoe, he nudged the shirt cuff up.

Travis shook his head, rejecting what he saw.

He moved a little closer to verify.

The tips of Miguel's fingers were missing. They had disappeared into the rock. Travis gathered his nerve and used his shoe to nudge Miguel's hand. The fingers were stuck there.

Travis stood up. He circled Miguel's body. The blood stains on the rock were beginning to disappear. The toe of Miguel's shoe was embedded in the rock as well.

Travis shuddered. He backed away and then realized that he was moving downhill, towards the white floor of the giant room. He turned and began walking away quickly. This time he didn't look back.

Travis was almost around to the other side of the outlet when he saw a way out. The smooth bowl of the cave was broken by a crack that was a few inches wide. Its jagged path offered just enough of a handhold for Travis to climb up to one of the holes.

He walked as high as he could and then jammed his fingers into the crack. His feet pedaled at the smooth rock until he found enough friction to push himself upwards to the next grip. When he finally got his foot up high enough to reach the crack, the going was easier.

Travis finally pulled himself up over the lip of the hole and exhaled as he flopped down on his back. He looked back over the massive cave with its white floor. Somewhere, across the expanse, Miguel's body was being absorbed into the floor. Travis shook away the thought and turned his attention to the new tunnel he had reached. He prayed that it didn't peter out.

He followed the tube, always watching hopefully down to the next bend. One of these would exit to the mine, or even better, out to the night sky. He was sure of it.

The tube stretched out into a straight section. His light couldn't find the end of it.

He ducked into a crouch reflexively when the blast of air hit him from behind. It was warm and smelled like rotten eggs. The breeze was gone as quickly as it had appeared. Travis stood back up slowly and continued down the passage.

He slowed again when he saw a black spot on the wall. As he got closer, he saw another, and then a third.

They were portraits. The one on the far right was signed.

"Robert Clyde, 1896," Travis read aloud. In the portrait, the boy's eyes were beautiful, but sad. Travis moved away from the wall as he continued walking. He didn't like the way the faces watched him as he moved by. He kept expecting their open mouths to call to him, or their eyes to blink. A crack opened at his feet along the other side of the passage. Travis struck a balance, walking between the crack and the portraits. He was driven forward by the thought of that putrid air from behind. He felt like he was being driven, like a steer into a killing chute.

The portraits finally ran out. He hadn't bothered to count, but glancing back he saw that they stretched as far as his light.

Travis continued on and stopped at a mark on the floor.

Someone had disturbed the cave dust—it was unmistakable. Shining his light down into the crack, he saw that there was enough room to easily fit down into that space and there was a ledge down there. Even more interesting, there was half of a footprint on the ledge.

He glanced around, trying to decide what to do.

If there was someone else in the cave, he wanted to know who it was. Travis lowered himself over the edge and dropped down to the ledge. Once he ducked through he shone his light through to another big cave. To some extent, all these caves looked alike. Still, there was something familiar about this cavern. Travis looked back to make sure he could remember where he had been. He climbed down the rocks.

Something white and rectangular caught his light in the distance. Travis picked up speed.

He dropped down to the sandy bottom of this big cave and saw more footprints. He spotted the second white rectangle and then the third. They were paperback books, and they were spread out up the stone wall on various ledges.

He stooped and picked one up.

It was one of the paperback books that Carlos had found in the moldy bag.

Travis looked up and down the cave and began to realize where he was. He had traveled all that distance and lost a friend just to come back to the same shitty cave that they'd started in. It was too much. He felt like his head was going to explode with frustration. Travis put his hands on either side of his helmet and turned his face up towards the ceiling.

"FUCK THIS CAVE!"

Chapter Thirty-Two — Reunion

JUSTIN COUNTED OFF THE seconds.

"Twenty-one, one-thousand, twenty-two, one-thousand."

He slipped the end of the match between the gap.

"It's not the same," he said. He sighed and leaned back. The spread of the walls was measurable, but it wasn't consistent. He had no way of predicting how long he would have to wait before the crevice was passable again. To be fair, he didn't know if the whole crevice moved at the same rate.

There was nothing to do but wait.

Justin turned down his lamp until the flame sputtered. He lowered his head.

"...ck this cave," echoed from the rocks.

Justin sat up. His eyes were wide open.

"Hello?" he called. "HELLO?"

He waited a few seconds.

"Justin?" Travis called.

Justin jumped to his feet. He pulled the straps of his bag tight and glanced at his scattered matches before he rushed back down the crevice. It wasn't until he was nearing the edge that his paranoia kicked in. What if this was yet another way that the cave was screwing with him?

"Travis?"

"Yeah! I'm right here," Travis called from somewhere beyond the gap.

Justin saw his light but couldn't see his face.

"Be careful," Justin said. "There's a big hole there."

"Yeah, okay. Jesus, I'm glad you're here. I thought you might be dead. Wait..."

Justin shifted his eyes and tilted his head as he waited. "Wait for what?"

"How do I know it's really you?" Travis asked.

Justin smiled. "Because you let Hilary Cramer's brother touch your balls for a..."

"Okay," Travis said. Justin heard the laugh in his voice. "That's fine. No need to dredge up the past. How did you get over there?"

"I braced myself between the walls. I stretched out like Superman, you know? I wouldn't recommend it now though. The gap is getting bigger every minute."

"Seriously?" Travis asked.

"Wait—how did you get back there? We were in opposite positions the last time we talked."

"It was a long hairy trip around," Travis said. "Listen—Miguel didn't make it. He breathed in poison or something."

Justin didn't know what to say. He wanted to object. Travis had to be wrong. People their age didn't just die. But there was something in Travis's voice that made him bite his tongue.

"Hey, how are we going to get you back from there?" Travis asked.

"No," Justin said. "We need to get you to this side. This is the way out."

"I've been that way," Travis said. "The crack that leads back to the mines is closed. You just go up and around and wind up back here. Besides, there's dangerous shit over there."

Justin nodded even though Travis couldn't see him.

"The crack is opening again. I see what you're saying—it's definitely closed now—but I've been measuring it. It's reopening as we speak. I don't know how long it will take, but if we wait for it, we can get back to the mine. I've got to ask you something. Don't think I'm crazy, okay?"

Travis took a second before he answered. "Sure."

"When Miguel went, did it seem like the cave was eating him."

There was no answer from Travis. Justin realized that he should have waited until they were face to face before he asked such a weird question, but his theories were consuming him.

Travis's voice finally came. "Yeah. It did."

"Are you sure about this?" Justin called. He had his end of the rope looped around a sturdy rock. After that, the rope was looped around his own waist. He was leaning back to put tension on it.

"It's solid on this end. Just keep your end tight."

"We can wait until the gap closes," Justin said.

"How long is that going to take?" Travis asked. "Besides, as far as we know, this gap will only close when your crevice closes again."

Justin shrugged. It was a good point. He leaned back a little more and the rope creaked. He had no idea how long the rope had been in the cave. Justin didn't even know what Travis had connected the rope to on the other end. But Travis was desperate to make it across the gap. Truth be told, Justin was pretty desperate to see another living face again.

"I'm ready," Justin called.

Justin was pulled forward as Travis put his weight on the rope. He raised his foot and braced it against the rock he was using as his anchor. The rope creaked even more, but it stayed taut. Justin glanced over his shoulder to see where the rope was pulled over the rocks. The whole thing would have been much easier if not for the curve in the tunnel over the gap. Instead of a straight shot, Travis was forced to climb around a corner. Justin had no idea how his friend was going to pull it off.

The rope bounced and tugged as Travis moved. It dug into Justin's skin as he resisted the pull.

He heard Travis grunting his way around the corner. When he looked to see Travis's progress, he barked out a laugh and almost lost his grip.

"You said I was crazy when I wanted to stop and get my jeans," Travis said between panting breaths.

He had taken off his pants and tied the legs together. Travis was using the loop of denim as a sling to keep himself tethered to the rope.

"No," Justin said, laughing, "I said you were a pain in the ass. I never said you were crazy. The rest of us had the decency to bring underground clothes with us."

"Forgive me for not keeping a change of clothes at Ryan's house," Travis said.

Justin secured the rope with one hand and put his other hand out for Travis. When he was close enough, Travis reached over and pulled himself up to the ledge. The slack came off and Justin let go. He inspected the rope burns around his midsection.

Travis was taking off his shoes so he could put his jeans back on.

"Everyone else gets Ryan's mom to do their laundry. I don't know why you don't do that," Justin said.

Travis stood up and fed the end of the rope back around the rock.

"She won't do mine anymore," Travis said. "You remember the incident?"

Justin shook his head.

"The summer after graduation? We got blitzed on rum behind the Downtown Market?"

Justin nodded. "Right. Yes! Didn't you have a little accident that night?"

Travis made a flourish with his hand.

"You tried to get Ryan's mom to wash your shit-pants?"

"They were my only pants," Travis said.

Justin doubled-over laughing.

Travis flicked the end of the rope, sending a wave around the corner of the rock. While Justin got control of himself, Travis flicked the rope a few more times.

Justin wiped his eye and straightened back up. Still catching his breath from the laughter, he asked, "What are you doing?"

Travis gave one more flick and the rope went slack. He reeled it in, looping it around his arm. Justin's mouth fell open as he watched. The end of the rope was fashioned into a noose.

Justin stammered with disbelief. "You didn't have the end tied to anything?"

"It was over one of those sticking-up things. One of those rocks."

"A stalagmite? Are you serious?"

"Yeah, why?"

"Those aren't sturdy. You dumbass," Justin said.

"It worked," Travis said.

Justin shook his head. "Come on. I'll show you the matches."

"Okay. Cool," Travis said. He nudged his foot towards Justin's line of matches on the rock.

"Don't touch!" Justin said. He put his hand on Travis's arm.

"I don't get it."

"I put these down some time ago. I don't know exactly how long it has been. When I started, I could only fit three matches across there. Now it's up to six and a half. The gap is getting wider. You see where that footprint disappears behind that rock? When I came here, that footprint wasn't even visible. In fact, I think you and Miguel got stopped at least ten feet back."

"No," Travis said. "We backtracked to there because we couldn't go any farther here. We had to back up to a spot where we could reach both sides and there was somewhere to go."

"Oh," Justin said. "Still—this is the way we came in, and as soon as it gets wide enough, this is the way we can get out."

"What makes you think it's going to keep getting wider. Maybe it gets wide for a bit and then contracts. Maybe it only gets wide enough to pass through like once a month or something. It could be based on the moon—you don't know."

Justin slumped a little. "Yeah. True. I'm desperate to get out of the cave and back to the mine. At least then we would have a chance."

Travis fished a finger up under his helmet to scratch his head. He glanced around. "We'd have more than just a chance—we'd be out. I remember exactly which mine shafts to take to get out."

"Yeah, but that might not be the only problem," Justin said.

"There's this book I found."

"The paperbacks?"

"No. It's a diary," Justin said. He shifted the pack from his shoulder and dug through until he found the journal. He began to explain its contents to Travis.

Chapter Thirty-Three — Tracking

"Up there?" Roger asked.

"Yeah."

He shrugged. Roger wished that he had half the confidence that Florida possessed. She was always one-hundred percent convinced that she knew what she was doing. Decisions were a snap for her.

She was already climbing. Roger did have confidence in one thing—he knew that she had better upper-body strength than he did. Since she was struggling with the climb, he had little hope that he would be able to follow her.

Florida reached the hole and turned back.

"How about you make sure it goes somewhere before I climb?"

"This is the way we saw the movie-guy go," she said.

"So?"

Florida turned and then disappeared.

Roger sat down on the sloped wall and looked out across the huge room. From what he'd seen of the skeleton across the way, the floor beneath him wasn't to be trusted. He kept that in mind as he leaned back. Looking across the enormous cave alleviated his claustrophobia.

"It goes," she called from above.

"Got it," he said. Roger mumbled to himself as he climbed. "Damn, Alaska, you're always looking for something to climb."

"Don't touch it," Florida said.

"Why not?" Roger asked. He brushed the soot line that made up the portrait's hair.

"You've ruined it," she said.

"Do you think anyone is ever going to be this deep in this cave ever again? Do you think we're getting out of here alive? Who did I ruin it for?"

"This guy," she said, pointing to the signature. "Carlos Garza."

"If he cared about it, he should have done a better job making it," Roger said.

"I'm sure he did the best he could," she said.

"Now this guy," Roger said. He moved across the tunnel to the opposite wall. "Robert Clyde was a real artist. You think this actually dates back to 1896?"

"I don't see why not. This mine was in service well before then. It's not unrealistic to assume that one of the men found his way up here and made those drawings."

"He had real talent. He was wasting his time digging up rocks for a living."

"Maybe this kind of drawing wasn't popular back then," Florida said. She moved down the wall like she was at an art gallery. "Modernism was becoming popular at the end of the nineteenth century, I think. These types of drawings might have been considered passé."

"Forgive me, but I think that beautiful drawings are always beautiful, regardless of what's in fashion."

"You just don't realize how you're affected by the current..."

Florida was interrupted by the echo of a yell.

Roger moved around her and limped quickly down the tunnel. He stopped when he found the spot where there was a crack between the floor and the wall of the passage.

"I think it came from down here," he said.

Florida angled her light down through the gap. "More voices," she said.

"We're chasing ghosts," Roger said.

Florida nodded. "And I'm starting to wonder if it's the best idea. They don't seem to be leading us anywhere useful."

"There aren't a lot of choices," Roger said. He pointed his light farther down the cave. "You don't have very many batteries left. Flares are going to be a bear to navigate with, and I can't imagine they last very long. We have to figure this out pretty quick. What's the plan—chase the voices or keep going down this tunnel and see what happens?"

For once, Florida didn't have a quick decision. She glanced both directions and then back the way they had come. Her light settled on the first portrait. The woman's face was horribly sad.

"What do you think?" Florida asked.

Roger blinked. He was surprised by the question, and equally surprised that he didn't have an answer.

"I've never believed in ghosts," he said.

"I don't either," she said.

"But I'm starting to," he said.

She raised her eyebrows and then gave a little nod.

"So," he continued, "if we assume that we're following some kind of spirit or something, it might also be safe to assume that the guy didn't make it, you know?"

"That's why he's a ghost," she said, completing his thought.

"Why would we follow someone who didn't make it?"

"Up until this point, we didn't have a whole lot of options," she said. "How about I run ahead for a second and give you a break? I think better when I'm running and your foot looks like it could use a rest."

"I'm not sure it's a great idea to split up."

"I won't take any turns. I'm just going to see if this goes anywhere. For all we know, there's an exit right up ahead and Robert Clyde just wandered in here to draw his portraits and then he wandered right back out."

Roger was nodding along with her idea. It was an interesting thought.

"I *am* slowing you down, and we *are* running out of light. Yeah, okay."

"Good. I'll be right back," she said.

Roger eased himself down to a seat on the rock floor. He looked up and saw Florida do something amazing. She slipped her arm out from the strap of her pack and handed it down to him.

"I'll go faster without this bouncing around. Keep it on, would you?"

"Yeah," he said. He put the backpack on. "Stay safe."

"Will do," she said. Florida ran off down the cave.

Chapter Thirty-Four — Hope

"THIS IS FAKE," TRAVIS said. He closed the journal and handed it back to Justin. "Forget about it."

"It's not fake," Justin said. "You remember where we found Miguel's knife? I found it in one of those things."

"So? I'm saying that anyone could have written this. Someone is just screwing with you."

"People don't write like that anymore," Justin said. "With big flowery letters like that."

"Bullshit. It's not impossible. I could do something like that if I tried."

"Wait a second. I'm saying that there are things in this mine that can kill us. You saw Miguel die. We're saying the same damn thing."

"Miguel was an accident," Travis said. He stared at Justin. "He kicked up some of that powder stuff and breathed it in. As long as we stay away from that, we'll be fine."

"This cave is expanding and contracting," Justin said. "I put books back there on the rocks and they're moving on their own. It's like they're flowing down an invisible stream. Our possessions were stolen and then ended up being packed in that corrosive powder. We also found bones in there. All these things add up."

Justin thumped the journal like a Bible.

"Add up to what? What do you want me to do about it?"

"I think this cave is digesting people. It's like one of those sea anemones or something. People come in, they get trapped in the folds in here, and then they get digested. It's trying to feed on us."

Travis scratched his head again. He looked back towards the

matches.

"There's something you should know," he said. "Wait—two things. Miguel was sinking into the floor of that place where I left him."

"See!"

Travis was pulling his pack from his back. "And this."

He pulled out the chunk of ore and pointed to the hammered and polished part of the gold.

"What is it?" Justin asked.

"It's a wedding ring. This gold is recycled."

"See!" Justin said. He slapped Travis's shoulder. "I fucking told you. This cave eats people."

"So what do we do about it?" Travis asked.

"If you see darkness, run."

"Great. Great plan," Travis said. He shook his head.

"You remember that girl Mariah?" Travis asked.

"There were like five girls named Mariah in our class. Which one?" Justin asked.

"She was only here the year you came. After that she moved to Wyoming or something."

"No," Justin said. "I don't remember anyone from that first year. I mean, except people that I became friends with later. That whole school year is just a blur to me."

"Yeah, you were a weirdo."

"Me? That school was terrible. You guys were the worst. I was there like a week before a rumor went around that my family was part of a cult. Everyone said my parents were arrested for sacrificing dogs and old people and that I was being raised by my aunt and uncle," Justin said.

Travis laughed.

"And I know you were one of the people who made up that rumor," Justin said. "What's her name—that girl you dated in sophomore year—told me."

Travis covered his mouth, but kept laughing.

"Yes, it was all very funny," Justin said. "Ha. Ha."

"But you *were* a weirdo," Travis said. "It was wrong of us to start those rumors, but you were a total weirdo. Do you remember when you used to wear those purple socks and you would tuck your pants into them?"

"It was the style back east."

"There's not one chance in hell that I'm going to believe that."

Justin sat stone-faced for a second and then turned away. A small smile replaced his scowl. "Yeah, okay. I was trying to find some way of being cool so I made up that sock thing. It could have been a trend. If just one more person had picked it up, I could have totally started something. You had failures too. What was that song you tried to get everyone to like?"

"Let's not talk about that," Travis said.

"No, no. We should talk about it. We've talked about how I was such a weirdo. Why don't you tell me—what was the thought process behind singing that song at the talent show? After a month of everyone refusing to like that song, you thought you could finally make it popular by performing it at the talent show?"

Travis's laugh dropped into a chuckle. "My grandmother liked that song. I told her I would sing it for her in front of everyone and then she died. I thought I could talk it up and make it popular, and then it wouldn't be so weird when I performed it in the talent show."

They sat in silence for a second.

"Sorry, man, I didn't..." Justin couldn't finish the thought. He burst out laughing.

"Oh, fuck you," Travis said. He reached forward and swatted at Justin.

"No, seriously, that's tragic," Justin said. He kept laughing.

"Very funny. Make fun of somebody's dead grandmother."

Justin smiled. "I'm not making fun of her, I'm just thinking about you singing that goofy song in front of everyone. I bet she enjoyed it. It's sweet—her dying wish was to see her own grandson humiliated one more time."

Travis and Justin laughed together. The sound filled the

narrow passage.

When they fell silent, they realized that there was a new sound in the cave.

Justin scrambled to his feet and gave Travis a hand up. The walls were visibly moving. The crevice in front of them was growing wider.

"Go, man, what are you waiting for?" Travis asked.

"What if you're right? What if they fluctuate and we get crushed when the walls squeeze back together?"

"We have to take a chance on something. Go!"

Justin nodded and moved forward. They made it a few steps before the walls were too close together. Travis stayed right at his back. Each time Justin inched forward, Travis was right there.

"Watch out," Justin said. He pointed down at the floor. They passed by a couple of places were the ledge didn't stretch all the way over to the opposite wall. Travis tried to get a sense which wall was moving, but it seemed to be both. When he pointed his light at the floor, the walls appeared to part from the center out. It didn't make any sense. The sandy footprints exposed by the retreating walls should have been scraped away.

"Holy shit," Justin said.

"What?"

"I think I see the mine."

The walls stopped. The sound they had made was barely audible, but now that it had stopped, the silence seemed ominous. Travis could hear himself breathing.

"Can you squeeze through?" Travis whispered.

Justin gave it a shot. He wriggled between the rocks, pushing himself into the gap. His helmet got stuck and he grunted as he forced it forward.

Travis heard the sound again.

Justin screamed. "Fuck. Pull me back."

Travis grabbed his trailing arm and yanked. He pulled on Justin's arm as his friend twisted. Justin groaned and then popped free. They had barely enough room to turn in the space. Travis eyed the walls suspiciously, wondering if they would collapse back together.

"Come on, damn it," Justin whispered. "Just open a little more."

Travis put his hand on one of the walls. He felt a vibration, but couldn't sense any real movement.

"I don't want to die in here," Justin said.

"No," Travis said. "Me neither."

"Just a little more," Justin whispered.

When they heard the low rumble again, Travis was sure that death had found them. They were going to be compressed into paste between the collapsing walls. When they parted again, the only thing left of them would be their footprints on the sandy floor.

Travis realized that he was still holding Justin's hand when his friend jerked him forward.

"Come on!" Justin shouted. He let go of Travis's hand and moved fast.

Travis followed. He misjudged one of the gaps. Travis slipped through on his toes and his helmet fit through the space between the walls, but a sharp edge of rock scraped his cheek. He felt a line of blood rolling down his face like he was crying thick tears. He ducked through the next gap. He wanted to shed his backpack. It kept getting hung up on the walls. The space was so tight that he couldn't figure a good way to free his arms from the straps.

Suddenly, Justin disappeared.

A hand shot back through the crack and pulled him forward. Travis popped free and stumbled into the middle of the mine shaft. He turned back, expecting to see the crevice slam shut behind them, and he was right—the crack was gone.

Justin moved to the side a little and the shadow from his light showed Travis that he was wrong. The crack was there, it was just hard to see when he looked directly at it. He had to move to an oblique angle before it was really visible. The walls made a strange optical illusion that conspired to hide their crevice.

Travis hiked his bag up to his shoulders.

"Let's get the fuck out of here," he said.

Justin nodded.

211

They ran, pausing only a second at the turn to verify that they both agreed. They got to the shaft that led down and Travis threw himself to the floor. His foot found the rung while Justin leaned over and pointed his light down to the tunnel below.

The rung was bent. One side had been torn from the wall. Travis slipped down and caught himself before he could fall too far. His other foot found the next rung down and he was stable again.

"Careful with that first step," he said to Justin. "Keep your foot all the way over to the left side."

Justin's light bobbed as he nodded.

Travis found the next step and dropped his head below the lip of the shaft. He still held the edge of the rock. With one more step he could grab on to the broken rung.

Justin snatched his hand as his foot was feeling around.

"It's okay. I got it," Travis said.

Justin didn't let go. Travis looked up and Justin tore his eyes away from whatever he had been looking at. He looked sad and frightened as he shook his head.

"What?" Travis asked. He looked down. "Carlos! Hey, man, is everyone else..." Travis trailed off as he got a better look. Carlos was down there. His face was pointed up the shaft. His eyes were closed.

"Carlos?" Travis asked.

Carlos didn't answer.

Justin pulled on Travis's hand.

With both their lights shining on his face, Carlos turned and walked out of view. A cold chill ran down Travis's spine. He climbed back up a rung until he was face to face with Justin.

"What the fuck?" Travis asked.

"I don't know. I don't like it," Justin said.

"It's the way out. Like it or not, we have to go that way."

Justin took a look up and down the mine shaft. He turned back to Travis and nodded. Travis stood there on the rung. He figured it was just his imagination, but his legs felt colder down there. It was like the first time he'd gone swimming in the ocean. Below him was an unknowable deep. Anything could be down there in that water. Enormous creatures who barely ventured close enough to the surface to understand sunlight might be swimming beneath him, intrigued by the sight of his legs dangling. Travis fought the urge to climb up out of the shaft.

Travis reached down with his foot, feeling for the next rung again.

"Hold up," Justin said. He leaned over the shaft and opened Travis's pack. He lifted back up and tied the old length of rope around one of Joy's flashlights. The yellow beam seemed pathetic as Justin lowered it down into the hole. He set it down on the floor of the tunnel below and it shone like a lonely beacon.

Travis started down again.

He bent his legs and crouched low so he could see down the tunnel. When he had looked both ways, Travis pushed off and jumped down from the wall. Justin was right behind him. Travis stayed put until they were both down.

They looked up and down the tunnel, using their lights to chase back the darkness. Neither said anything for a minute.

"Carlos?" Justin called. "You here?"

Travis nudged his friend's shoulder. He pointed at the ground. Dark spots were dripped in a trail down the tunnel.

"Back to back," Justin whispered.

Travis nodded and kept his light pointing in the direction of the trail of spots. He saw the rope slithering in his peripheral vision as Justin coiled it up. Travis moved backwards as Justin walked forwards.

Travis studied the darkness. He watched the edges of his light against the wall, making sure that his beam progressed down the tunnel at the same pace they were walking. He remembered the journal. He remembered the description of the darkness swelling and flooding the tunnel, like a dark liquid.

Justin stopped.

"What?" Travis asked, over his shoulder.

"I thought I saw something move." Justin pressed back until their spines were touching.

"You thought you saw it, or you did? Which is it? Those are two different things."

"I saw something, but just the edge of something."

"Do you see it now?"

"No."

"Then keep moving for fuck's sake."

Justin started shuffling forward again, allowing Travis to back up once more. He felt Justin beginning to turn and glanced to his side to see that they were rounding a corner. That meant they only had two more straight sections and one more corner before they were out. At least that was the way that Travis remembered it.

"We should just run," Travis said.

"We'll keep going slow," Justin said. "Slow and safe."

At the edge of Travis's light, in the middle of the tunnel's floor, the shadow began to advance. Travis reached back.

"Give me that flashlight," Travis said.

"Why?"

"Just give me the fucking flashlight."

As Justin put it in his hand, the shadow grew. It was the shape of a man. It didn't make sense. For his shadow to be cast towards Travis, the man would have to be lit from behind. If he was, then where was the light?

Neither the flashlight nor his headlamp were able to chase away the shadow as it grew.

"I've got a shadow back here," Travis said.

"Yeah, okay. Let's move faster," Justin said.

Behind Travis, Justin's back pulled away. Travis kept his light trained down the tunnel, hoping it might keep the shadow at bay. He picked up speed, sneaking glances behind himself to make sure he was keeping on track.

When they got to the next turn, Justin spun and joined his light to Travis's. The two of them trained their lights on the shadow and sidestepped along the wall. They were at the last section of mine. To their right, the exit waited.

The shadow stalked forward. It turned the corner with them. For a second, Travis saw the shadow in profile. It was stretched out. He couldn't determine if it was thrown by Carlos or not.

"Should we run?" Travis whispered to Justin.

Justin's light whipped away as he turned to see where they were going.

"Yeah," Justin said. "Whenever you're ready."

Travis nodded. It was hard to turn his back on the advancing shadow. He kept expecting to see the man emerge from the darkness, but the form stayed just beyond the reach of Travis's light. Travis backed over a rock and nearly stumbled. He had to turn now, before it was too late.

He spun, turning his back on the shadow.

They sprinted. The flames of their headlamps were challenged by the rush of the headwind. The flashlight beam swung wildly in Travis's pumping hand.

Justin looked back at the shadow. He barked out a single word. "Faster!"

In the distance, Travis saw the white rectangle of a sign. It was the skull and crossbones posted at the entrance to the mine. They were almost there. He couldn't stand it. He had to look. With a glance over his shoulder, he saw the terrible truth. The shadow was nipping at their heels. It would be upon them before they got to the open sky.

He dug deep, pulling out a little speed he didn't know he possessed. For a second, he pulled beyond Justin. A terrible thought crossed his mind—he didn't necessarily need to outrun the shadow. As long as he outran his friend, that might be enough.

Travis didn't get the opportunity to test his theory.

Before they reached the exit, a figure sprung from the darkness.

Chapter Thirty-Five — Night

KRISTIN MADE IT TO the top of the pile of rocks and surveyed the desert. By the winding access road, the highway was miles away. It seemed smarter to cut the distance by walking a straight line through the scrub. Despite the logic, she wasn't convinced until she saw the lights of the cars. The rising air played tricks with the headlights. It made them dance and shimmer, but they were beautiful. They represented civilization and safety.

She began to pick her way down the rocks.

Kristin veered away from a dark bush. It could be hiding anything. She oriented herself with the stars before the highway dropped below the line of low hills she was going to have to cross.

"This is stupid," she whispered. "I'm five minutes into this and I'm already making bad decisions and second-guessing them."

She picked up her pace. The decision was made. It was time to commit and see it through.

Kristin couldn't keep her eyes off the stars. The sky was so deep and black, she could almost imagine that she could see which stars were closer to the Earth.

She ran into a bush and resolved to keep her eyes pointed at the ground. It was difficult though. After being in the cave, the idea of limitless space had an undeniable appeal.

Somewhere off in the night, a truck blared its horn and Kristin stopped.

She blinked and tried to figure out what she had just seen. She was walking downhill and still a bit elevated from her surroundings. Because of that, the desert floor spread out before her and she had a decent view of all the rocks and bushes in the starlight. That's not what confused her. There had been a few dark spots across the terrain and they had grown lighter when the horn sounded.

Any other night, she might have dismissed the phenomenon as a trick of her eyes. Tonight was different.

Kristin waited.

When nothing happened, she cautiously crept towards one of the bright spots. It didn't look any different than the surrounding desert. There were a couple of bushes in the center of the spot. Kristin gave them space, but kept her attention focused there.

The effect was so gradual that she would have missed it if she hadn't been paying attention. From below the bushes, the shadows began to pool and then grow. They seeped outward like water soaking into fabric. Kristin backed away. She turned and saw that she was backing near another spot where the shadows were growing. She had to change direction.

Kristin panicked and ran for a rock. She climbed its face and turned in time to see the shadows finish their expanse. Once they were done growing, it was impossible to detect them. Sure, the sand was a little darker, but it all looked perfectly natural. She could have wandered right into one of those shadows. It was just dumb luck that she hadn't.

Kristin glanced around. She found some loose rocks on top of her boulder. She lifted one and brought it to her shoulder. The distance was difficult to judge in the night, but she did her best. She flung her rock at the center of one of the shadows.

It hit the sand to the right of the bushes.

The impact was far enough away that she couldn't really even see it in the dark. Kristin was beginning to doubt the whole thing. Had there really been growing shadows, or was she just stressed out and over-tired?

She turned a slow circle on top of her boulder and realized that she didn't even really know where the shadows where. The whole scene just looked perfectly normal.

Just for safety, she picked up a much bigger rock. She aimed a bit more carefully and threw it at the bushes.

She heard a couple of things.

First, the rock tagged the branches of the bush and then fell to the sand. Right after that, it must have tumbled into a hole. She heard it ring against stones as it tumbled. The last sound it made—a big, reverberating thunk—sounded like it came after a decent drop.

The shadows retracted.

They all sucked down back into their holes. At the same time.

Kristin had an epiphany. She imagined the shadows like big nets, all radiating out from their holes. They waited—delicately triggered traps—for a sound, or maybe motion, and then retracted, pulling their prey. Once deployed, they were impossible to detect.

Kristin glanced back in the direction of the highway. She couldn't see it, but knew the direction once she oriented herself with the stars. The shadows were already beginning to creep their fingers back out across the sand.

She ran.

Chapter Thirty-Six — Darkness

ROGER LISTENED TO HER feet retreating down the cave. He lowered himself to the floor of the cave and leaned back against the wall. The sad eyes of the portrait kept drawing his attention. Roger reached up and shut off his light.

After a few seconds, he let his eyes drift shut. They weren't doing him any good.

He crossed his legs and wrapped his hands around his bare foot. The rock had been sapping the heat from his foot. His own flesh felt cold and foreign.

A breeze swept down the cave.

The air felt warm at first. When it cooled down, it brought a foul smell. Roger wrinkled his nose and tucked his chin to his chest. He pulled his shirt up over his nose and smelled his own sweat instead. It had been a long day. He tried to imagine how many hours he'd been in the cave and realized that he didn't have a clue.

Something brushed his foot.

Roger held perfectly still. He controlled his urge to turn on his light. As the sensation moved up his leg he squeezed his eyes shut and held his breath. As his oxygen ran out, Roger heard his heartbeat in his ears. He imagined fingers of smoke moving over his body, probing for weakness.

"Hello?"

He saw a red glow through his eyelids. Roger cheated one eye open and saw Florida standing there, shining her light at his face. He exhaled slowly.

"You're taking a nap?" she asked.

"No," he said, shaking off his paralysis. "I was... I was sitting here in the dark, and..."

She raised her eyebrows.

"I don't know," he said.

She put her hand out to help him to his feet. "While you were napping, I think I found a way out."

"Seriously?"

"Yeah," she said.

"Why did you come back?" he asked. He flipped on his light when she turned to lead the way. "Why didn't you leave and grab Dr. Deb's team for help?"

"It's not that simple. I need your help," she said.

The cave sloped down and to the right. Roger's bare foot landed on a rock. He hopped on his good foot for a couple of paces. Florida glanced back at him.

"You need help?"

"There's a rock in the way. I think that both of us can move it," she said.

"And it leads out?"

"Yeah. Well no, but yeah. It's easier if I show you."

It didn't lead out.

Roger understood what she meant, but it definitely didn't lead out.

The cave twisted and turned and it seemed to narrow each time. The floor was littered with jagged rocks that had fallen from the walls. He had to place his feet carefully. Florida stopped. She motioned him to squeeze by. He saw the issue.

Right in the center of their passage, a big rock was stuck between the walls. It was like a puzzle. It looked like if the rock could be lifted, they might be able to push it through to the other side.

"What makes you think we want to go through there?" he asked.

"Can't you see?" she asked.

"No."

"Here." She backed up and ducked by him so they could change places. Roger had to stand on his toes, but then he understood. The cave on the other side looked to be a decent size. The walls were rounded, but the floor was flat. In fact, it looked unnaturally flat. It looked manmade. His light picked up a different texture on the left. He had to squeeze his head into the narrow place between two rocks before he got a good look at it.

It was wood. It looked like a wooden door, or at least the edge of one.

"They blocked up some of the mine entrances," she said. "I think that's one of them."

"We'll need a lever or something to lift this rock," he said.

"Maybe. I was able to jiggle it. Maybe if you get down you can muscle it up?"

Roger put his hands on the rock and gave it a shove. It didn't budge.

"I don't know."

"I think it's kinda wedged right now. Just get down and see if you can lift it," she said.

Roger pointed his light down at the jagged rocks. He scanned the edges of the wedged rock and looked for any debris they might be able to move to give them more of a chance. There was nothing. Roger lowered himself carefully down.

Lying on the rocks was even worse than it looked, and it had looked excruciating. Sharp edges bit into every square inch of his back, and the pain was amplified as soon as he tried to exert upward force on the stuck rock.

Florida tried to straddle him, but her foot slipped. Her shoe pinched the skin of his shoulder and he grunted with pain.

"Sorry," she said. "Try to lift it."

"What do you think I'm doing?" he yelled.

He pressed even harder, using his own arm as a lever. A sharp edge bit into his elbow, tasting his blood.

"Higher," she said.

"How about you help?"

"You have to lift it so I can roll it out of the way," she said.

Roger arched his back away from the rocks, but it only pushed his shoulders down even harder. He planted his feet and tensed up his thighs, recruiting them into the effort. For the first time, he felt the thing shift.

Sand and debris tumbled into his eyes. He clenched his jaw and grunted through his teeth.

"That's it! A little more," she said.

Roger's muscles seemed to hum with the effort. Florida started grunting too. At first he thought she was making fun of him. She gave one more triumphant grunt and the rock rolled through the gap. Roger pulled his fingers back too late. The rock had tumbled over the tips of two of his fingers. The stinging pain filled up his head. He sucked in a breath and pulled his hand to his chest.

"Yes!" she said.

Her foot brushed his nose as she climbed over him.

Roger sat up and saw her light exploring the room. Behind them, the cave seemed to eat his light. He didn't waste any time crawling through the hole to join her. She was already working on the door.

"I think it's nailed into place," she said.

"Nailed into rock?"

"I don't know. I'm not a carpenter."

"Kick it down," he said. He flexed his fingers as feeling started to return to the crushed tips.

Florida stood back from the door and thrust her foot forward. She planted her heel in the center of the door. It shook from the impact. Dust rained down from the frame. Florida kicked several more times while Roger stood back and watched.

The room was small enough that it didn't warrant exploration. A simple sweep of his light was enough. Aside from the hole where they'd come in and the rock on the floor, the door was the only feature.

Florida kicked one more time and gave up.

She backed away. Roger scanned the door with his headlamp. There was not much to it. The wood was old and deeply grained. The frame didn't look particularly thick. The hinges on the left extended into bands of black metal. It didn't have a latch or a handle.

"Wait a sec," he said.

She turned and let him by.

It was the hinges that tipped him off. If he could see the hinges on the side, then kicking the door might not be the best approach. He worked his fingers into the tiny gap between the top of the door and the frame. His recently-crushed fingers flared with pain, but he did his best to ignore it as he pulled. The rusty hinges groaned as the door swung inwards.

He opened the door and revealed what was on the other side.

"Are you..." Florida began. She didn't finish the question.

They were looking at a solid face of stone. The door had opened inward to reveal nothing but flat rock. Roger slapped his palm against it. It was as solid as the walls around them.

"I don't believe it," she said. "It doesn't make sense."

"You expected something in here to make sense?" Roger asked.

Chapter Thirty-Seven — Survival

THE BODY HIT TRAVIS'S midsection and plowed him into Justin. The three of them stumbled into the side passage. Justin spun to push back against the assault. His legs twisted and he tripped himself. As he fell backwards, he recognized the attacker—it was Carlos.

Travis screamed.

Justin was on the bottom of the pile. Travis and Carlos were stacked on top of him.

Carlos tapped their lamps in quick succession, snuffing the flames. The only light left was the weak glow from the flashlight that Travis still held. Justin watched his two friends wrestle over that light.

"Close your fucking eyes and shut up," Carlos whispered.

"What the hell are..." Travis started.

Carlos slapped a hand over Travis's mouth. "Just fucking do it."

Just before Carlos won the battle and the flashlight went out, Justin saw Carlos shut his eyes.

It went against his instincts, but Justin closed his own eyes. He was still buried under the other two. As he caught his breath, he heard the hiss of the acetylene lamp. The unlit gas was escaping to the mine.

Above the sound of his carbide lamp, and above the sound of Travis panting, Justin heard a new sound. It was air rushing through the main shaft. The gust lasted several seconds and was followed by a low rumble. They laid still in the dark for more than a minute. Justin squeezed his eyes shut to resist the urge to open them. Something was moving in the mine, but it wasn't moving with footsteps.

After what felt like forever, Carlos rolled off of the top of the pile.

"Thank you," Travis whispered.

"You can turn your light on now," Carlos said. "But shut it back off if I tell you."

Justin cupped his hand over the bowl of the reflector to let the gas build up. After a second, he spun the ignitor and his headlamp came back on. The light comforted him.

"What was that?" Justin asked Carlos. "Jesus, what happened to your hand?"

Carlos looked down at his hand and frowned. Travis backed away when he saw it. For the moment, his own light was forgotten. Their friend's hand was wrapped in a strip torn from his shirt. The makeshift bandage was stained with dried blood. His pinky and ring finger were missing.

"Forget about it," Carlos said, folding his arms to hide his hand. "There are things in this cave that kill people."

"We know," Justin said. "It's like chemicals that digest people."

Carlos shook his head. "No, man. This thing hunts. It tracks people down and finds them. The only way to get it to overlook you is to close your eyes and stay quiet."

Justin looked at Travis. They both looked in the direction of the mine's exit. Carlos has pushed them towards the tunnel that led to the emergency shelter room. Somewhere back there were canned biscuits and emergency water. But just a quick sprint from the mouth of their passage, the exit to the night was incredibly close.

Justin nodded to Travis and then took Carlos by the arm. "Let's get out of here, okay? We'll get you help for your hand."

Travis lit his lamp and took Carlos by the other arm.

Carlos shrugged them both off. "You go out there and you'll die. It scoops people up when they try to leave. It sucks them back in. It might not get both of you, but it will get at least one. We have to find another way out."

"It's right there," Travis said. "I'll grant you that there was something in the dark chasing us, but it looks like it's gone now.

Let's make a run for it."

"No, man," Carlos said. "You can't outrun it. You gotta believe me."

"We'll go together," Travis said. "Me and Justin. When we get out, we'll get help, okay?"

Carlos turned to Justin and grabbed him by the shoulders. "Listen, man, that thing knows everything. This is where it hunts— at the entrance. It's not stupid. You only got this far because it wanted you to get this far. You go out there and it will just suck you back in."

"If we hear something or see something, we just close our eyes, right? If we close our eyes and be quiet, it passes us by," Travis said.

Justin nodded. That plan had just worked minutes ago. Surely it would work again.

Carlos shook his head. "No. Closing your eyes only works on the chaser. The chaser drives you to the hunter. You can't fool the hunter."

"What do you think?" Justin asked Travis.

Travis glanced at Carlos and then led Justin a couple of paces away. He spoke into Justin's ear.

"We have to get him help. He's not looking good," Travis said.

"He was right about the thing though," Justin said.

"Maybe that thing was just headed outside. We just thought it was chasing us. Who knows what happened when our eyes were closed?" Travis asked.

"Yeah. Okay," Justin said. He turned back to Carlos. "Okay, man—stay here. We'll be right back with help, okay?"

Carlos backed away from their lights. He inched backwards towards the emergency shelter room. "You're going to die." Before he backed out of their lights, they saw Carlos close his eyes.

"Well that was fucking creepy," Travis said.

"You ready?" Justin asked.

Travis nodded. "Just a quick right turn and a short sprint. Then we're out."

"Yup," Justin said.

He counted to three and they ran. It wasn't the crazy panic of earlier. They sprinted side by side and kicked-in even faster when they saw the sign again. Justin didn't slow as they passed by the skull and crossbones. He didn't slow until they moved away from the entrance of the cave and saw the lights of the Jeep.

They were tipped up towards the sky, pointing at nothing.

"What the fuck?" Travis asked. He caught up as Justin slowed.

They both looked back towards the entrance of the mine.

"Let's move farther away," Justin said. I don't even want to be close enough to *see* that thing. He waved at the hillside.

"Agreed," Travis said.

They approached Joy's Jeep and slowly circled it.

Travis peered through the windshield and then touched the hood. He backed away quick when the thing rocked under his touch.

"Maybe we could roll it to roof, side, and then back to tires?"

"It would just keep rolling," Justin said. "We'd have better luck if we winched it back up to the road."

The vehicle was on a slope. That slope ran downhill for at least fifty yards before the terrain flattened again. And down there, there was nothing but loose sand and rocks. Justin glanced back towards the mine, just to be sure it was still behaving.

"She has a winch on the front," Travis said. "Nothing to hook it to though."

"If we looped it around, we could hook it to that that big rail over by the mine. The winch might spin the Jeep around and then drag it up."

Travis looked in the direction that Justin was pointing and then locked eyes with him again.

"Yeah, but..." Travis started.

"Right," Justin said. "Fuck that."

"Exactly."

"All right. If we're walking, we might as well start walking. Wait—where's Ryan?" Justin asked.

"He's probably off trying to figure out which type of cactus will get him fucked up. We're missing Joy, Kristin, and Ryan. If we head towards the highway, I bet we find at least two of them," Travis said.

"Sounds like a plan."

Chapter Thirty-Eight — Stuck

KRISTIN RAISED ONE FOOT. The snake was coming right for her.

She had a rock in her hand, but it was the last rock she had. She wasn't about to waste it throwing it at a snake. Besides, she would probably just make the snake angry if she hit it with a rock. She waited. There was almost nothing in the world that creeped her out more than snakes.

As it slithered, the snake moved it's coils up the sandy slope just enough so that when it slipped back down it would stay on the path. This wasn't a marked path, it was the tiny gap between two of the shadow traps. Kristin knew where it was because she had seen the traps deploy. She didn't know how the snake sensed it.

The snake was ten feet away when it stopped. She couldn't see it in the starlight, but she imagined its tongue flicking out, tasting the air, wondering what she was doing there in the middle of its desert.

The snake reached some decision and started moving again.

Kristin didn't have a choice—she couldn't move.

Her last few rocks had missed the mark, but she wasn't sure they would have done any good anyway. Even when she hit the hole dead on, it didn't seem to trigger the shadow traps anymore. They were growing accustomed to her trickery. They were figuring her out. The thought was chilling.

When the snake was only an arm's length away, Kristin couldn't stand it any longer. She threw her rock down at the thing.

She missed.

The rock hit the sand right in front of the snake. It jerked back, arching its neck into an S, and preparing to strike. They stared at each other for a few seconds. At least she assumed that the snake was staring at her. She couldn't see its beady eyes in the starlight. The snake began to shift its body to the side, forming a coil so it could stretch out. It was big—probably big enough to reach her leg if it really stretched out.

Kristin glanced behind herself. She couldn't go backwards. She didn't have a good sense of where the shadow traps covered the ground back there. Kristin began to wonder if she could leap past the snake. Maybe if she could jump clear of it, she could balance on the same line that the snake had just showed her as it moved across the sand.

Whatever she was going to do, she knew she had to do it before the snake made its move.

As it drew its body beneath itself, one of the snake's coils intruded into the shadow space.

Kristin nearly mistook the snake's jerk for a strike. Instead of darting towards her, the snake was jerked backwards at a crazy speed as the shadow trap pulled it in. The trap on the other side was triggered as well. The desert brightened around her when the traps retracted.

Kristin ran forward. The trap that had taken the snake was re-deploying slowly. The other one flooded back out. Kristin pounded up the sand to get to the next ridge. The shadow traps didn't seem to like ridges. If she could climb it, she would be able to walk along it for a bit.

Kristin's feet churned in the sand.

She glanced back as she tried to ascend the sandy slope.

The shadow trap was lethargic after its capture of the snake, but it was still coming. It closed the gap towards Kristin's useless feet. Every time she tried to throw herself up the hill, she slid back down even more.

She forced herself to slow down and dig in her foot before she put weight on it. With that one step accomplished, she tried the other. She nearly fell over backwards. She would have tumbled right back into the shadow trap. Kristin caught her balance and climbed another careful step. She pulled her lower foot up just as the shadow trap began to overtake her.

She dug in again and took a big step.

As she pushed off to climb, her toe slipped down. When it touched the shadow, it felt like her foot had been magnetized and was being attracted to a giant piece of iron. The shadow tugged on her toe with a gentle but undeniable pull. The pull increased with each millisecond. Kristin threw herself forward and grabbed the branch of a thorny bush. She pulled on it, letting the spikes pierce her fingers. Her foot popped free and she clawed her way up through the sand. She reached the top of the hill and turned.

The shadow trap was fully spread out below her. It was no longer advancing. She sighed as she collapsed to the sand. She looked to the other side of the ridge. There was no telling where the shadows might have laid their traps. Until she saw them retract, the desert all looked the same. She pushed to her feet.

She was careful to keep her balance as she walked down the ridge of sand. In some places, the footing was solid. In others, the sand fell away and threatened her balance. When she found a few rocks, she gathered them eagerly, filling her pockets.

Kristin scanned the landscape, looking for a likely target.

It seemed like the shadows were darkest near one of the thorn bushes about thirty paces away. The distance was at the limit of her accuracy. She let the rock fly and listened to hear it hit. As with most of her throws, she never actually saw the rock land. It was lost to the dark when it left her hand.

She hit the bush! Its leaves rattled and the rock clunked down into the hole below it.

The shadow surrounding the bush didn't change at first. Kristin frowned. This is what she expected. The shadow traps had learned her technique and they were resisting reaction.

Something was changing though. She stared at the bush and tried to figure it out. Her eyes widened as the change made sense. The shadow trap was growing. It was deploying even farther and was actually climbing the hill that she was standing on. Kristin didn't have much time. She ran along the ridge of sand, trying to escape before the thing crested her hill.

The shadow trap didn't like the hill and it spilled to the side much faster than it climbed. Kristin was able to easily outrun it. She stood as it reached its limit. Now that she had seen it move, she understood the thing's boundaries. Unfortunately, there was no margin between it and the next suspicious shadow. She wouldn't be able to shoot the gap. Kristin continued down her ridge.

Up ahead, the hill fell away at a sharp angle. Sand gave way to rocky scree. At the bottom, she saw the access road. All of her wandering in the desert had finally led her back to the damn access road. She had tried to save time and had only managed to add hours to her trip.

Kristin shook her head and laughed at herself.

She started a small avalanche as she began to descend. Rocks tumbled down the slope. Kristin paused and let them fall. She saw something terrible. A few of the rocks bounced into the road and the shadows down there grew. One of the shadow traps was actually intruding on the road. From what she could tell, the thing pooled across, blocking her exit.

She eased down until she was sitting on the slope. She tried to memorize the outline of the shadow trap. This one was huge. It would be nearly impossible to navigate around, and it spanned the road. She put her head in her hands.

Chapter Thirty-Nine — Trap

FLORIDA PACED IN A tight circle. She gestured with her hands as she talked.

"This just can't be," she said, shaking her head. "This room was cut from the rock, right? I mean, look at the floor. You can see the marks where they made this flat floor. And someone took the time to frame and hang that door. Why the hell would you do that?"

"Maybe they were going to cut a passage through there, but they hadn't gotten to it yet?" Roger asked. "We'll just go back the way we came. There has to be something we missed, right?"

"People have been here," she said, pointing down. "More than that—they've spent time digging and building here. There has to be an exit around here somewhere."

"Don't rocks move? Maybe there was an earthquake that caved something in, right? Maybe it used to connect but doesn't anymore. Let's not get obsessed."

"I don't think a cave-in looks like that," she said, stabbing her finger towards the solid rock on the other side of the door.

"Okay," Roger said. "I know you're frustrated. I am too, but there's nothing more to do here. Let's turn back and we'll head back towards those portraits. I'm sure we'll see something we missed."

Her eyes practically sparkled with frustration. She balled her fists and swung them down.

"Damn it," she said. "When I saw that door, I was so sure that this was the way out. I can't even tell you how mad it makes me."

"Come on," Roger said. He began to move back towards the passage where they'd entered. The rocks over there were jagged.

He had to place his bare foot carefully. It was getting tender from all the abuse.

As Roger squeezed his way out, Florida was slapping her palms against the flat rock. He paused for a second and then decided that she needed a moment alone. Roger inched through the gap. Bracing his hands against the walls helped. It took some of the weight off his foot.

Roger's hand slipped. One of the jagged rocks scraped his palm.

"Shit," his whispered. He turned his hand towards his face and saw the white edges of flesh just before his blood began to seep. It wasn't a bad cut, but it served as a good warning. There was no sense in favoring one body part just to injure another.

When Roger looked back up, his heart stopped beating in his chest.

The man was standing just a few paces away. His face looked serene in Roger's headlamp. His clothes were dirty tatters—the front of his pants were yellow with urine stains. His armpits were circled with crusty-white salt. His hair hung in greasy clumps.

The man's beard was gray with brown and yellow streaks. It reached down to his chest.

To Roger, the most alarming thing were the man's eyes—they were closed.

When Florida put her hand on Roger's back, he screamed.

"What?" she asked.

He pressed himself to the side.

"What? What's wrong?"

"You didn't see him?" Roger asked.

"Him? Who?" Florida asked.

"That guy. There was a guy right there," Roger said.

"Where?"

Roger threw up his hands. He moved his light around wildly. The passage wasn't very large, but Roger's light was getting dim and didn't penetrate far into the darkness.

"I don't see anyone," Florida said. "Do you still see him?"

"I'm not crazy, Florida," Roger said. "There was a man here."

Roger began to hop forward. Florida hung back a bit and moved her light around to try to see past him. When he got beyond the jagged rocks of the narrow passage, Roger started moving his hands over the walls, searching frantically. Florida caught up with him as he spun and shifted to the walls of the other side.

"What are you doing?"

"He must have some secret here. Maybe we can't see it for some reason. Maybe you can't see it with your eyes, you know?" Roger asked.

"Hey, Roger?"

He stopped and looked at her. His eyes blinked compulsively. It looked like a mixture of excitement and fear in his eyes.

"What?"

"You remember when you told me to not get obsessed a few minutes ago?" Florida asked.

Roger turned back to the wall, feeling the surface for some mysterious passage.

"I think you're getting a little freaked out here," Florida said.

"I just saw a guy," he said. He didn't turn to address her. He began feeling along the floor.

"Right," she said. "We both have seen things that don't make sense. Remember the climbing guy. He looked like a movie or something being projected on the rocks as we got closer. Maybe there are gasses down here that create hallucinations. Maybe we're just going a little crazy because we've been cooped up underground for too long. Our lights are getting pretty dim. It's easy to see weird stuff in low light when you're freaked out."

"I could *smell* him," Roger said. "He smelled like a homeless guy who has been out in the sun for too long, you know. He smelled of piss, and sweat, and shit. Whoever it is, he's been down here a long time."

Florida nodded. She moved beyond Roger and started to walk up the passage as he massaged the rocks. "What was it you suggested earlier? Maybe we should head back to the portraits and see if there's something we missed? That's a good idea. Let's do that. There was that one crack that looked like it might go somewhere. You remember that?"

She forced herself to keep walking. She needed to establish her independence again. She was starting to feel too tied to Roger. If he went off the rails, she didn't want to be dragged down with him.

Still, she felt more comfortable when she heard his lopsided footfalls behind her. Roger kept up well, despite his footwear issues.

"I'm still encouraged by that door," she said, turning. "At least it means..." She trailed off. Roger was still back there on the floor, feeling up the wall. She glanced around herself with quick, jerky motions, wondering where the sound of footsteps had come from. She shook off the question. It must have been some weird echo. "Come on, Roger. Let's get out of here."

He got up slowly and came after her with slumped shoulders.

"I saw someone," he said.

"I believe you," Florida said. "I was saying—I'm still encouraged. That wood came from somewhere, so there must be a pretty easy way out. They wouldn't have dragged it too far in here for no reason."

She glanced back.

Roger nodded, but she didn't have any sense that he had been listening.

"You were fine a minute ago," she said. "I was the one who was freaking out. What happened to you?" She turned and walked backwards.

Roger had been looking at the floor. He raised his head slowly and met her eyes as he shuffled forward. "There was something about him. He *knew* things. And he was real. He wasn't a ghost or something. He was real and then he just disappeared."

Florida turned her back on Roger and picked up the pace.

"Florida," he called.

"What?" she asked. She didn't slow down.

"There's something I have to tell you."

"What?"

"Could you... Do you have to walk so damn fast? I want to tell

240

you something."

"What?" she asked. She turned around and walked backwards.

He picked up his speed and gained ground on her.

"I don't have much to live for," he said. He looked down as he spoke, like he was ashamed to meet her eyes. "I don't want to be one of those old, helpless people you see begging on the street. I'll kill myself before it gets to that."

"What are you..." she began.

He cut her off.

"If we get out of here, I'm going to make a change. I'm going to find some way to better myself."

"Okay," she said.

"Will you hold me to that? Will you remind me of that when we get out?"

"Sure," she said, shrugging. She turned around again. "Why would you say that right now?" she asked over her shoulder.

"That guy I saw," he began. His voice was quavering, but it gained conviction as he continued. "He looked like what I fear I might become, you know? He was dirty, old, had no self-respect, and he had his eyes closed. He was blind to what he has become. I'm not going to get like that. I've had some hard times. You can blame it on circumstances, or you can blame it on me. Both things are true. Regardless, I'm not making any excuses. I'm not giving up anymore."

"Okay," she said. She didn't have any idea what he was talking about, but his speech seemed to require an answer.

"Just remind me of that?" he asked.

"Okay."

Chapter Forty — Road

THEIR FEET FELL INTO a rhythm as they walked down the road. Justin's light sputtered out first.

"You want to stop and refill?" Travis asked.

"No," Justin said. "I don't think we need the light, honestly. Stars are bright enough to find the road."

Travis shrugged and shut off the water to his own headlamp. After a few more minutes, his light failed as well. Their eyes adjusted quickly and it was actually easier to see farther with them off. The headlamps only reached so far. The starlight went on forever.

They crested a hill and saw the road winding off ahead of them.

"We could cut off the corner and save some time," Travis said, pointing.

"No. If we leave the road, we're just going to risk missing those guys. Best to stay on course, you know?"

"Yeah. Honestly, I don't know what we're going to say to Miguel's mom anyway. I guess I'm not too eager to deal with that," Travis said.

"Yeah," Justin said. "You think you can lead the cops to where he's at?"

"Fuck no," Travis said. "I'll draw them a map. I'll be damned if I'm ever going in that fucking mine again."

"Yeah," Justin said. "Good point."

"Besides, that crevice thing ebbs and flows. Maybe we wouldn't be able to get back there anyway."

"True."

They walked in silence down the hill and around the bend. Occasionally, the road crested a hill and they could see all the way to where the mountains met the stars. Then they'd drop into a dip and they would only be able to see the next turn or the next rise.

"Maybe we ought to hide the gold, you know?" Travis asked. "Hey—did I tell you that I found a diamond in there? I hope it doesn't get lost in the pack."

"You might be right," Justin said. "It might look like we were grave-robbing or something. Then again, there's no sense in hiding the stuff until it looks like the others are coming back with the authorities, you know? If we see headlights or hear an engine, we'll ditch the pack behind a rock and come back for it in the daylight."

"That's a plan," Travis said.

Neither of them spoke for a minute.

"We should give the gold to Miguel's family," Justin said.

"I was just thinking the same thing. Is his grandfather still alive?" Travis asked.

"I don't know," Justin said.

"If he is, someone should smack that old man in the face. That's bullshit, talking your own grandson into risking his life for some gold."

"He talked him into it?" Justin asked.

"I think so."

Travis put his hand out and caught Justin's arm.

"What?"

"You didn't hear that?" Travis asked.

"Shit. What now?"

"I think it was Kristin."

They both heard it the second time.

"Staaaaaaahp!" she yelled.

They stopped walking and listened.

"Where are you?" Justin yelled.

"I'm up here," she yelled back.

They both looked around. Justin couldn't see her. There was desert off to the right and hills to their left.

"There," Travis said.

Justin followed his pointing arm and finally saw the outline of her distant arms, waving over her head.

"Come on," Travis said. He began to head off the road, towards the hill.

"No!" she screamed. "Don't come any closer."

Travis stopped and turned around to look at Justin. He put his hands up with an unspoken question.

"What's wrong?" Justin yelled.

"Back up about twenty paces," Kristin yelled.

They did, but they took small, hesitant steps. While they moved, they studied her distant outline.

"More," she called.

They kept moving until she yelled again. "Okay, now turn hard to your left and come about halfway up that hill. They followed orders, but it was difficult going. The path she dictated moved them right up a steep edge of rock. The terrain was difficult enough. In the dark, it was nearly impossible. When Travis tried to move a little closer, to get around a particularly tall rock, Kristin yelled again.

"No! Back. Back. Right there."

By the time they got halfway up the hill, as she'd ordered, they were both panting and irritated. She coaxed them forward. They walked along the side of the hill. Their feet slipped on the loose rocks and sand, but she wouldn't let them move any higher or lower on the slope.

"Okay, straight to me," she said when they were about a dozen paces from her.

"What the fuck is this all about?" Justin asked.

"I'm sorry, but I couldn't trust that shadow there. You see?"

He turned and looked in the direction she was pointing. The road snaked out below them. There were tons of shadows, but none of them looked particularly untrustworthy.

"What are you talking about?" Travis asked.

"It's hard to explain," she said. Kristin bend over and picked up a big chunk of rock. Travis shied back. Kristin looked like she meant business. "Just watch, okay?" she asked. She made sure that they were both paying attention to the road. "I don't know if this is going to work yet. They forget after a while, but this one might be smarter than the others. The bigger they are, it seems like the smarter they are."

"What the fuck are you talking about?" Justin asked.

Instead of answering, Kristin cocked back her arm and let the rock fly. She had a good arm and was aided by the way the terrain fell away from their position. The rock sailed. It went over the road and came down near a clump of bushes on the other side. Justin blinked when the thing clunked to the ground.

His eyes adjusted. The world seemed a little brighter.

"What the hell?" Travis asked.

"Keep watching," Kristin said.

"What are you guys..." Justin started he didn't finish his question. Something was flowing across the road.

"See? It comes back quick. This one is smarter. I knew it would be," Kristin said.

"Holy shit. What is it?" Travis asked.

"Did you ever go to the aquarium down in Apple Valley?" Kristin asked.

"No," Justin said.

"Yeah, I went," Travis said.

"They had a coral reef down there, and there was this one thing..."

"Anemone," Justin said.

"Yes," Travis said. "That's what you said before. He had the same idea."

"No," Kristin said. "Not quite. An anemone will sting things and then slowly contract them back to its mouth. The thing I'm talking about was called a 'feather duster worm.' It would spread out like an umbrella and then when it would come in contact with food, it would collapse in the blink of an eye. That's what these things are like."

"And rocks are food?" Justin asked.

"No," Kristin said. "I was using a rock to trick it. It won't fall for a rock again, not for a while. Give it a try."

Travis knelt and picked up a rock. He lobbed it towards the same bushes that Kristin had hit. The rock crashed through the branches and then thumped the sand. The shadow didn't stir.

"There's actually a hole somewhere in there. There's always a hole in the center. It's where they come out from," Kristin said. She bent and picked up another rock. Her next shot missed the bushes.

Justin threw the next rock and his passed right through the branches and echoed as it fell down into the hole. Justin nodded.

"See? It didn't react that time," Kristin said.

"It did," Travis said. "Just a little at the edges. It flinched."

"So you're saying that if we went down there..." Justin began.

"Or over there, or there, or up even a little higher on that hill you climbed. Yes, if you went into one of those spots, you'd trigger a retraction and it would suck you down into its hole. I saw it happen with a snake. One instant you're there. The next, you're gone."

"I'm a lot heavier than a snake," Travis said. "Are you sure it would be able to take us?"

Kristin shrugged in the starlight. "Is it worth taking the chance?"

"That depends," Justin said. "If we can find a way around them, then I guess it would make sense to avoid them."

"Yeah, okay," Travis said. "What's the best way around?"

"That's the problem," Kristin said. "I can't find a way around this one."

Kristin described the extent of all the shadow traps that she knew about. They followed her pointing finger and tried to get a sense of the area. Then she told them about how she'd reached the spot they were at.

"Some of the other ones were slow enough that I could trigger them, and then make a run for it. But you've seen how fast this one is. We wouldn't make it halfway down the hill before it came back out. And we don't know what's on the other side of that rise. We might crest that hill just to find that the trap overlaps with the next one," she said.

"Have you seen that?" Justin asked. "Have you seen two overlapping traps?"

"I guess not," she said.

"You described how the snake seemed to know the path between them. I'm guessing that if all these traps were able to overlap, there wouldn't have been a snake at all," Justin said.

"Wait a second," Travis said. "This is the road we came in on. How did we get by this road in the Jeep if these things are as powerful as you think?"

"That's a good question," Justin said.

"I don't know," Kristin said. "Maybe we were moving too quickly, or maybe it doesn't like metal. I saw a few of them retract at the sound of a truck horn before. Maybe all the noise made them pull in before we came through, you know? It doesn't matter anyway. The Jeep is toast."

"Yeah, we saw that," Justin said. "Joy must be pissed."

Kristin looked down.

She told them about Joy and Carlos.

Travis swallowed hard at the news. "That sucks about Joy, but we've seen Carlos."

"What?" Kristin asked. She grabbed Travis by the arms. "Where is he?"

"He was near the entrance," Justin said. "He was convinced that he couldn't leave because he thought something would get him. We figured we would go get help and then come back for him."

"We have to go back," Kristin said. "Maybe we can yell to him. Do you think he's close enough to hear?"

Justin and Travis looked towards each other in the dim light.

"I guess," Travis said. "He was a little disturbed though. I think he needs some time to settle down, you know?"

"We have to go," Kristin said. "We have to tell him to stay away from the exit."

"What?" Justin said. "Why wouldn't we just try to get him to come out?"

"Because he's right," Kristin said. "I don't know how you two made it out, but there is something that will get him if he's not careful." She moved away from Travis and Justin and began to work her way down the slope.

The men watched her descend towards the road for a second and then they went after her.

Chapter Forty-One — Observation

"WE'RE GOING TO BE here forever," Roger said. He hung his head and looked down between his swinging feet. His bare foot looked swollen and purple in his dim light. They had been wandering in the cave for what felt like days. After dropping down through the crack from the portrait tunnel, they had found endless winding caves, but none of them seem to lead anywhere. It was a giant collection of dead ends.

"Probably," Florida said.

Roger looked up at her. It was unlike her to show any emotion besides determination. He was surprised by her candid response. She was collecting scraps of paper. One of them was sitting on the rock next to Roger. It was a page out of a paperback book. They were scattered everywhere in the long cave. For some reason, Florida had taken it upon herself to collect them.

She had a big handful of them when she sat down next to Roger.

She sorted through them.

"We ought to make a plan," Roger said. "I don't want to live much longer than our lights, you know. Before this thing goes dark, I want to find a way to kill myself."

"You could probably jump from one of those high ledges down into the white floor we found earlier." She looked down at her hands as she spoke. Her tone was distracted and matter-of-fact. Her entire demeanor was confusing. "The fall would probably kill you. Try to land on your head if you can. Actually, I think there's a reflex that will make you put your hands out, whether you want to or not."

Roger raised his eyebrows.

When he looked over at Florida, she was pointing emphatically at one of the pages she was holding. Roger followed her finger. She was pointing at the word, "He."

"What are you..." Roger started.

Florida cut him off. "I'm just trying to be pragmatic." She moved her finger over to the next word. He read the word there. "You've got a good point. Maybe suicide is the only solution."

Roger watched her finger and read the sentence she had constructed from the pages of words: "He is listening to us."

Roger looked in her eyes. She nodded.

He covered his mouth with his hand.

Florida flipped pages and found the words she was looking for. She pointed out another sentence. "Don't say anything."

Roger nodded.

As Florida flipped through, Roger stopped her. He pointed at a single word: "Who."

She raised her shoulders and then put a hand over her eyes. Roger understood. It was the man with his eyes closed—the one he had described earlier. He *was* real. Roger wanted to ask if Florida had seen the man, but she was busy constructing a new sentence.

It took some time. She had to rifle through her pages to find the words she was looking for. While she did, it occurred to Roger that he should be padding with a dummy conversation, so the blind man wouldn't grow suspicious.

"I've never been much of a religious man, but I still believe that suicide is wrong," Roger said.

Florida grunted her agreement.

"Still, walking around in the dark until I get dehydrated or maybe I fall into a crevice isn't going to be my fate. I'm not going to go out like that, you know?"

Florida was ready. Roger watched her finger move from page to page and word to word.

"I want to catch him. The man knows his way around. We can make him take..."

Roger nodded emphatically. There was no reason for her to continue.

"What's wrong with your neck?" she asked.

Roger understood. The man was probably attuned to even the smallest sound of movement. He would be wondering why Roger was nodding.

"Just a crick in my neck, I guess."

Roger padded more as Florida spelled out her plan, word by word.

Roger continued his one-sided conversation as he ducked through the next hole. It felt eerie to talk to himself in the cave. He tried to listen between his own words to see if Florida needed help.

"And then when I moved out of the city, I couldn't believe how hard it was to hold down a job. I'm not trying to sound like a victim. I take responsibility for my own actions, you know?"

"Roger!"

He ducked back through the hold and sprinted back towards the sound of her voice. She had chosen well. Earlier, they had found the narrow passage with the mineral deposits on the walls. The minerals smelled terrible, and they were very powdery, so they muffled the sound. It was the perfect place for Florida to split off from Roger and hide. And the trap must have worked. He could hear her struggling with someone before he even rounded the corner.

His light went out.

There wasn't a flicker, or any sign that his batteries were about to fail. It just went out.

Roger could see the dancing glow of her light around the corner, but that barely helped him navigate. He had to make his way around the rocks with one bare foot and no light.

Roger's knee crashed into a ledge. He ignored it and limped around the corner.

The man appeared to be much stronger than Florida, and he outweighed her as well. She had her arms looped around his chest and was clinging to his back. As he thrashed, she flopped from side to side. Her helmet flew off and bounced off a wall. Through all this, the man's eyes remained closed.

Roger tripped as he raced forward to help. He tumbled down and grabbed the man around the knees. Roger's chin came down on a rock and his teeth slammed together, radiating pain up through his jaw.

The smelly man kicked and twisted. He nearly got away when he bashed Florida back into a wall. Without her helmet, Florida's head hit the rocks and she appeared crosseyed for a second before she got her wits back. Roger held firm.

The man in the tattered clothes tumbled to the ground. Florida landed on his chest and Roger pinned down his legs.

"Who are you!" Florida demanded.

The man didn't make a peep.

"Get the short rope from my pack," Florida said over her shoulder.

Roger stayed sitting on the man's legs as he dug in to the backpack. In a few minutes, they had had the man immobilized.

"Tell us who you are and why you've been following us," Florida said. She pulled the man to a sitting position on the rocks. His hands were tied in front of him.

"Fuck that," Roger said. "Tell us how to get out of here."

In response to the order, the man smiled.

"He understands us," Roger said.

"Of course he does," Florida said. "He's been following us and listening to us for an hour, maybe more." She turned back to him. "How long have you been down here?"

Roger went and fetched Florida's helmet. She put it on and pointed her light at the man's weathered face. He flinched back from the light. Roger moved to his side. Careful to stay out of bite-reach, Roger used his fingers to force open one of the man's eyes. They saw his wild pupil dance around and take in the sight of the cave.

"NO!" the man screamed. He pulled away from Roger's touch and slammed his eye shut again.

"You tell us what we want to know or we're going to force your eyes open," Florida said. "We're going to shine this light right in your eyes. And we have brighter lights, too."

As she spoke, he grew more and more agitated. The man began to squirm, trying to free himself of the ropes, or maybe just trying to escape from his own skin.

"She's not joking," Roger said. He placed his fingers on the man's forehead.

"Okay!" the man said, letting out a foul expulsion of air. "Don't make me look."

"So answer me," Florida said. "Who are you, and how long have you been down here?"

"My name is Carlos Garza. I don't have any idea how long I've been down here."

"From the portraits," Roger said.

Florida ignored him and pressed forward with her questions. "Why are you following us?"

A look of sadness and fear settled on Carlos's face. He shook his head back and forth. He kept his eyes closed, but he turned his head towards Florida when she spoke.

"Why are you following us?" she demanded.

She tilted her head at Roger and he understood. He put his hand on Carlos's forehead again and prepared to force his eye open.

"I'm waiting for you to die," Carlos said. "I can't help it."

Roger pulled his hand back when he saw a tear escape from the corner of Carlos's eye.

"Do you know the way out?" Florida asked.

"There is no way out," Carlos said.

For a second, he almost looked happy.

They marched him back to the main cave. Carlos had to take small, shuffling steps with his feet tied together. Florida picked up more of the paperback pages and spelled out a simple question for Roger—"What now?"

Roger took the tether and led Carlos away. The man's eyes stayed closed, but he still seemed to know where both Roger and Florida stood. He tilted his ear to one and then the other. When they had moved away from Florida, Carlos seemed to relax a little. He clearly had already figured out that Florida was in charge.

"Listen, man, we'll leave you alone if you just tell us how to get back to the regular mine shafts, you know?"

Carlos tilted his head. "There's no sense in going back there. That's where they hunt."

"Who hunts?"

"The shadows," Carlos said. "Even when you learn about them, they'll still get you if you stay out in the mines."

"You're here," Roger said.

Carlos reached up and pointed to his eyes. "Sometimes even I forget. If you peek, they find you. The only reason I get away is that I've been here so long. They think I'm a part of them."

"What the hell does that mean?" Roger asked.

Carlos didn't answer.

"You're going to show us how to get back to the mines, or we're going to leave you tied up," Florida called from her position.

Roger leaned in close. The man's smell was so strong that Roger thought he could almost see the odor radiating out from Carlos. "She's serious," Roger said. "She'll kill you if you don't help us."

"You can't threaten me with death," Carlos said. "I'm not afraid to die."

"Then I'll let her hold your eyes open until the shadows come," Roger said. Carlos didn't say anything, but Roger saw him shrink back. His threat had scored a hit. "You don't have to go with us into the mines, you just have to lead us there."

"It's the same thing," Carlos said.

Roger turned to Florida. "I don't think he's going to help us. I'll pin him down while you hold his eyes open."

Carlos shook his head. "I'll show you. You'll have to untie my feet. I can't show you with my feet bound."

"Good," Roger said.

Chapter Forty-Two — Searching

"CARLOS!" TRAVIS YELLED. HIS voice was beginning to sound ragged around the edges. Justin tapped him on the shoulder and took his place at the rock.

"Carlos!" Justin yelled towards the opening of the mine.

Travis retreated to the overturned Jeep, where Kristin was standing with her arms folded.

"We're just not close enough," Kristin said.

"We all agreed," Travis said.

"I know," she said. "It's just so frustrating. I felt so bad when he was taken away. I managed to..."

"Carlos!" Justin yelled again.

"I managed to block it out until you guys said you'd seen him. I guess I figured there was nothing I could do. Now I feel so guilty again."

"Don't," Travis said. "We were right with him and we couldn't get him to leave. It's not your fault."

"I would have been able to talk sense into him. He always listens to me."

"Don't be so sure."

"Carlos!" Justin yelled. Justin turned away from the mine and walked to the others. "I don't think we're doing any good here."

"Regardless, I think it's too dangerous to try to cross the desert or walk down the road," Kristin said. "So we might as well wait here until morning."

Justin looked to Travis.

Travis was studying the Jeep.

"Maybe there's another option," Travis said. "There is the

winch. Maybe I was too hasty when I said there was nothing to hook it to."

"What are you thinking?" Justin asked.

"We pretty much have to winch in the direction of the mine, right?" Travis asked. He lined up his arms and judged the angles. "That's the only way we're going to have a shot at rolling the Jeep over or getting it back up to the road."

Justin scratched his chin. Kristin took a step back and took it all in.

"We can't get any closer to the mine," Kristin said. "Ryan was several steps out when the thing pulled him back in. It was horrible."

"The Jeep is too big to fit in the mine," Travis said.

"So?" Kristin asked.

Justin started nodding. "Yeah. Let's test this thing."

"Exactly," Travis said. He moved to the back of the Jeep and opened the rear hatch. With the Jeep on its side, the hatch opened sideways. Joy had a blanket and some tools back there. Travis found what he was looking for—there was a pillow he had sat on when they made him sit in the back of the Jeep. He removed that and shut the hatch again.

Justin worked his way around the front of the Jeep, holding onto the bumper as he slipped on the loose rocks. He figured out the winch and began pulling the cable from the spool. When he had enough, he tossed the hook up to the road and continued to play out more slack. When he had enough, he locked the winch and climbed the bank.

Travis was hooking the pillow to the end of the hook.

"What are you guys doing?" Kristin asked.

"We're going fishing for monsters," Travis said.

Kristin shook her head. "This is a terrible idea. We should wait for sunrise. It can't be much longer. Look—the sky already looks brighter over there."

"You're pointing west," Justin said. "The sun rises over there."

Kristin turned around.

They had placed a rock on the path to the front of the mine. Before they started calling, they had all agreed that they wouldn't go beyond that rock. Travis stood at the rock and coiled the winch cable in one hand. When he was finished, he took the hook in his other hand. It was attached to the pillow.

"Don't get tangled in the line," Justin said.

Travis nodded. He played out a little cable and started swinging it in a big vertical circle. When the hook was coming up and around, he let it fly and dropped the coiled cable. It sailed about five feet before the cable bunched and the hook dropped to the ground. Travis started reeling it back in.

"Move," Justin said. He took the hook from Travis's hand.

"I was about to get it," Travis said.

"Stand back," Justin said.

He swung the hook much faster, and held the coils when he launched it. He opened his fingers and let the hook take the cable from his hand, coil by coil. The hook landed just a couple of paces from the mine entrance.

"Beginner's luck," Travis said.

Nothing happened.

Justin looked back to Kristin.

"It's close enough," she said. "That's where Ryan was standing. Maybe it knows the difference between a person and a pillow?"

Justin frowned. He began to reel in the cable.

"Wait," Travis whispered. "Hold up."

Justin stopped pulling and studied the darkness. He had no idea what Travis was whispering about. The mine looked just the same as it had before. Kristin approached him from behind and took the cable from his hand. She motioned for him to move out of the way and she set the cable down on the ground.

"What do you see?" Justin whispered.

She put her finger to her lips.

Travis had moved back to the Jeep. Justin turned at the sound and saw Travis climbing down to the front bumper. A second later, he heard the sound of the winch motor. Travis kept pulling until he had taken up the slack.

Kristin held up her hand and Travis stopped the winch.

Justin squinted at the dark to try to see what she was looking at.

After another second, she made a motion and Travis started the winch again.

She stopped him.

Justin looked back. He couldn't see the pillow anymore. It was lost in the darkness. The change had been so gradual that he hadn't noticed it before, but the pillow was now part of the shadows. Kristin backed up from the cable. Justin followed her lead. She signaled to Travis and had him tug the hook another foot.

The line straightened and then jerked.

Kristin and Justin both took another step back.

The cable tightened and made a strange springing sound as it snapped past the Jeep's tire. The vehicle groaned. Justin saw Travis. He was standing on top of the Jeep's quarter panel, so he could see Kristin's signals and work the winch. When the Jeep jolted, Travis fell off and disappeared on the downhill side of the vehicle.

"Get out of the way!" Justin called.

They heard Travis scrambling on the hill. The Jeep began to turn. It pulled a quarter of the way around before it started to move up the hill Justin cringed as he saw the angle the Jeep was taking. They hadn't envisioned this—the way it was spinning, there was no way it would stay on its side.

He was right. The metal screeched and ground against the rocks. He heard the body taking a beating as it pulled. With the moan of bending metal, the Jeep tilted and then finally flipped. It came down on its roof. Meanwhile, it inched up the slope and towards the mine. The cable vibrated in the starlight. It hummed with the effort.

Justin took another step back. He saw Travis's head pop up on the other side of the Jeep as he climbed back up to the road.

When the Jeep reached the road, it picked up speed.

Travis ran forward.

"What are you doing?" Justin had time to call out.

Travis was trying to get in front of the Jeep.

The Jeep was unstoppable, grinding forward on its roof. The noise made Justin's teeth hurt. There was a tension in his guts as well as Travis stumbled and was nearly overtaken. Travis leaned down and hit something on the front of the winch. The Jeep stopped immediately, but the winch started turning. The spool revved up quickly and deployed the rest of the long cable.

It flew off the spool like a whip, and sailed through the night. The hook, pillow, and cable disappeared into the mine.

"Perfect," Travis said. He walked over to where Kristin and Justin were standing. "Now we just have to flip it onto its wheels and we're good to go."

Kristin put up her arms and started to herd them backwards. Justin looked in the direction of her stare, but he didn't see anything.

"Oh shit," Travis said.

"Run," Kristin whispered.

Not seeing the threat, Justin fell in behind Travis and Kristin. He would have to trust them. They stuck to the road and sprinted away from the mouth of the mine. They finally stopped about twenty paces beyond the Jeep. Travis ducked behind a boulder and Kristin and Justin fell in behind him.

It was disconnected from the cable, but the Jeep began to rock. One of the windows blew and something pounded on the upside-down hood.

"What is it?" Justin whispered.

Kristin put her hand over his mouth.

He couldn't see what was doing the damage, but he heard it. Ripping and tearing that he assumed was the upholstery was followed by a screeching. The destruction ended with the sound of something punching repeatedly through the sheet metal.

When it was over, Kristin removed her hand and then slumped back against the rock.

"Wow," Travis said.

"I guess it doesn't like pillows," Kristin said.

"Or Jeeps," Travis said.

"We're just lucky that the thing didn't come out after us when we were screaming. It could have easily reached us. It might be able to reach us now." At the idea, Travis poked his head above the rock again. He settled back down after verifying that they were safe.

"We wait for daylight. Once the shadows are gone, we walk for help," Justin said.

"Assuming the shadow traps are chased away by the daylight, you mean," Travis said.

Justin exhaled and nodded. He looked to Kristin.

"Unless you've got a better idea?" Justin asked Kristin.

"Maybe," she said.

Chapter Forty-Three — Passage

THEY TIED A LEASH around Carlos and attached it to Florida's wrist. Roger hung onto her belt. It was the only way. At times it seemed like Carlos was moving through walls.

Florida was out of fresh batteries, so they cobbled together some that were mostly dead. As a result, Roger's light was just a whisper in the darkness. Florida's was a little better. Still, even with the full power of the sun, Roger doubted that Carlos's navigation would have made sense.

He led them down a winding passage and then took a left. He angled his body in a strange way. At the last second, Roger understood why. A crack seemed to appear and swallow Carlos as he approached. The rope led Florida in. Roger watched his own hand disappear. If he hadn't been pulled ahead by Florida's belt, he might have stopped and just stood there, looking at the wall of rock.

As they slipped into the crevice, their dim lights were swallowed by the close walls. As far as they knew, Carlos was leading them towards a hole in the floor where they would plunge to their deaths. He didn't. The disgusting man appeared to be trustworthy and led them through another room that led to another invisible crevice.

They walked for way too long, twisting on an unknowable path. Roger was beginning to think that they would come out exactly where they had started. Carlos didn't slow and didn't seem to fatigue. Roger stumbled over a rock with his bare foot and had to hop to keep up. He dragged on Florida's belt and she stopped.

"Sorry," Roger whispered.

"It's okay. He stopped," she said. "Why did we stop?" she asked Carlos.

"This is it," he said. "You go straight through here and you'll be back in the mine. I won't go any farther."

"Why?" Roger asked. "Why don't you come with us? We can find our way out."

"There is no way out," Carlos said. "Once you come here, there is only death."

Roger saw her light swing as Florida shook her head. The passage was so tiny that her light just lit a small area of rocks on either side of her head. Roger couldn't even see beyond her to where Carlos was standing.

"Teams come here every year," she said. "Dr. Grossman has brought tons of teams through the mines. They've never lost a single person."

"And you're still alive," Roger said.

"You're wrong on all counts," Carlos said.

"Shit!" Florida said. She grunted in frustration as she tried to move forward through the twists of the rocks. "He's gone."

"What?" Roger asked. "Where did he go? Follow the rope."

With difficulty, she turned around and held up the end of the rope. It was still looped into the noose that they had used to bind Carlos's hands. He had shed the leash and disappeared.

"Fuck," Roger said.

"Maybe it's okay. He said the mine is straight ahead. There's a chance he was telling the truth, right?"

"Yeah," Roger said. "There's a chance."

Without their guide, navigation was excruciating. Florida had to contort her body to fit between the rocks. Roger had it even worse. He was bigger and had to take care with his foot. His body felt sore all over. Each movement was a study in pain.

"Why did you stop?" Roger whispered.

"I think I see it," Florida said. There was desperate hope in her voice. Roger felt his heart beat faster and primed himself for disappointment. He was ready to believe anything.

She struggled forward. Roger felt her belt pull from his fingers.

"Hey," he called out. She wasn't slowing down. Roger mashed his bare foot into the unseen rocks and tumbled forward in his attempt to keep up. He lost his way. His light only showed the rocks directly in front of his face and he couldn't see Florida's weak light at all. Roger tried to get back to his feet, but he was stopped by a jagged rock poking him in the middle of his back. He was inexplicably pinned in his position and couldn't find any way out. Roger couldn't even back up. He was wedged in a crevice.

A hand appeared in front of his face.

He got his own hand free and managed to take hers. Roger squirmed through the gap and pulled himself from the crack in the wall. He emerged to the floor of the mine. He kissed the dusty floor.

"We're looking good," she said.

Roger followed the direction of her pointing finger.

At the next intersection, he saw one of the little flags posted.

Tears of relief welled in his eyes.

Chapter Forty-Four — Rolling

"WHAT DID SHE SAY?" Travis asked.

"She said that they fatigue," Justin said.

"What the hell does that mean?"

"I guess she thinks there's a safe period after they go back in," Justin said.

They were still perched behind the rock. Kristin, moving in a low crouch, was all the way over at the Jeep. When she reached the bumper of the overturned vehicle, she turned back and waved to them.

"Is she crazy?" Travis asked.

"Yup," Justin said. He moved around Travis and began his own shuffling run to Kristin. Behind him, he heard Travis whisper a curse and then follow too. They grouped behind the Jeep.

Kristin kept one eye on the mouth of the mine as she spoke.

"The jeep was starting to tip when that thing was beating on it. Let's see if we can get it to roll."

"Fuck that!" Travis whispered. "If we make noise, that thing is going to come back out here and snatch us. It can move a damn Jeep. You think it's going to have a problem taking the three of us?"

"Have you heard of a refractory period?" Kristin asked. "It just expended a lot of energy. If we have a chance, it's now. You'll notice—it never got *inside* the Jeep. Ryan was safe in there for hours. I don't think it can get in."

Travis looked to Justin for support. "She's crazy, right?"

Justin nodded. "She's crazy, but she might be right. I think we should push on the driver's side."

267

Kristin nodded. She and Justin began to move around the Jeep.

Travis followed. "You're both crazy," he whispered.

"Get it rocking," Justin whispered. They followed his lead as he pushed and released. He coaxed the Jeep into a rhythm. Kristin joined him and then broke off once the rocking began to make noise. She studied the front of the mine and then returned to push again. The top of the Jeep had been crushed by the earlier molestation. The square edges of the roof were caved-in and it wasn't very difficult to get it moving. The terrain helped as well. The makeshift road was crowned and the Jeep was balanced on the high spot.

Justin was wrong about the side to push on. After it picked up speed, the Jeep wanted to tip towards the three of them. They rushed over to the other side to help it along. It took a few pushes to get it going again, and then the Jeep paused at its balance-point. Justin dug in and really shoved. He wanted the Jeep to have enough momentum to carry it back to its wheels.

The Jeep began to fall. Travis and Kristin understood. They threw their shoulders to the roof along with Justin. They got lucky. The wheels fell into the depression on the far side of the road and the Jeep kept rolling.

Kristin pulled back when the Jeep was nearly back on its feet. She studied the front of the mine as Justin and Travis clutched the top of the Jeep and used their weight to keep the thing from rolling too far.

The crashing noise dispersed and the night was quiet again.

Travis pulled at the rear door handle. The hinges groaned and metal squealed as he opened the door.

"Shhh!" Kristin hissed.

"After all that," Travis whispered. "You're afraid of a door opening after all that?"

"I guess it's okay," she said. "I don't see anything."

"You think it will start?" Justin asked. He tugged at the driver's door, but his fingers snapped the handle and the door stayed closed. It wasn't going to budge. Travis crawled between the seats. Justin got in back.

Kristin held her ground as Travis cranked the engine. It sounded tired at first but it sputtered to life.

"Shut it off," Kristin said. She slid in back next to Justin and closed the door.

"Why?" Travis asked. "Let's see if we can get out of here."

"Just do it," she said.

Travis cut the engine and they were dropped into silence again. After being outside, the interior of the car felt claustrophobic. Justin itched to get back out. He felt trapped in there.

"I'm with Travis," Justin said. "I say we see if we can get out of here. Like you said, it doesn't look like they want to get inside the Jeep, and we got here just fine."

"What happens if we break down?" Kristin asked. "This vehicle has been put through the ringer. Half the windows are busted out. You think we'll last if the engine gives out while we're driving through one of those shadow traps?"

"I don't know," Travis said. "Maybe."

"Yeah, and maybe not," she said.

"Why do you think it's any safer to stay here?" Justin asked. "As far as we know, we're better off hiding behind that rock like we were. I don't get what the point of this is." He tried to open the other rear door, but the crushed roof was holding his door shut. Justin knocked away the broken glass and began to slip through to the night.

"She wants to wait," Travis said.

Justin dropped back in. "What?"

"She wants to wait for Carlos. She still thinks he's coming out," Travis said.

"But we yelled forever," Justin said. "Seriously?"

Kristin looked away. She didn't meet their eyes as she answered. "Don't you think we have an obligation to see if he comes out? We have to warn him about the thing, don't we?"

"He knows about the thing," Justin said. "He's the one who told us. He's got his eyes shut and everything. Trust me, he's fine."

"I don't want to leave him," she said.

Justin and Travis looked at each other.

Travis was the one who spoke first. "Then don't. You wait here behind that rock. We'll drive out and get help, right? We'll be back as soon as we can."

"You guys would seriously leave me here alone?" Kristin asked. "That's cold."

"It's practical," Justin said. "I mean, it's a risk either way, right? We will increase our odds of survival if we try both things."

"Yeah. That makes sense," Travis said.

Kristin covered her face with her hands. "Why did I let you guys talk me into this? This whole trip was a horrible mistake."

"Hey," Justin said. "This was everyone's mistake. Don't blame us. Are we going to split up or stay together?"

"I don't want to split up," Kristin said. "I don't want to be alone out here again, okay?"

"Fine, but we're going to try driving away," Justin said.

Travis scratched the side of his nose while he squinted. "I don't know. Maybe we could stay for just a little bit. We could see if Carlos gets up the nerve. If we see that thing coming out of the mine again, we'll back away in a hurry, right?"

Justin let out a disgusted sigh. "You guys are crazy."

"Twenty minutes. Half-hour, tops," Travis said.

Justin shook his head.

Chapter Forty-Five — Reality

THEY STOOD OVER IT.

"Whose flag is that?" Roger asked.

"Purple and red is J-2. Aaron and Kevin," Florida said.

Roger turned his weak light to the wall where the drop stamp was mounted.

"Hey!" he said, turning. "Try the..." he cut himself off.

Florida was already pushing the switch on the radio. "Command, this is team J-6. Request radio check. Over."

Roger raised his eyebrows as he waited. Florida wouldn't meet his eyes.

"Command, this is team J-6. Request radio check. Over."

The radio crackled with static. "J-6 this is Command. Where have you been? We're ready to pack up for the day. Over."

A radiant smile broke over Florida's face. They locked eyes. Roger beamed his own smile back. His headlight winked out. He slapped the side of his helmet and it came back on with one last gasp of electricity. Roger shook his head and smiled again.

"Command this is J-6. We're a little lost. We're at a flag of J-2 at the moment. Can we get some help here? Over."

"J-6 stay put. We're going to send a team out on J-2's path. Confirm—J-2's path. Over."

"Yes, we're on J-2. That's purple and red. We're going to stay put. Over."

"J-6, we will check in by radio on the fives. Over and out."

Florida's shoulders fell as she let out a big sigh.

She wandered over to the wall and pressed her back against it. She slowly eased down to a seat. Roger limped over and eyed the floor. He decided to stand.

"You think we can move a little farther away from that crack?" Roger asked.

"Nope," Florida said. "I'm going to stay within an arm's length of that flag and I'm not going to stop looking at it until help arrives. And you're going to stay right here with me."

Roger nodded. "Yeah. Okay." He didn't settle to the floor, but he leaned back against the wall next to her. "They're going to shit their pants when we tell them about Carlos and everything."

Florida nodded. "We didn't run. We didn't panic."

"Well, you ran a little, but it wasn't out of panic," Roger said.

"When they ask, we stayed together. We followed protocol and stayed together," she said. "We'll tell them that someone took your pack. Maybe it was Carlos. Hell, it was almost certainly Carlos. He was probably tracking us all day."

"What about measurements and stuff? We didn't take any readings past the hangman's cave," Roger said.

"Maybe we did," she said. "Maybe the readings were stolen with your bag. Maybe we followed every protocol. Then you get paid and I get credit."

Roger nodded. "That's a good point. I hadn't thought about it that way."

The radio crackled. Florida jumped and then smiled. She picked it up.

"J-6, we are en route. Confirm that you're still on a J-2 flag. Over."

She pushed the switch. "That's right, Command. We're sitting on a J-2 flag. Over." Florida looked up to Roger as an idea occurred to her. She whispered to him without triggering the radio. "You can get the ID from the drop stamp. They'll know how far along we are."

Roger turned and looked at the drop stamp. His light flickered and went out again. He hit the side of his helmet and it came back one more time. He read the ID and Florida relayed it by radio back to Command. They waited for a response.

"J-6, did you say 7812-217? Over."

"That's right, Command. 7812-217. Over."

They waited. Florida whispered, "That's it, right?"

Roger confirmed the stamp ID and then nodded.

"J-6, that's not a valid stamp ID. Are you sure you're reading it right? Over."

Florida got to her feet quickly and joined Roger. He beat the side of his helmet as his light went out again. Florida shushed him and read the ID for herself.

"Command, I'm looking at the ID. It is absolutely number 7812-217. Over."

Her statement was met with a long silence from the radio. Florida held it up with both hands, like she was about to begin praying to the thing.

It finally crackled again and the friendly voice came from the speaker. "No worries, J-6. We'll get everything sorted out when we get to you. Over and out."

Florida ran her fingers over the raised numbers on the drop stamp. She looked at Roger and then looked back at it.

"Weird," she said.

"I wish they would hurry up and get here," Roger said.

"It can't take more than a few minutes," Florida said.

Roger took off his helmet. In the faint light from Florida's headlamp, he took out the batteries. He blew on the ends, flipped them, and stuck them back in.

"You didn't honestly think that was going to work, did you?" she asked.

"Worth a shot," he said. He flipped the switch on and off. Nothing happened. "Maybe we should light a flare or something?"

Florida shrugged and then took off her pack. She began to sort through it. "You know, it's not a terrible idea. They'll definitely be able to see us from a distance with one of these. They don't last too long, but they are really bright."

She handed a flare over to Roger. He moved closer so he could read the instructions.

"Huh. It expired," he said. "Typical. Put my back to the wind— right. This burns about fifteen minutes. Is that long enough?"

"I've got three. Go ahead."

Roger followed the instructions and struck the abrasive cap

against the tip of the flare. It was like lighting a giant match. The flare burned with a bright, noisy, red flame. Roger set it down and waved his hand in the air to disperse some of the smoke.

Florida put her arm across her nose and shrank down to the floor. Roger moved next to her.

"That's a lot of smoke," he said.

"And a lot of light."

Roger turned and looked up the length of the tunnel. Aside from the smoke, he decided that the flare was a very bad idea. The shadows danced in the red light. The tunnel looked like a decent approximation of what Hell might look like.

"Look at that," Florida said. She sat up straight.

"I know. It's creepy, right?"

"No, I mean look at the flag," she said.

Roger shrugged. "What about it?"

"With the red light from the flare, the colors look black and white. That's the flag of group F-6, I think."

"So?"

"How yellow were our lights when I looked at the flag before? I told them purple and red. Maybe it was blue and orange or something. Maybe the dim color of my headlamp was making me see the colors wrong."

"You're crazy. I saw purple and red too."

"Yeah, using the same yellow light."

"Calm down," Roger said. "I'm sure that they're on their way."

"But what if that's why they didn't recognize the stamp ID?"

Roger exhaled. "Okay. Get on the radio and tell them that the color might be wrong. Maybe they have another way for us to identify which path we're on. Better safe than sorry."

"Yeah," she said. She nodded. "Exactly." She keyed the radio. "Command? This is J-6. We're unsure about the flag color. When we spoke earlier, we said we were on a purple and red flag, but our lights were pretty dim? We're unsure of the color. Is there another way to verify the color?"

She turned up the radio and waited for a response.

Roger whispered, "Color is a silly way to identify anything underground. You'd think they would put braille or something on the flag, you know?"

"Do you know braille?" Florida asked.

"No, but..."

Florida held up a finger and raised the radio when it began to crackle. She narrowed her eyes when no voices emerged from the device.

"Command, this is J-6? Over."

She put the radio up to her ear. At first, the sound was so faint that it was indiscernible from the background static. A single note emerged. The voice swelled from the speaker. Florida pulled the radio away from her ear. Roger drew close and they listened as the moan broke into a chorus of screams. They couldn't identify individual words or voices in the din. The radio emitted sounds of horrible torture and chaos.

"Command?" Florida asked. When she let go of the button, the screams came through even louder. They filled the mine.

Chapter Forty-Six — Gone

ACCORDING TO THE CLOCK on the dashboard of the Jeep, they only waited five minutes. Travis was bouncing his knee, Kristin was compulsively turning her head to look in every direction, and Justin counted off the seconds.

"Okay, we gotta go," Travis said.

"Yeah," Kristin said. "Okay, I changed my mind. Let's go get help. We can come back for him."

"Good," Justin said. "You're finally making some sense."

Travis turned the key. The Jeep fired right up. The engine seemed to be okay, but when Travis put it in gear, it was clear that the Jeep had taken some damage. They heard a grinding noise as he backed away from the entrance of the mine and turned the Jeep around.

Kristin spun in her seat to keep an eye on the entrance as Travis pulled away.

Justin climbed over the seat and brushed away debris so he could sit in the passenger's seat. Kristin kept watch behind them. Travis drove in silence, sitting forward in his seat and concentrating on the dirt road ahead of them. Each time the Jeep bounced, one of the headlights flickered. Finally, it went out. Travis found the switch for the high beams. The remaining headlight did a decent job of showing their path.

"What happens when I get to the shadow trap?" Travis asked. "Should I drive right through it?"

"We made it through before," Kristin said.

Travis and Justin looked at each other.

"Yeah. Fuck it," Justin said. "Go fast."

Travis nodded. He increased their speed. On the next bump, a crack split the windshield. Travis leaned to the side to see better. Justin pulled his seatbelt across and then thought better of it. They saw the turn ahead. The road descended into a little dip and then rose again. On the other side, next to the hill where they'd seen Kristin, they saw the place where the big shadow trap stretched across the road. Kristin leaned forward and Travis sped up a little more.

They all studied the road ahead, trying to guess where the shadow trap began.

When the Jeep bounced over a bump in the road, Justin gave a shout at the sound. The Jeep sped on. Travis guided the vehicle around the turn and down another hill. When they started to climb again, Kristin spun around and looked at the hill they had just passed.

"We're by it," she said.

"Yes!" Justin said.

Travis nodded and didn't take any of his focus from the road ahead. They bounced over a rough patch of road and the backend of the Jeep began to get a little squirrelly. Travis eased off the accelerator and loosened his death-grip slightly. Over the crest of the next hill, they saw lights in the distance.

"That's the highway," Justin said. He banged his hand down on the dashboard. Justin moved up to the edge of his seat. "Holy shit, I was starting to think we would never make it, you know?" Justin turned back to smile at Kristin.

Her jabbing finger nearly poked him in the eye.

"Look out!" she screamed.

Justin whipped around. Travis was already reacting. He hauled the wheel over to the side and stomped on the brakes.

Justin almost didn't recognize the man in the road as the headlight swerved away from him. He was standing there, right in the path on the far side of a small hill. Carlos was standing there with his eyes closed and his hands down at his sides. The Jeep's tires locked up and they spun halfway around in the loose gravel.

The Jeep rocked as it came to a stop.

Kristin was staring out the back at Carlos.

Justin tried his door. It banged against the bent frame and wouldn't open. Instead of getting out, Justin turned in his seat.

"I knew he would come to his senses," Kristin said. She put her hand on the door.

"Wait!" Travis said. "What if it's a trap?"

"What?" Kristin asked. "What are you talking about?"

"What if the thing can't get us while we're in the Jeep, so it's using Carlos to lure us out?" Travis asked.

"No," Kristin said. She didn't argue or come up with any tortured logic. She simply repeated the word again. "No."

She pushed on the door and the metal groaned.

Travis didn't try to talk her out of it. Instead, he dropped the Jeep into first gear and ground the transmission again. The Jeep lurched back into motion and she fell back against the seat. Travis spun the vehicle in a tight circle until the headlights were pointed around to Carlos again. He approached Carlos at a quick pace, but angled the Jeep so they would pass to his left.

Travis slowed as they approached.

Justin heard Kristin working at the door again. He reached into the back seat and grabbed her arm.

"Hold on," Justin said. "He's right—let's just see." Justin reached back and grabbed Kristin's arm. She stopped tugging at the handle.

When the Jeep pulled to within a few feet of Carlos, he began to back away.

Justin craned forward to see Carlos's feet. When he figured it out, he started yelling. "No! Back up! Back up!"

Travis slammed on the brakes and dropped the Jeep out of gear. He shifted to reverse and goosed the engine as he lifted his foot from the clutch. The tires began to spin, but the Jeep still slid forward. The ground swallowed Carlos. The Jeep kept sliding. The loose gravel didn't offer enough resistance against the momentum of the Jeep.

A crack appeared in the surface of the road. As the Jeep slipped downhill, the crack widened until it was big enough to consume the Jeep. Travis tried to steer against the slip, but nothing he did seemed to slow their creep. His spinning tires had no consequence.

Justin threw his shoulder to his window. The glass was already cracked. In the seat behind him, the window was already knocked out. He threw his shoulder against the window one last time and then began to crawl over the seat again.

The Jeep started to tip forward. The headlights showed the jagged sides of a chasm. The engine whined and the rear tires spun freely as they lifted from the ground.

Justin climbed through the window and kicked himself away from the Jeep as it disappeared into the widening hole.

Justin landed on the sloped surface of the road and began to slide after the Jeep. He pedaled his legs against the gravel. Using his hands and feet to propel himself upwards, he began to make progress against gravity.

When he got back to flat road, Justin didn't stop. He turned to his right and scrambled up the gentle slope. He stumbled at the peak and landed on the sand. He flipped over in time to see the taillights of the Jeep disappear. The chasm closed. The road appeared passable again.

In the distance, a set of headlights cruised down the highway, unperturbed by the drama in the desert.

"Help me!" Justin screamed. It didn't do any good. The highway was still at least a mile away. He might as well have been on the moon, yelling at the turning Earth.

Justin's senses adjusted to the night. He slid down the sandy hill and stepped onto the surface of the road. He took a couple of cautious steps forward. He glanced back over his shoulder and then looked towards the highway.

Kneeling down, he could see the tracks of the Jeep. He could see where they got chaotic and then ended with lines carved into the dirt road.

Justin backed away. He retreated to his sandy hill.

He looked to the sky and the highway and used both to make his best guess about which direction was north. With that settled, he lowered himself to the ground facing east.

"Wait until dawn," he whispered.

He pulled his legs under himself and propped his head up with his hands. Gradually, his heartbeat returned to normal. The adrenaline coursing through him relinquished its hold. He exhaled and tried to not think about his friends and the Jeep, somewhere below the dirt.

Justin was tortured with the idea of seeing Carlos. He couldn't stop looking over his shoulder. Each time, he was convinced that he would see Carlos there, standing with his eyes closed. The idea made Justin's stomach turn.

Justin waited for the dawn.

Chapter Forty-Seven — Abandoned

FLORIDA DROPPED THE RADIO. Roger rushed forward and scooped it up. He found the volume control and turned it down, until the din was barely audible. Still, it was terrible. He was hearing people screaming for their lives. He was hearing the desperation of people who were facing certain death.

One particular scream was louder than the rest.

Roger was tempted to shut off the radio completely, but he couldn't do it. There was a chance, however small, that the people on the other end of the connection might still help them escape. He wasn't willing to give up on that chance.

The scream echoed and swelled even though he turned the volume down even more.

Florida's head jerked to the side and Roger finally realized why the voice was getting louder. It wasn't coming from the radio—it was coming down the mine shaft.

"Put it out," Florida whispered. "Put the flare out before it finds us."

Roger moved forward. He didn't know how to extinguish the flare, but he was pretty sure he didn't want to anyway. There was someone else down there, and the person sounded like they needed help. After all that time alone with just Florida, Roger wasn't about to turn his back on another human being in need.

He set down the radio and moved another few steps towards the sound. The flare was behind him. It cast his own shadow on the floor.

Roger's shadow stretched forever. The edges danced.

He took another step and finally saw movement and a white

light. A figure stumbled forward. Roger ran to the person.

The person's screams were wordless, but they conveyed undeniable emotions. He heard fear, anger, and despair. As he approached, virtually all he could see was the headlamp as it turned towards him. Compared to Florida's light, this one was as bright as the sun.

As he reached the person, the light finally turned away and he saw the person's shape. The face angled towards him and bellowed one more agonized scream. Roger flinched. Beyond the glare of the light, he could see the rip in the man's skin.

It began just below his eye and continued through his cheek and down his neck. The skin and muscle were pulled apart to reveal the jagged white edge of bone. The man flopped over on his back and his helmet bounced from his head. When it came to rest, the light was pointed down the length of the man, revealing the devastation of the cut.

He had been opened, from cheek to thigh. Despite the severity of the wound, there was precious little blood soaked into his clothes. The light left the man's eyes as Roger knelt down.

Roger heard Florida scream. He looked back and saw her a few paces away. Her yellow headlamp was dwarfed by the light from the flare behind her. She was covering her face with her hands as she looked down at the man who was sliced open.

"That's Jacob," Florida said. "He is part of the command team."

Roger reached out and touched the man's wrist. He was dead.

"Not anymore," Roger said. He picked up Jacob's helmet and traded it for his own. The bright light felt like a weapon on his head. He pointed in the direction that Jacob had come from. He didn't see anything except a few scattered drops of blood on the rock.

"We know which way to go," Florida said. "There will be flags."

Roger nodded.

Before leaving Jacob, Roger bent the man's arm and fed it through the strap of his pack. He pulled it up over Jacob's head until he freed it from the other arm. Roger ignored the blood on the pack. He slipped his own arms through the loops and started down the tunnel. He and Florida walked side by side.

"What are we heading towards?" she asked.

"I'm not sure I care," Roger said.

Chapter Forty-Eight — Under

As the Jeep slipped into the hole, Kristin fell forward. She got her hands out in front of herself and managed to absorb the bulk of the shock before her face slammed into the dashboard. Next to her, Travis had been thrown to the side and was compressed in the space between the steering wheel and the door.

The Jeep ground at first and then tumbled weightless for a second. It rotated as it fell and crashed down on the roof. The battered roll bars held up for the most part. Kristin landed on the interior of the crumpled roof and pulled her legs to her chest so she could rotate her body. As soon as she got upright, she began to crawl between the upside-down seats so she could get to the rear of the vehicle. In the front, rocks and debris were coming through the windows. In the rear she could see empty space through the back window. That's what Kristin headed for.

She heard Travis moan behind her. Kristin ignored him.

To get to the back, she had to squeeze between the rear seats and the crushed-in roof. The bags were in her way. She pushed aside the moldy canvas bag that Justin had liberated from the depths of the mine. As she crouched in the cargo space, she moved the bags and realized that she couldn't see anything but black beyond the shattered window. She rooted through the bags and came up with one of the silver flashlights.

Kristin turned it on and shined it into the darkness.

"If you're coming, then come on," she said to Travis.

"My leg is caught," he said. He punctuated the statement with a pathetic moan.

Kristin didn't answer. She pressed herself down and slid

through the window. Her shoulder was in tough shape. She transferred the light to her other hand and tried to get a sense of the place. She pointed the light upwards to get an idea of how far they had fallen. It was impossible to tell. She couldn't even see the night sky. The walls pinched together up there. Gasoline was dripping down the back of the Jeep. The fumes stung her eyes.

Kristin began to climb the overturned Jeep. It was wedged between the rocks. There was no way that the side doors would ever open.

"You have to go out the back," she said as she balanced her weight between the muffler and the differential. She looked up. She could touch the walls where they came together. There had to be a space between the rocks, but she couldn't find it with her light.

"Carlos!" she yelled. "Where are you?"

Below her, Travis moaned again.

Chapter Forty-Nine — Battlefield

THEY FOLLOWED THE TRAIL of blood back to the next flag. From there, they could see the next turn. Florida began to rush ahead and realized that her headlamp was barely putting out any light. She slowed back down to Roger's pace.

When they saw another body, they both came to a stop.

It was a young woman with blonde hair. Her head was split in two.

"Oh, no," Florida whispered. Roger's light sparkled on the halves of her brain. The cut went right down her spine.

Roger stepped around her on one side, Florida on the other.

Florida bent to pick up the woman's helmet. She dropped it quickly and wiped her hands on her pants. The helmet had been split as well. Battery acid leaked from the bisected headlamp. As she stood back up, Florida's headlamp flickered and then finally went out. She was now at the mercy of Roger's lamp, and the man was moving on. Florida rushed to catch up.

At the next intersection, they took a right. Roger stepped carefully over a severed arm. Florida didn't take any time to investigate it. Her head was already full of disgusting images. She didn't need any more.

Dr. Grossman was surrounded by papers. She held a clipboard to her chest. Florida couldn't see any wounds on the woman, but her eyes were open and lifeless. Her chest didn't rise and fall with breath. Roger nudged Dr. Grossman's foot with his shoe and she didn't react.

Static burst from a radio on the floor and Florida almost ran. She reminded herself that she would be sprinting into the darkness.

"The entrance has to be close," Roger whispered.

"Who did this?" Florida asked.

Roger shook his head. "More like 'What.'"

They stood as Roger played his light over the black rectangle.

His eyes moved to Florida and then back to the end of the tunnel.

"That's the exit," Florida said.

Roger shook his head. "Not anymore."

"We should at least *try* to leave," Florida said.

"We'll flip a coin," Roger said. "Loser tries to walk through that blackness to see if we can get out. Maybe it's just camouflage, you know? Maybe we can just walk right through."

"Maybe," Florida said. Her eyes turned back to the bodies. They had walked by a pile of corpses to get to the mine's exit. Some of the people were students who Florida knew pretty well.

"That Carlos guy always keeps his eyes closed, right? Maybe if we keep our eyes closed," Roger said.

"Call it," Florida said. She had a quarter in her hand. Roger's light tracked it as she flipped it up in the air.

"Tails," he said.

She caught the coin and smacked it down on the back of her hand. She lifted her hand slowly. It was tails.

"I'll go," he said.

"No," she said.

Florida started walking. Behind her, Roger's light shifted as he moved to the wall of the tunnel. Her shadow stretched out ahead of her, meeting the black curtain that separated her from the outside world. As she approached, she remembered the haggard old man from the mine—Carlos. She closed her eyes.

Roger watched as Florida walked. He hated himself for his own cowardice. It should have been him walking into danger. Then again, the evidence of the mine's danger was all around him. Maybe it was more brave to stay there with the corpses while Florida took a shot at getting out of the damn mine. It was impossible to know the correct course of action.

She slowed as she approached. Her hand went up. Roger guessed that she had closed her eyes. It might not mean anything, but Carlos seemed to be a survivor, and it was the strategy that he employed.

The darkness that was stretched across the mine's exit seemed to envelop her. She was walking into a curtain of tar. Roger held his breath as her final step took her into blackness. The back of her shoe was the last thing to disappear. Florida didn't make a sound.

As he watched, the black curtain began to grow a little brighter. Points of light poked through from the back and Roger realized that he was seeing out to the night sky.

He ran forward. His light picked up something shiny on the floor of the mine. Roger realized that it was Florida's headlamp. He jumped over it and kept moving.

As he passed beneath the rock overhang, Roger emerged to the desert night. The world opened up around him in a vast expanse.

He skidded to a stop when he realized that someone was standing there under the stars.

Roger's light hit the old man's face. His eyes were closed.

"One stays to keep the secrets," Carlos said.

Roger scanned the terrain with his light, looking for Florida. "Did you see my friend come through here?"

"Everyone else becomes part of us," Carlos said.

Roger stepped to the side to get around Carlos. "I thought you said there was no way out."

Despite his closed eyes, Carlos reached out an arm and settled his hand on Roger's shoulder. Roger ducked from under the hand.

"Goodbye," Carlos said.

Carlos started walking forward, towards the entrance of the mine. Roger didn't stick around to see what happened. Instead, he began to run towards where the bus was parked. The helmet bounced from his head as he rounded the corner. The light shut off as it hit the ground, but Roger could still see fairly well by the moonlight.

The bus wasn't there.

Roger kept running. He pointed himself down the road and settled into a fast jog as he tried to master his breathing. He wasn't cut out for jogging, but he was going to do his best. He slowed even more as the road crested a small hill.

Florida's name came to his lips, but he held back on yelling for her. If she made it out, she would be fine. She was a survivor. Now that he was outside, he wasn't going to waste any time looking for her or anyone.

Roger slowed to a fast walk as he rounded a corner. His panting breath tasted sour in the back of his throat. Any more running and he would start to throw up.

There was a person standing in the middle of the road. He recognized Carlos by smell this time.

"You're like a bad penny," Roger said. He spat to the side.

"One stays to keep the secrets," Carlos said.

"Good luck with that," Roger said. His legs were twitching and hot, but he found the strength to sprint around Carlos and continue down the road. When he glanced back, Carlos was gone. Roger began to wonder if maybe Carlos was just in his head. Maybe he was feeling guilty about leaving Florida behind and Carlos was his brain's attempt to exorcise that demon.

He saw him, standing at the crest of the next hill.

Chapter Fifty — Escape

KRISTIN SPIT OUT THE dirt that fell in her face. She wiped sand from her eyes and jabbed the sharp end of the crowbar up into the darkness. His hand reached for the flashlight that she had wedged into the frame of the Jeep.

Kristin kicked at the hand.

"Ow!" Travis said. "Fuck. You kicked me."

"Get your own damn light," she said. "I need this one." She stabbed up into the dirt again. More of it spilled down.

"It's impossible. You're never going to dig your way out. It's solid rock above us," Travis said. "But I see a passage. We can find our way out."

"Fuck passages," Kristin said. A clump of dirt came down. She dodged back and managed to avoid it hitting her face, but a bunch of sand went down the front of her shirt. She ignored it and kept tearing at the soil above. Her arms were getting tired.

"I can't find any other lights in there," Travis said.

"Then you can explore in the dark. It's going to be the same result either way," she said. When the next clod of dirt fell, Kristin was digging at the end of her reach. There was only a narrow column of dirt—the rest was all hard rock. She needed something more to stand on if she was going to dig much higher.

"It has to go somewhere," Travis said. "Carlos had to have come from somewhere."

"Good luck. You're not taking my light."

Travis reached for it again and she swung without thinking. The crowbar hit him in the forearm and gave a hollow ring.

"Fuck!" he said. He withdrew and disappeared back inside the

Jeep.

Kristin found a loose rock in the wall. She managed to knock it out and rolled it into position. She stood on top of the rock and got a little more height so she could continue her digging.

Travis reappeared from the back of the Jeep.

"I found this candle. Trade me a candle for the flashlight," he said.

"No," she said.

"Come on. You're staying in one place. A candle would work fine for you."

"Why don't you help me dig? Are you allergic to work? Are you so lazy that you won't dig to save yourself?" she asked. More dirt came down into her mouth. She spat it to her side.

"Why are you so convinced that you're going to be able to dig your way out of this? You didn't help me when my leg was pinned, why the hell should I help you with your stupid digging? I'm going to find whichever way Carlos went and go that way."

"Don't you get it?" Kristin screamed. "He's not trying to get out. Something has changed about Carlos. I could see it from twenty feet away. If we hadn't slowed down to avoid hitting him, we would be out of here by now. Whatever is trying to keep us down here, Carlos is helping it."

"No way," Travis said. "I don't believe that."

He began fumbling with the matches.

"Don't light that here," Kristin said. "There's gasoline everywhere. Can't you smell it?"

"Then give me the flashlight," he said.

"No."

Travis climbed slowly until he was standing directly over the Jeep's gas tank. Kristin stopped digging and picked up the flashlight. She pointed it at him. Travis had taken out one of the matches and was holding it against the striker.

"You give me that flashlight or I'll drop a match right on this gas."

The tank was cracked or there was a hole punched in it. Gas had been leaking from it since she had climbed out. There was no telling how much had pooled on the rocks below them.

"Don't do it," she said.

He held out his hand.

Kristin glanced once more at the dirt above her and then back to Travis. The flashlight picked up hints of madness in his eyes. She wasn't eager to find out how much chaos that madness would bring.

She handed over the light.

"Thank you," he said. He tossed the matches and they bounced off her chest and fell down into the upside-down workings of the Jeep.

Travis tucked the flashlight under his arm and began his clumsy climb down from the Jeep.

"Don't leave, Travis. We can dig our way out. We didn't fall that far. It can't be much farther to the surface."

He was already climbing over rocks and leaving the scene. The taillights from the Jeep gave the cave somewhat of a red glow. The hole above her was just black. She looked at the crowbar in her hands. She might have hit him with it again. She might have knocked the flashlight from his hands. But she suspected he wouldn't get far. He would be back and they would dig their way out together.

She watched for a few seconds as the flashlight wound around another rock and then disappeared down a side passage.

"Good luck," she whispered.

She jabbed upwards with the crowbar and another cascade of dirt and sand tumbled down.

Chapter Fifty-One — Confrontation

"ONE STAYS TO KEEP the secrets," Carlos said as Roger approached.

"You said that already. How do you keep appearing? Are you a dream? Are you a figment of my imagination?"

"We've been together forever," Carlos said. "We feed each other. It's your turn to take my place."

"Get out of my way," Roger said. His anger rose. There was something smug about the way that Carlos kept his eyes shut. It was the ultimate form of disrespect.

Carlos shook his head. "One stays."

Roger advanced on the man. Carlos opened his mouth to speak again and Roger hit him. He planted both hands on Carlos's chest and shoved. Carlos never saw it coming.

His stringy gray hair flew as Carlos stumbled back. His feet tangled and he fell to the gravel road. Roger landed on top of him. Roger punched down at the old man, bashing his rotten teeth. Carlos still didn't open his eyes. Roger clasped his hands around Carlos's throat and began to squeeze. In the moonlight, he saw Carlos smile.

Roger grew even angrier.

In an effort to knock the smile from Carlos's face, Roger lifted the old man's neck and slammed it down into the gravel. He repeated, again and again, but Carlos still smiled. Roger yelled out his rage. His fist closed and he raised it. Roger beat the man's face and then closed his fingers around his throat. He squeezed until it seemed that his own bones would snap from the effort.

The smile on Carlos's face began to disappear. The old mans eyes finally began to open. Roger leaned forward to make contact.

Carlos didn't focus on him. His eyes were glassy and unresponsive. Roger moved even closer. He took his hands away from Carlos's throat and had to pull them from the sand. His hands had sunk in during the choking.

Carlos wheezed. The gentle sound turned into a breathy laugh. Carlos finally met his eyes.

"It's an honor to be chosen," Carlos said. As he finished the word, sand ran into his mouth. He tilted his head back and his face disappeared below the surface of the road.

Roger pushed himself away from Carlos, but he didn't get far. His lower legs had sunk down into the sand, along with Carlos's body. Roger clawed at the road surface, trying to free himself, but the sand gripped him and dragged him deeper. He was being absorbed by the road.

Roger placed his hands down and pushed. He tried to roll on his side to get more surface area against the sand. No matter what he did, he only sunk more. Carlos had disappeared and it felt like his body was wrapped around Roger's legs. Carlos pulled at him like an anchor.

When Roger screamed for help, he was already buried up to his ribs. The expulsion of breath let the sand compress around his chest. He focused all his effort on trying to draw a full chestful of air. His head and arms descended quickly.

Roger was gone.

Chapter Fifty-Two — Bomb

THE HEADLIGHTS WERE BEGINNING to dim by the time that Kristin climbed down from the back of the Jeep. Travis's candle was still sitting on the frame of the Jeep. She threw it off into the darkness and lowered herself down so she could slip through the back window. She climbed through the gas fumes, all the way to the driver's seat where she had to turn her brain around to figure out where the controls for the headlights were. She shut off the remaining light and then turned the switch to just parking lights.

When she crawled back out, she stayed in the fume-filled rear of the Jeep long enough to paw through what was left back there. Travis had taken anything that looked like a light source. She found an old t-shirt and a plastic bottle. The shirt had soaked up some of the dripping gasoline.

Kristin sat up straight with an idea.

She grabbed her stuff and crawled out of the Jeep.

The crowbar was still sitting atop the overturned Jeep. She grabbed that and headed off in the direction that Travis had gone. It was tough going after she left the red glow of the taillights. Kristin took her time. The last thing she needed was a twisted ankle.

The path narrowed quickly.

Kristin turned around frequently, making sure she still had a decent trajectory to the Jeep.

She reached a place where she was going to have to duck under a low rock. Kristin put her head through and verified that there was somewhere to go. She knelt down in the darkness and chewed the inside of her cheek as she considered her plan.

It was rash and impulsive. There wasn't a backup plan if it went wrong. She couldn't think of any other way.

Kristin tore the shirt and began stuffing it into the bottle. She had no idea if her idea would even work. When she got the first half in, she left a foot of t-shirt dangling from the mouth. She moved by touch—the taillights were too far away to do her any good.

Kristin found the matches in her pocket. She was about to strike them when a horrible image streaked across her mind. She imagined her pants catching a spark. They were likely still soaked in gas from her crawl. She pictured her burning legs lighting up the last agonized moments of her life.

Kristin moved her hands away from her lap before striking the match.

The shirt burst into flames immediately. Kristin lifted the bottle carefully and used the light from the flame to illuminate her shot. When she was sure she had a sense of it, she threw the bottle towards the Jeep.

Nothing happened. She could see moving shadows. The bottle was still lit, but it was too far from the vehicle to catch.

The plan was terrible—she was willing to admit that. She hoped for some giant Hollywood explosion that would somehow blast a hole right out of this underground dungeon, but she hadn't even managed to catch the Jeep on fire. Kristin sighed and began to crawl over the rocks so she could retrieve her bomb.

"It's a fuse, not a bomb," she whispered.

She crested the last rock and paused. A persistent yellow flame was burning away at the end of the bottle. It was lying on its side on one of the few flat parts of the cavern. Kristin blinked and then stared. The thing wouldn't stay still. As the shirt burned, the rock under the bottle swelled and tilted and then shifted again. The movement was slow, but it was visible because of the moving bottle. The bottle rolled back and forth. Kristin held perfectly still and realized that she could feel the rocks grinding underneath her.

The bottle finally gained enough speed to bounce up over an edge and tumble in the direction of the Jeep. Kristin watched for a second, mesmerized, before she realized the implication.

She scrambled back over the rocks.

She crawled as deep as she could and wrapped her hands around her head. Nothing happened. She waited another minute and then crawled under the low rock. She saw the dancing flames—something had caught. It could only be a matter of time before the gas tank blew.

She waited.

At one point, she heard a big expulsion of air and she ducked into her protective crouch again. Still, nothing happened. She straightened up and watched the flickering light grow. The light played strange tricks with the shape of the cavern. The walls themselves seemed to be undulating. Kristin imagined that she could feel the floor shifting.

Air began to rush past her from deeper within the cavern. It was feeding the flames. She put her arm up over her mouth and nose so she could breathe through the fabric. The air was getting thick and acrid. Only the fresh air from deeper in the cave was really breathable.

When Kristin coughed the first time, she realized what a horrible mistake she had made.

She slipped and fell to her butt.

Kristin whipped around, looking all around her in the yellow glow from the flames.

It wasn't a trick of the light—the floor *was* moving. Dirt filtered down on her head. She realized that the whole cavern was moving. She moved forward, even though it was towards the heat of the flames. She didn't want to be caught under one of the low rocks as the space grew and shrank. It seemed like the cave was trying to chew her up.

Chapter Fifty-Three — Quake

IN JUSTIN'S DREAM, HE was falling. His eyes flew open and he realized that the dream was true. The ground was shifting beneath him and he was slipping down the side of the hill. He flipped over and clawed at the hillside, but it was no use. The loose sand and gravel flowed like a river and he was caught in the current. He was sliding back down towards the road.

Justin looked over his shoulder and saw hungry shadows waiting for him. The sun was beginning to color the sky in the East. He imagined that the light was magnetic and was drawing him towards it.

His foot caught a solid rock and he steadied himself. Just as he exhaled, the rock slipped. It became part of the avalanche. Justin rolled as he fell. He tumbled back towards the road.

He landed on the shoulder and dirt cascaded down onto his legs. Justin scrambled to his feet. He couldn't stand the thought of being buried again.

The road itself began to shake and Justin dropped into a low crouch to stay upright.

His head whipped to his right when he saw a new shadow appear in the middle of the road. He ran. Another shadow was spreading behind him.

Justin stopped and spun in place, looking for a safe direction to flee. There was nowhere to go. A crack started to form in the dirt. His patch of road began to tilt. This was just how the Jeep was taken, and now he was going to be consumed by the same ravenous patch of road.

Justin saw one chance—he could jump the new hole and

maybe escape down the road. Yes, there were shadows down there, but anything was preferable to the chasm in front of him. He ran, even as the ground was falling away.

A new light, even brighter than the emerging dawn, was coming up from the hole in the ground. It was a child's conception of hell—a burning orange light coming from a crack in the soil.

Justin leaped.

The ground betrayed him. It shifted again and his momentum was sucked down by the falling earth. He didn't clear the gap. He crashed into the far ledge with his upper body. His legs were dangling down into the chasm.

Justin dug his fingernails into the dirt and pulled.

A hand closed around his ankle.

Chapter Fifty-Four — Lesson

ROGER TRIED TO OPEN his eyes, but they were filled with sand. He coughed and spat out a mouthful of dirt. When the hand closed around his wrist, he screamed.

The voice in the darkness was gentle.

"Organic goes to the right. Metal goes in the middle. Synthetic goes to the left," the voice said.

"Let me go!" he yelled he pulled his wrist from Carlos's grip and tried to get up. His head hit the rocks above and stars swam across his closed eyes. He blinked, scraping his eyes with sand, and saw nothing. There was nothing but blackness around them.

He heard a smile in Carlos's voice. "Organic to the right," Carlos said. Something cold was pressed into Roger's hand. He ran his fingers over it until he recognized the shape. The toes were what tipped him off. It was a foot, severed at the ankle.

Roger screamed and dropped the thing.

"No," Carlos said. "To the right."

Roger felt the tickle of Carlos's foul breath when he whispered into Roger's ear. "If there's still some flesh, you can eat it." Carlos smacked his lips.

Roger forgot about the rocks and tried to pull away again. He slammed his head a second time.

Roger bellowed with fear and frustration.

Chapter Fifty-Five — Free

THE SHADOW WRAPPED AROUND Florida like a sticky membrane. She kept walking the best that she could, but it suddenly felt like she was moving through molasses. She leaned into the thing and drove her legs forward. There was weakness in the center. Florida pushed her hand forward and felt it pierce through the darkness and touch fresh air on the other side.

The shadow began to withdraw, pulling her back into the mine. Florida didn't waver. Her running coach had told her a simple fact that she applied to many aspects of her life—a marathon was two races. The first race was twenty-one point two miles, and it was the hardest thing she would do. The second race was the last five miles, and it was twice as hard as the first part. Florida was accustomed to digging in. She was accomplished at perseverance. With that in mind, she flexed her muscles and fought the shadow.

She punched her other hand through the hole and felt the shadow weakening.

Florida lowered her shoulder and fought.

The shadow snapped away. It gave up and she tumbled out into the night. She looked around, confused. It had been daylight when she went in, and there had been a table set up with equipment. It was all gone.

She didn't wait for an explanation.

She ran.

The first few turns were uneventful. Florida settled into an easy jog down the dirt road. She wished she had been paying more attention when they pulled in. It was tough to make out the twists and turns by moonlight.

In the next depression, she saw a flowing creek. With her next few strides, Florida realized she had been mistaken. It wasn't a creek—it was a shadow flooding into the low part of the road. She didn't stop or turn back.

She ran faster.

Florida jumped at the last second, hurdling the growing pool of shadow. She imagined that she could feel it tugging at her feet as she soared over it. Florida increased her speed. By the top of the next hill, she was panting for air, but she kept accelerating.

Florida felt the ground move underneath her and ran as fast as she ever had in her life. This wasn't her long-distance pace. This was her sprint. Her form suffered and her breath burned her throat, but she didn't allow herself to slow.

She could feel the desert gathering around her. Something was mustering all its strength for one last attempt at taking her life. Florida used the thought as motivation to pump her legs even faster. Her breath evened out as she poured on speed.

She saw the place ahead where the dirt road became asphalt. The black line of pavement ran all the way to the highway. To her, the solid road mean civilization. It was the border where human achievement had conquered nature. If she could just reach it, she thought she might be okay.

There was one more dip in the road between her and that freedom.

At the bottom of that dip, the shadows had flooded. She couldn't see anything of the gravel road down there.

Still, she ran towards it.

It was way too far to jump, but she tried.

Florida planted her foot at the edge of the shadow and threw herself into the night. She pumped her legs and her arms, trying to get every last inch out of the leap. It wasn't going to be enough. She saw the swirling shadows beneath her and knew that she was going to come down in that pool of darkness.

On the hill above her, at the edge of the pavement, a set of headlights pierced the darkness.

Florida yelled her frustration as her feet came down in the black. She tipped forward, grabbing useless handfuls of sand and rocks. With one glance down, she saw the awful truth. Her legs were submerged up to her knees. When she tried to pull a leg free it was black, like it had been dipped in oil.

Chapter Fifty-Six — Fight

JUSTIN KICKED AT THE grip that was pulling him down. He could feel the hot flames wafting up on rising air from below. He pulled with all his strength. If the demon holding onto his ankle refused to relinquish its grip, it was going to be pulled above ground with him.

Justin got lucky. His fingers caught a hard edge buried in the soil.

His fingers felt like they would rip from his hand as his fear powered his muscles. Every inch was agony.

"Let go!" he screamed. He thought that if the weight were just removed from his leg, he could easily make the climb.

The hand around his ankle only tightened. It was soon joined by a second hand.

Justin's fingers trembled with the effort. His grip was just about to fail.

He imagined slipping backwards and tumbling down into the pits of hell. He clenched his teeth and banished the thought.

Something soft hit his face.

Justin looked up. A rope was hanging down the slope. He couldn't see its source, but at that point, he didn't care. Justin grabbed the rope with one hand and then the other. As soon as his weight was committed, the rope began to pull.

It lifted him with agonizing patience. His fingers slipped against the rough fiber and the grip on his ankle never relented. When his thigh crested the edge of the chasm, Justin thought that his leg would be broken in two from the weight. He rolled, taking the pressure from his thigh and shifting it to his knee.

Justin cried out from the pain. He thought for sure that his flesh would be ripped in two between his grip on the rope and the claws holding his ankle.

As his shin carved a groove in the edge of the pit, he saw the fingers for the first time. He heard a woman's groan.

From above, he heard a delighted cackle. Justin looked up. He couldn't see the person's face, but he saw a hunched form silhouetted by red lights from behind.

Justin's fingers slipped. A layer of skin stayed put on the rope and was torn from his hands. He bit the rope to take some of the pressure from his hands. It smelled of tar and gasoline. He was dragged upwards at the same slow pace.

Below him, the person attached to his ankle began to crest the lip. As the weight diminished on his leg, the hands began to climb him. One hand moved to his calf and the other reached up to his knee. Justin looked down and saw her head for the first time. Kristin's face was blackened with soot. Her eyes were crazy. Her hair was backlit by the flames. She had been transformed into a demon and she pulled as she climbed.

Justin tried one more time to shake her loose. His hands slipped again on the rope. He found a knot at the end and he dug his fingers into it.

"Two for one," the voice above him said. The statement was followed by another cackle.

They continued to rise.

Justin could hear an engine idling above him. He could hear a grinding motor that vibrated down the rope. The ground beneath him began to level off, but he didn't let go of the rope. Kristin tugged at his legs again and then she climbed up beyond him.

She ran past the hunched man and his vehicle. Justin pushed up to his knees and climbed the rest of the way up the slope. He looked down at his bleeding hands and then met the eyes of the old man.

His silver beard was draped around his smiling mouth. His eyes were nearly lost in a million wrinkles. The old man pulled something from a back pocket and tossed it to Justin. It was a red rag. It looked clean enough. Justin dabbed it on his rope-burned palms.

"I suppose we better catch up to the lady before she falls into more trouble," the old man said. He began to shuffle towards the driver's door of his old truck. The truck was backed up to the sloped road. The man hit a switch on his way by and shut off the motor that had been winding the rope onto the reel.

The door creaked as the old man opened it.

"Are you coming?" he asked.

Justin didn't even glance back. He ran for the passenger's door.

The old man drove slowly and they gradually caught up to Kristin, who was running down the road.

"Who are you?" Justin asked.

"My name is Bertrand Ulrich," the old man said. He held out his hand and then saw that Justin had the rag wrapped around his right hand. Bert withdrew his hand and cackled.

Justin's brain immediately tried to place the name. When it did, he blurted out what he had read without thinking. "You killed Charles."

A cloud passed over the old man's jovial expression. He reached forward and shut off the radio with a click.

"You better talk to the lady," Bert said as he pulled alongside Kristin.

Justin found the crank for the window.

"Kristin, get in."

She looked at him with her crazy eyes. He noticed that her hair had been burned in the back. Her shirt was burned, too.

"Get in," he said again. Justin turned to the old man. "Can you stop for a second?"

The truck skidded to a stop on the gravel road and Kristin kept running. Justin opened the door and realized that he didn't want to get out. If he got out, the old man might drive away and they would be left to contend with the shadows again.

"Will you wait for me?" Justin asked the old man.

The sparkle had returned to his eyes, and the smile to his lips. Bert nodded.

Justin stepped down out of the truck and moved around the door. He began to jog after Kristin. His heart fell when he heard the truck drop into gear behind him. He knew what would happen next—the old man would speed past him, abandoning them once more.

He was wrong.

The truck kept pace, but didn't overtake him as he chased after Kristin.

"Kristin!" he yelled.

She glanced back but kept moving.

"Kristin!"

She jogged on, towards the highway. Justin wasn't able to match her speed and she gradually pulled away. Until she tripped, he was sure that she would run forever. Her spill didn't look too bad, but it took her to the ground. When Justin caught up, she was on the ground, curled into a ball.

"Kristin?"

Justin reached down and touched her leg. She pulled away from his touch.

"Fuck you!" She flailed her arm in his direction. "Just leave me here. That's what you're going to do, so do it."

"Kristin, I'm not leaving. Bert is waiting to give us a ride. We can get out of here now."

"Why should we trust some dirty old man in the desert?" she asked. "Just go away."

Justin tried to straighten back up, but his legs gave out. He fell back on his ass.

"Because I've been exactly where you are," the old man said. He stepped in front of the headlights and cast his hunched shadow over them. "I sat on this very stretch of road and wept. It wasn't tears of joy that were falling from my eyes—it was pure guilt. Why was I the one who made it out, and how could I have left all my friends? Hell, I killed my own cousin down in that wretched hell."

"What are you talking about?" Kristin asked.

Justin was relieved to see that she was beginning to sit up.

The old man scratched his white beard before he continued. "I was a miner from '91 to '93. In three years it felt like I spent a lifetime down in that hole."

"You can't be that old," Kristin said. She wiped her eyes with the back of one of her blackened hands. The motion left clean streaks in the soot on her face.

Bert cackled again. "I turned ninety-six last February, and with a little luck I'll live to see ninety-seven. And after all those years, I was beginning to think that I would never repay the favor. But I made a promise, and I've been out here on June 1st every year since."

"What promise?"

Bert nodded and cast his eyes over towards the rising sun. "There's always one who stays behind, and always one that gets away. That's what the man told me, and that's what I'm telling you. I didn't figure on two of you. I always have been extra lucky."

"Can we go?" Justin asked. Rolling onto his knees, he pushed back up to his feet. He put out his hand and was surprised when Kristin took it. He helped her up.

"That's a good idea," Bert said. "It would be a shame if the ground opened up and took one of you back in."

Justin and Kristin rushed back to the truck while the old man laughed.

He slowed as the truck neared the highway. They watched a car go by and Bert brought his truck to a stop.

"Now before I take you away from here, I need a promise," Bert said.

Kristin and Justin looked at each other, and then turned their attention back to the old man.

"Someone else is going to need your help. I can't say if one or both of you should come. Maybe you could take turns." The thought brought a smile to Bert's face for some reason. "But someone has to be out here for the next poor soul who tries to escape."

"Escape what?" Kristin asked.

"The mine," Justin whispered.

"No, I know *that*. I'm asking what the hell is down there. What killed our friends?"

Bert shook his head. His constant smile evaporated. "I can't say. Something lives down there, and it feeds. It feeds off of the unlucky desert animals who stumble into one of the holes. Every now and again it has a feast of foolish men who venture underground. That patch of dirt is inhabited."

Justin nodded his agreement.

Kristin glanced out the back window at the desert road. "Can we leave?"

"Not until you promise," Bert said. "I helped you, and I'm not going to be around to help the next poor soul."

Kristin looked down.

"I promise," Justin said.

Kristin kept her eyes down. "Yeah. I promise."

Chapter Fifty-Seven — Shadow

FLORIDA PULLED ONE LEG from the shadows, but the blackness covering her lower leg stretched back, connecting her to the pool. Meanwhile, she sunk even more.

"Hey!" a voice called.

She looked up. A person was standing there, right on the edge of the asphalt. The form moved and something tumbled out of the darkness. Florida covered her head with her arms and the shadows pulled her down.

It was a thin white rope. Florida grabbed it and looped it around her hands. She tugged on it and greedily took up the slack as she started to climb.

"Hold on." It was a man calling from above.

A second after he yelled, the rope began to jerk upwards. Florida stopped pulling and focused her effort on simply holding on. She looked down as she was dragged up the gravel. The shadows stretched and then receded. Her legs pulled free. They no longer looked covered in ink. Florida pumped her legs and got to her feet. Using the rope, she ran up the slope.

The man had a car parked on the edge of the asphalt.

He looked to be about her father's age.

"Thank you. Oh my God, thank you so much," she said. She shook the coils of rope from her hands and reached out to shake the man's hand with both of hers. "You won't believe what happened. We all went in there to do some experiments for my class, but I think they're all gone." She gestured behind herself and stopped to catch her breath.

"I know," he said.

Florida stood straighter and took a slight step back.

"The thing in the mines—It digests," the man said.

Florida took another step. The interior lights in the car came on. Florida saw a woman in there. She pushed the door the rest of the way open and stepped out.

"You're scaring her," the woman said. "It's okay. We're here to help you."

"I don't know you," Florida said. She knew it was a stupid thing to say, but it was what came out.

"I know," the woman said. "Listen—I was you. I was right in the same position you're in now. It was twenty years ago, but I was you. You don't know us, but please, let us drive you out of here. You don't have any other choice."

Florida glanced back in the direction of the mine. She'd seen no living sign of her group. The equipment was gone. Even the bus had disappeared.

She turned back to the woman. Her eyes were sad and kind. She looked at least as old as the man, and she looked like life had been a struggle for her. Most of all, she looked trustworthy.

"My partner," Florida said, gesturing over her shoulder. "He's still inside."

The woman nodded. "It always keeps one, and it lets one go. In our case, it let two of us go."

The man had already moved back to the driver's door. He slipped inside and closed the door, leaving the woman to persuade Florida.

"Can we go get help?" Florida asked.

"Of course," the woman said. She shook her head slightly as she said it. Somehow, even that was comforting. Florida knew that the woman was lying, but she was at least being honest about it.

"Okay," Florida said.

The man backed the car around and pointed it towards the highway. Florida looked at the seat beside her. The white rope was coiled next to her. That simple piece of cotton had saved her life.

"Honestly," the woman said, "we didn't expect you. I found that rope in my garage and I brought it along at the last minute. Justin didn't even think to bring one."

The man interjected over his shoulder. He defended himself. "We talked about it, but we thought it would be years before we ran across anyone."

"What are you talking about? Are you from the university?"

The woman shook her head. "No. We're just keeping a promise."

Florida saw the woman reach out and put her hand on the man's shoulder. He nodded and slowed to a stop. Florida's hands curled into fists. She had fought for her life plenty in the past twenty-four hours, and she was ready to do so again.

"You have to make a promise," the woman said. She looked Florida in the eyes.

"What?"

"We saved your life, and someday there's going to be someone who needs you to save theirs."

"A poor soul," the man whispered.

"That's right," the woman said. "Some poor soul is going to try to escape and they're going to need your help. We helped you, so our job is done. It's your turn now." As she said the words, some of the sadness began to leave the woman's eyes. She actually began to smile.

"I don't get it," Florida said. "What is this, some kind of joke?"

"No," the woman said. She shook her head, but there was still the ghost of a smile on her lips.

Chapter Fifty-Eight — Choice

ROGER WAS A CHILD in the darkness. The world didn't make any sense to him until Carlos showed him the way. He had to learn where to find water, where to shit, and the sorting places. Sorting was his job. His payment was the occasional mouthful of stolen meat. Carlos would eat anything—snake, scorpion, spider, or coyote. Roger was picky at first, but as the days turned into weeks, his standards sank into the subterranean depths.

He spent much of the time yelling. He yelled for help, and yelled against the injustice. He was convinced that someone would hear him eventually.

When Carlos got too close, or had the temerity to touch his shoulder or his arm, Roger attacked. Carlos was slippery in the dark. Before Roger could do any damage, the old man was gone. Eventually, he encountered Carlos less and less. Roger moved between the sorts, doing his work and claiming his reward. He would protest—refuse to work and sit sobbing in the darkness— but hunger would eventually propel him forward.

As sight became useless, Roger could feel his own brain reallocating resources to his other senses. The echo from a drip of water would give him a clear idea of his surroundings. The texture of the rocks would tell him where he was in the cave. Roger even started to understand how the caverns shifted and breathed. Nothing was static in the dark. Passages opened and closed. Everything moved in the living rock.

Roger woke from a dream of a picnic on a summer day. His eyes had been shut so long that his eyelids were crusted over. But the dream of the sun had been so happy that tears were running down his face. He forced his eyelids open for the first time in an age.

He saw light.

Roger crawled towards it, climbing the ledges up and up. The light was just the tiniest flicker in the distance. He moved in complete silence. His eyes had almost forgotten how to see.

Roger saw the old man in the distance. The dim light was flowing down the long tunnel, illuminating the portraits. The light didn't seem to come from anywhere in particular. It simply flowed down the rocks, like spring runoff.

Anger formed as a hot ball in his stomach as he approached Carlos.

The old man was scratching a new portrait into the wall. It was a crude representation, but Roger recognized Dr. Deb.

"I'm no good," Carlos said. He stood back to assess his drawing.

"I'm going to kill you," Roger said.

Carlos nodded. "I know."

The light faded as Roger attacked.

Chapter Fifty-Nine — Duty

FLORIDA WOKE BEFORE HER alarm, bathed in sweat.

She didn't know if she had contained the scream or not.

In her dream, the rope had never come. The shadows had dragged her down into the darkness to be digested by the soil. The dream had come every night for a week. It happened the same way every year. No matter what she did—pills, booze, sleep deprivation—the dreams always came in the days leading up to the anniversary of her escape.

Florida got out of bed and gathered up the sheets.

The phone rang as she was stuffing them into the hamper.

"Hello?"

"Good morning!" he said. He was always so chipper in the mornings. Florida both loved and hated that about him.

"Hey," she said.

He paused, reading her mind over the phone. She loved and hated that too. It was nice to be with someone who could understand her state of mind from a single word, but it also made her feel naked.

"Nightmare?" he asked.

"Yeah. It's okay. They'll end today."

"You say that every year."

"And it's true every year," she said.

He laughed at her. "I think you and I have different definitions of what 'end' means."

"Is there a reason for this phone call?" she asked. Florida did her best to sound angry, but he knew her too well.

"Hey, hold on," he said. She could hear the smile in his voice.

"I was just calling my lovely lady to see if she wanted to have dinner with me tomorrow night. But if you're going to get all crabby about it, I'm sure I can cancel my reservations."

"Tomorrow sounds good, but it has to be early."

"Give me some credit," he said. "I remember—you'll be sleep deprived. What I've got planned is a nice dinner that will be over long before your bedtime. Can I mark you down as a yes?"

"Yes."

"Wonderful! I will swing by and pick you up."

They said their goodbyes and hung up.

Florida sat on the stripped bed and looked at the phone. Her alarm went off.

The call wasn't really about dinner. He was checking up on her. It was sweet, but it was also a little constrictive. She still wasn't convinced that she wanted anyone to know her that well. Florida shook off the thought and headed for the shower.

She parked her truck on the shoulder of the highway and watched the access road. There were concrete barriers erected to keep anyone from trespassing, but it would be easy enough to circumnavigate them.

One time, a few years earlier, she had chased off a group of thrill-seeking teenagers. They had hitchhiked out there. They laughed and joked with each other as they began to hike across the desert. Florida had stopped them by firing a rifle in the air.

After collecting themselves and yelling obscenities in her direction, they made themselves scarce.

Most years, Florida didn't see anyone except the cars gliding east and west on the highway. They never bothered her. The police didn't even bother to stop and ask her if she needed assistance. The area seemed to give off a vibe that most people weren't interested in getting involved with. That was Florida's theory, at least.

Justin and Kristin had warned her.

"You can go to the cops if you want," Justin had said. "I bet they won't even care."

"He's right," Kristin had said. "Bert Ulrich told us the same thing. We tried. We told everyone we could think of. I got down on my knees and begged Carlos's mom to go to the police. She kept saying, 'He'll be back. He wanders sometimes, but my Carlos always comes back.' She never gave up on him."

"It's a self-defense mechanism," Justin had said. "The thing knows how to make people ignore it. It's how it has survived all this time. I bet there are tribes of Indians who lived near the thing for centuries and they never acknowledged it."

"It doesn't have mind-control powers," Kristin had said.

At the time, Florida hadn't really been interested in following their conversation too closely. She was simply concerned with getting home alive.

As it grew dark, Florida sat up straight. She poured her first cup of coffee from the big thermos strapped into the seat next to her. It was going to be a long night of sitting, but it was worth it. One night in the truck would mean the end of the nightmares for another year.

She had tried to skip the promise once. She had never made that mistake again. The guilt and worry left her frantic and unable to breathe. She had driven out to the access road in a panic. Ever since, she didn't take a chance. She could only hope that her duty would be over sooner rather than later.

Then again, the only way for her responsibility to end would be if someone were to die. It was impossible to wish for that.

Just before midnight, a car pulled up behind her.

She recognized her boyfriend as he approached. When he knocked, she unlocked the door and moved the thermos so he could get in.

"You don't mind if I keep you company for a bit, do you?" Eric asked.

The interior light shut off as he closed his door.

"Don't you have to work in the morning?"

"I caught a nap earlier. I'll be fine," he said.

He was smart enough to not ask too many questions. Still, his presence seemed to demand that she explain herself.

"I can't tell you why I come out here," she said.

"I know," he said. He put his hands up. "Can you tell me which direction I'm supposed to be looking though? Are we watching the highway, the sky, or this blocked-off side road?"

She didn't say anything.

"Stupid question, I guess," he said. "You wouldn't come out here to look at the sky or the highway. You're clearly looking at this side road. What is it, an old bomb testing site?"

She sighed.

"Sorry. I won't ask again."

They sat in silence for a long time. Florida made a point of never looking at the clock while she waited. When the sun was completely over the horizon, she would leave. That was all the clock she needed.

"When we have kids someday, we can get a camper and make an excursion of this trip every year," Eric said. "At least until they start school."

"You want kids?" she asked.

"A whole houseful," he said. "You?"

"Yeah."

"It's settled. We'll have a whole houseful. We can name the first one Abby and then work our way through the alphabet," Eric said. "We'll have to be creative when we get to number twenty-seven."

Florida laughed.

Eric reached out and touched her hand.

"That's the first laugh I've heard in a week," he said.

She looked down. She pictured Roger's face and wondered what it would look like now. Was he still alive? Kristin had jolted like she'd suffered an electric shock when Florida had mentioned Carlos. Florida should have never brought up the name.

"Abby, Brad, Carlisle, Deborah," Eric began.

"Stop!" Florida said. "I'll have your kids if you just shut the hell up, okay?"

Eric made a motion that she could barely see in the darkness. He twisted a lock at his lips and threw away the key.

Florida returned her gaze to the desert.

Somewhere down that blocked road, the mine was still open. Nobody ever talked about the people lost anymore. Dr. Grossman had taken in several groups who had emerged just fine. It wasn't until the June 1st trip—Florida's trip—that they'd had any trouble.

When the department head—Dr. Grossman's boss—had called, Florida had lied. She told the man that she had missed the trip. She regretted it almost immediately, but there didn't seem to be a good way out of the lie. The investigation had evaporated as quickly as it started.

Headlights appeared from the other direction. Before the big truck reached them, it veered off the road. The truck eased by the barricade and continued down the access road towards the mine.

Florida sat up straight. The gun was in the trunk, but the big truck was already disappearing. It was too late to warn them off.

"Holy shit!" Eric said. "Where are those guys going?"

Florida sighed. She broke her own rule and checked her watch. It was almost one in the morning. Sunrise would begin just after five-thirty. She had counted three heads in the truck. There could have been more—it was a big cab. A strange mixture of emotions began to rise in her chest. She was anxious, sad, and a little relieved. In six hours, her responsibility would likely be over.

"You should go," she said to Eric.

"Are you going to go after them? Is that why you're here?"

"No," she said. She shook her head slowly. "They're on their own."

Eric studied her in the dark. He was probably reading her mind again. She needed to learn that trick.

"Call me when you get home safe, okay?" he asked.

"Yeah."

He got out.

Eric took his time getting back to his car and turning around. She jiggled her leg impatiently as she waited. When he was finally gone, she didn't know exactly what to do.

Florida released some air from her tires before she attempted to drive around the barricade. It was probably unnecessary, but she didn't intend to take any chances. She crept down the cracked asphalt until she could see the end. Where the pavement ended and the road was dirt, it looked like the end of the world.

She imagined Roger ahead, underground, waiting with closed eyes for the new visitors.

Florida shut off her lights and killed the engine.

She had a thick rope in the back of the truck. She had gloves and a hook below the front bumper to attach the rope. She had less than five hours until sunrise. She remembered the promise that Kristin and Justin had exacted from her.

Some poor soul was going to find his or her way out, and she was going to be there to rescue them. With that, her duty would be done. Maybe someday when they had a houseful of kids, she would tell Eric about that night. Maybe she would tell him about her journey underground.

Maybe she wouldn't.

Ike Hamill
June, 2015
Topsham, Maine

About *Inhabited*

Thank you so much for reading *Inhabited*. I hope you enjoyed reading it as much I enjoyed the writing. This was one of my favorite books to write. The idea for *Inhabited* came after I watched several videos of people exploring abandoned mines. It's easy to think of those places as haunted. In those videos, the mine itself seems to have a personality, and it seems pretty pissed off. As I dropped these people into jeopardy, I began to think of the cave as a sleeping giant. The characters had unwittingly stepped right into the thing's mouth.

I stepped lightly around the mythology of the cave creature. What you read in this book is no more than what the characters themselves could deduce. Yes, I have some ideas about where this thing came from, and its life-cycle. I'm sure you've formed your own ideas as well. The story isn't about the development of this complex and heartless organism though. It's about the struggle of people to survive.

Could you do me a favor? Could you take a second and leave a review for *Inhabited* wherever you happened to pick it up? Also, please tell a friend about my books. Anything you can do to help spread the word would be amazing. I feel lucky that I have the chance to write books, but without reaching readers, there's really no point.

Hit me up on Facebook, Twitter, or email if you want to talk about *Inhabited* or any of my other books. I'm easy to find, and there are links below. If you sign up for my mailing list at ikehamill.com, you won't regret it. I'm in the habit of offering a free download of my new titles as they come out. Everyone on the list gets a chance to download for free before the book is even announced to the public.

Thanks for reading,
Ike
http://www.ikehamill.com
http://www.facebook.com/IkeHamill
@IkeHamill on Twitter
IkeHamill@gmail.com

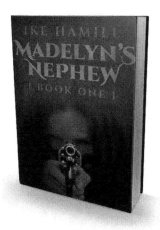

Madelyn's Nephew

After the sun turned, Madelyn fled north to escape the riots and the encroaching glaciers. As long as the world was ending, she wanted to live her final days in the one place she had always been happy—her grandmother's cabin. She survived the Roamers, the scavengers, and the wildlife, but she can't escape her fear of dying alone.

She left behind this note:

"Gather my bones, if you find them. If a bear hasn't dragged them off, or a wolf cracked them for my marrow. My skull goes on the wall with the others. Any other remains can be planted near Sacrifice Rock. That's where my grandfather is buried, and where I dug up the skull of my beloved grandmother.

Her sweet eyes were still wise and kind, even when I only imagined them from their hollow sockets. She taught us so many things—how to hunt, trap, and fish. She should have taught me how to live alone. I never learned the trick of scaring away the ghosts. They won't shut up and leave me in peace. I guess it's time to join them."

—Madelyn

The Claiming

It wasn't her fault.

It wasn't Lizzy's fault that she saw the cloaked people out in the yard. It wasn't her fault that she was drawn by the moonlight to watch them as they advanced on the house. And it definitely wasn't her fault when people began to die. Lizzy didn't want the strange dreams where she saw how they were killed. Even her sister was starting to suspect her.

It wasn't fair because it wasn't her fault.

Lizzy was claimed.

Extinct

Channel Two predicted a blanket of snow for Thanksgiving weekend—unusual, but not alarming for the little Maine island. What comes is a blinding blizzard, and a mass disappearance of nearly every person Robby Pierce knows. He and his family flee, trying to escape the snow and the invisible forces stealing people right from the street.

Miles away, Brad Jenkins battles the same storm. Alone, he attempts to survive as snow envelops his house. When the storm breaks, Brad makes his way south to where the snow ends and the world lies empty. Join Brad, Robby, and the other survivors as they fight to find the truth about the apocalypse and discover how to live in their new world.

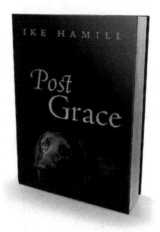

Post Grace

Grace Anne Orlov died peacefully in her home on Thursday, the 7th. Her husband, John, survives her in body if not in spirit. John studied killers and death, but failed to learn how to live alone after more than forty years of marriage.

Along with two daughters, a son, two grandchildren, and a stray bastard, John has a lot to figure out.
What he doesn't know might kill him.

Kill Cycle

The town I grew up in is dying, and I know who's killing it. At least I think I do. But he's a master manipulator and nobody will believe me. It's up to me to prove that he's the serial killer who has been stalking the streets. I have to stop him before he targets me, or worse, my family.

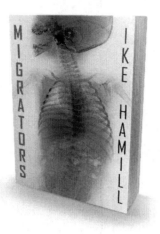

Migrators

Do not speak of them. Your words leave a scent. They will come.
Somewhere in the middle of Maine, one of the world's darkest secrets
has been called to the surface. Alan and Liz just wanted a better life for
themselves and their son. They decided to move to the country to rescue
the home of Liz's grandfather, so it would stay in the family. Now, they
find themselves directly in the path of a dangerous ritual. No one can
help them. Nothing can stop the danger they face. To save themselves
and their home, they have to learn the secrets of the MIGRATORS.

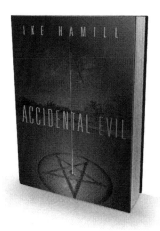

Accidental Evil

Kingston Lakes is a quiet town. During long summer days, the residents barely have a care. They almost never have to worry about the rise of a bloodthirsty demon who wants to feast on their flesh and enslave their immortal souls.

Almost never.

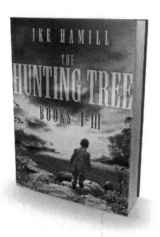

The Hunting Tree

For thousands of years a supernatural killer has slept in the White Mountains of New Hampshire. An amateur ghost hunter has just woken him up. Now that he stalks the night once more, he's traveling east. Although the monster's actions are pure evil, he may be the only thing that can save humanity from extinction.

Transcription

Thomas has found the biggest story of his career, and he can't believe his luck. He's sitting in the prison cell that at one time housed each of The Big Four, the state's most notorious murderers. There's only one problem: he's beginning to understand what drove them to commit their crimes. He's beginning to feel their madness.

Years later, his son suffers a curse. Every night, he's compelled to transcribe his father's stories. If he misses a single night, he'll do something terrible. It has happened before. James has given up everything to his curse, and it controls every moment of his life. James can only imagine what will happen if one of the stories gets out. In the worst case, people will die.

And the worst case is coming.

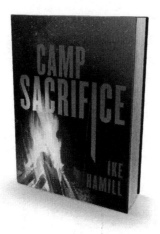

Camp Sacrifice

Welcome to Camp Sacrifice.

You'll find your cabin clean and comfortable, but please bring the following items to get the most out of your vacation this summer:

    1 - personal story of bone-chilling fright

    1 - mirror for summoning spirits

    1 - sharp knife for things that stalk the night

    1 - shovel to dispatch the undead

Oh, and be sure to cancel your autumn plans.

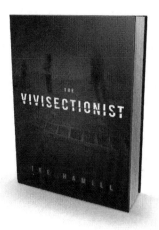

The Vivisectionist

The boys have the perfect summer planned. They'll camp out in the back yard for their last vacation before high school. There's only one problem —even though they're just a hundred feet from the safety of the house, they're being hunted by a serial killer.

Join Jack, Ben, and Stephen as they strap on their backpacks and go out looking for adventure. The woods behind Jack's house contain endless trails to explore, and the boys have weeks to investigate them all. Their neighborhood finally seems at peace again, now that the man who snatched the kid from down the street has been caught. But there's still danger in those woods, and the boys are about to stumble into it...

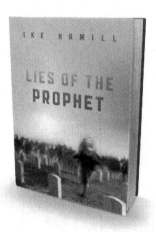

Lies of the Prophet

Gregory was the first to rise from the grave. With no organs and no pulse he burst from his coffin demanding to know why he'd been buried. His subsequent book made him a billionaire and encouraged others to follow in his footsteps. Unfortunately, the decayed, mindless undead who rose after him were nothing like him.

Lynne, Carol, and Marta are on a collision course with the same goal: they must stop Gregory. Join these three women as they battle supernatural forces and discover their own paranormal powers. They each have their own reasons for fighting Gregory, but the fate of the world rests in their hands.

Skillful Death

Deep in an Old World forest, an unnamed village lies hidden. Decades pass as the village waits for its special son to return. The boy challenged the lion, bested the snake, and defeated the elephant. He possessed an unearthly skill. His return will bring back balance to the village.

High in the Tibetan mountains, a monk waits for death behind a stone wall. For this last journey, he prepared his body over the course of one-hundred days. Outside his little tomb, another man is learning the secret of immortality.

In Seattle, an old man learns a new skill and finds unimaginable fortune.

It's my job to document these lives, keep my boss safe, and find that unnamed village. At one of these tasks, I will fail.

Punch List

Jeff doesn't want to think about the future. He's not even sure he can deal with the present. High school, friends who aren't friendly, and his crumbling family are hard enough. It's time for him to make a change. Maybe, with a little luck, he'll survive the summer.

Wild Fyre

The perfect technology would anticipate our every need, solve our problems, and answer questions we hadn't thought to ask.

The perfect technology would defend itself.
It would spread everywhere.
It would kill if it had to.

In this unique blend of Sci-Fi and Horror, Ike Hamill will bring you into the world of Fyre. The question is, will she let you live?

Made in the USA
Columbia, SC
17 September 2017